Turning Purple

Chris Gallagher

Purple – the calm stability of blue and the fierce
energy of red

Chapter One

I enjoy waking up early on the weekends and watching the sunrise. It's so peaceful. My wife and two girls are asleep and I feel like I'm the only one in the world watching that sun peak up over the horizon. The stress from life's everyday issues is gone for those quiet moments I spend on my patio. No pain in the ass boss telling me what to do. No annoying employees needing me to hold their hands through every trivial item at work. It's just that sunrise and me.

This morning isn't like any other mornings though. My life is about to change dramatically. A few weeks ago I went to see my doctor on what I thought was a routine visit to diagnose a dull pain that I was experiencing in my stomach. After multiple tests, MRI's and blood work I finally received my diagnosis yesterday. Pancreatic cancer. I didn't know much about pancreatic cancer other than the fact Patrick Swayze and Steve Jobs fought it and lost. Yes, those two guys with all of the resources they had at their disposal weren't able to beat it. In essence, pancreatic cancer is a death sentence. There aren't a lot of stories of people beating it. I'm hoping I have better luck than most, but only time will tell. I forced my doctor to give it to me straight when I asked him how long I had. In typical doctor fashion, he was non-committal at first and tried to do his best to keep the conversation positive. He started out with the old, "treatment has advanced", "with a positive attitude and support from your family", blah, blah, blah. I've always been a straight shooter in my personal life and in the business world and I expect the same from others that I deal with. Well, I got what I was looking for, the doc was as blunt as possible. "Maybe one year". My heart sank and I began to feel sick as those words came out of his mouth. So many emotions ran through me, but surprisingly enough, guilt was the overwhelming feeling that came over me. I immediately thought of my six and eight year old little girls and my wife. How dare I leave them? Who would care for them?

The connection between a father and daughter is truly unmatched. The day my first daughter, Lynnie, was born my life was changed forever. I had always been a pretty selfish person and was so focused on my career and put that first in my life. Yes, unfortunately, my career came before my wife too. The day that little girl was born everything changed. I was a father and there wasn't anything I wouldn't do for that little baby. I even became a better husband. Go ahead, ask my wife, she agrees. A couple of years later we were blessed with another little girl, Reilly.

So here we are, the family of four, living in a nice house in the suburbs, happily enjoying the lovely paradise that South Florida has to offer. Well, that's about to change, but other than my doctor, I'm the only one that knows that. I'll sit here this morning and watch the sun rise on the final chapter of my life. I'll be forty-three in five days. Life shouldn't end at forty-three.

Twenty years ago, wow, it goes fast. The four of us had just graduated from Florida State University and decided to jump in a car for a cross-country adventure. It was your classic college guy road trip.

No money, lots of drinking, fast food diet and of course, no sleep. It was our last hoorah before the real world started for us. We all knew it too and actually talked about it during the trip. We knew we'd never have the freedom that we had at that very moment. We knew what awaited us after we returned…life with jobs. No more waking up at noon for a 12:30 class, Tuesday nights were no longer "regular" nights out and our falls didn't revolve around college football season.

Well, we were right. The jobs, the marriages, the kids soon came along and our freedom was officially gone the minute that road trip ended. Life will never be as simple as it was in college and we all cherish those moments. We'll always look back at that road trip and smile remembering how much fun we had and that's why we all agreed to make an attempt to do it again.

Frank woke up earlier than usual that Friday morning. His motivation was simple, it wasn't a workday. It was the first day of our two-week "rewind" to our college days. He never believed we would pull it off and you could see the elation on his face that morning because he knew it was going to happen. Twenty years later, we're doing it again. The four of us managed to convince our bosses and our wives (the real bosses) to let us do this. Two weeks, just the four of us.

Frank lives just outside of Houston with his wife, two boys and a little girl. The law firm he works for is a monster. Oil, oil and more oil. They represent the interest of several oil companies in Texas providing regulatory guidance and counsel as the industry continues to be scrutinized thanks to the BP spill several years ago. He isn't a partner and probably won't ever be, but that's OK with Frank. They pay him plenty of money and he really doesn't have the passion for the work. In other words, he's fine doing what he is doing, collecting a paycheck and leaving his work life behind him as soon as he walks out of the office each day.

"Daddy, where are you going?" Frank's youngest, Samantha or "Sam" as she's referred to, asked while producing the saddest little face you've ever seen.

"You remember Sammy, Daddy's going on a trip with Uncle Kevin, Uncle Sal and Uncle Nolan."

"Mommy is sleeping, I'll go tell her."

"Hold on Sammy, don't wake your mom up yet, let her sleep for a little while longer and by the way, Mommy knows that Daddy is leaving today, but thanks for the offer," Frank said with a big smile. He has three kids, but only one girl and there's nothing like Daddy's little girl to put a smile on your face.

"Well look at you, bright eyed and bushy tailed," Frank's wife Erica observes as she makes her way down the stairs.

While Erica didn't go to school with us, we've known her for a long time as she and Frank started dating a year after we graduated. She's an amazing person, great mom and a wonderful wife to Frank. She has that "cute" look that would win any guy over. You know what I mean, she doesn't turn heads when she walks in a room, but her attractiveness goes through the roof once you get talking with her and her infectious personality and smile takes over.

"Boy, I'm starting to wonder if you'll even miss us on your boys' trip. What time is your flight?"

"I have to leave in about a half-hour and yes, I'll miss all of you, but you know what this means to all of us. I still can't believe we're actually doing it. The four of us getting our schedules straight and being able to get away for two weeks is a miracle."

"Listen, have a great time and don't worry about us, I have it covered, like usual," Erica convincingly stated with a devilish smirk. This wasn't the first time Frank has been away and won't be the last. He's had plenty of road trips representing his oil execs over the years.

20,000 square feet, yes, 20,000. That is the size of the palace that Nolan lives in just outside of Nashville. This house has it all. Fitness center, movie theater, 8-car garage (which, of course, is filled) and a must-have for any multi-millionaire, a bowling alley. Some might say its overkill, but if you know Nolan like I do, this is just about right. He has one of those larger than life personalities that has worked for him throughout his career. He went straight to New York as soon as he graduated and to his credit, worked his ass off in the finance world and made it big. When I say he worked hard, it is no exaggeration. Twenty-hour days, yes on Saturdays and Sundays too. You always hear about the hours guys put in on Wall Street, but now that I've actually seen it through Nolan, it amazes me. He has earned every penny and then some. I can't even keep track of his business deals. He seems to have his hands in everything, including politics. Not as a candidate, but as someone who has an interest in his pushing his business agenda forward. I've never asked him whether he is a democrat or a republican. I don't think he knows or cares. He's only interested in the party that can help his business interests the most and he opens up his check book when they come calling for campaign contributions. After all, how many people do you know that have had dinner with President Bush and President Obama? Trust me, he didn't get those dinner invites due to his charming personality.

"Son of a bitch, I'm going to shoot that little mutt," Nolan grumbles as he's lying in bed.

"That's what you get for trying to win your children over with a puppy," Nolan's wife Sophie fires back.

"Yep, my fault, I know I'm an idiot," Nolan agrees.

"You're the idiot? I'm the one who married you," Sophie says as she rolls over and lies on top of Nolan and smiles. "You're lucky I love you so much."

"Can you feel on your leg how much I love you?" Nolan laughs as he taps Sophie on her backside.

"You have a little dog to take care of, so keep it in your pants mister. Get down there and let him outside and I'll help you finish packing."

Sophie, Sophie, Sophie. Let me paint the picture for you. She is Nolan's second wife and let's just say that money can buy happiness, if you define happiness as 5'10", blond, blue eyes, big tits and a perfect ass. That's Sophie. Not a lot between the ears, but who am I to judge? She's twenty-seven years old, hasn't worked a real job in her life and Nolan didn't have her sign a pre-nup. Translation: if Nolan is a multi-millionaire, which he is, half of that is Sophie's. Pretty smart if you ask me. They met six years ago at a restaurant that Nolan frequents in New York. Sophie was the typical "actress, model, dancer" trying to find her way in the big city. Well, taking that job as the hostess in that fancy NYC steakhouse to make ends meet was the smartest move she ever made. Nolan was married when they met and he tried to have his cake and eat it too. The affair went on for a year until Nolan's first wife, Carrie, started snooping around on his laptop. It was ugly. Nasty divorce, Carrie won full custody of the kids, but Nolan got to keep the majority of his money. Carrie let him off easy because all she cared about was the kids. Nolan, unfortunately, cares more about his money. After all, he had another kid on the way with Sophie while his divorce was being finalized. They've added another since then and have a boy and a girl. They also squeezed a marriage in between the two pregnancies. Just your typical American family.

"What time are they getting here?" Katie yelled to Sal in a frustrating tone of voice.

"Do we really need to go through this again Kate?" Sal fires back. "I told you that Nolan will be here first and should arrive around noon."

"Well then you have a lot to do because I'm not cleaning up this house by myself so you and your friends can mess it up and take off for two weeks," Katie snapped back.

"That's it, isn't it? You're just pissed off that I'm going on this trip and that is bullshit! I do plenty around here and all you ever do is bitch and moan, I'm so tired of it Katie!"

This type of dialogue is, unfortunately, the only dialogue that has occurred between Sal and Katie lately. To say they've had better times is an understatement.

The two college sweethearts met when Sal was a senior and Katie was a freshman. They were once a great couple, had so much fun together, but those days are long gone. Their life together is now just one argument after the next. The stress of their relationship has begun to hurt other areas of their life. Sal is in sales for an auto parts manufacturer and spends a lot of time on the road. He hates his job and his attitude at work is getting worse as he and Katie's relationship spirals out of control.

Katie has also let her home life affect her work. She's an IT consultant and a pretty darn good one at that. She had built a great reputation in the industry, specifically with the major accounting firms, but things have changed recently. About two months ago she and Sal got into a terrible fight.

The verbal jabs turned into a physical encounter and they were both arrested for domestic violence. It happened on the morning of an important meeting for Katie that she ended up missing because she was sitting in a jail cell. Needless to say, she was removed from that consulting job and word spread fast throughout her industry as her absence resulted in a major embarrassment for the firm that she was representing. Landing jobs has been difficult for her since that day and the stress has taken its toll on her. She's dipped into a deep depression and blames Sal for everything that has gone wrong in their lives.

Fortunately, I've never personally experienced it, but I've seen relationships like Sal and Katie's deteriorate before. The mental abuse that exists on a day-to-day basis is too much for either person to handle and then it escalates into a slap, a punch or sometimes, even worse. It is sad to see a man and a woman that once loved each other so much develop hatred for one another. I am very concerned for their future together, but I'm more concerned about the negative affect it is having on their five-year-old daughter Hannah.

"Daddy stop!" Hannah screams as she runs into the kitchen and grabs him around his leg. Hannah was an innocent bystander during the fight a couple of months ago that sent her parents to jail. Seeing her father and mother involved in a physical altercation and then taken away from the house by the police has already damaged her psychologically. Now, every time a voice is raised in her house, which happens too often, she immediately thinks it will escalate into a fistfight between her mom and dad.

"Don't hurt Mommy, please!" Sal removes Hannah's arms from around his leg and storms out of the room. He knows the memory of what he did a few months ago will never go away and he is both saddened and frustrated by it. He was once his daughter's hero, but now all she sees in him is fear.

As his big Mercedes rolled through the winding roads of the Atlanta suburb Nolan's phone rang.

"John, what's up?" John is one of the many attorneys that Nolan deals with on a daily basis.

"We need to get together and discuss this right away," John says as his voice cracks a little.

"I fucking told you John that I'm not discussing shit for the next two weeks. That bullshit will be waiting for me when I get back, don't call me again!" Nolan hangs up and throws his phone down on the passenger seat.

A frustrated Nolan gathers his composure as he pulls into Sal's driveway. Sal sees Nolan pulling in and darts out of the house to meet him. He walks alongside of the car and directs Nolan where to park. Nolan rolls the window down, "You know I'm not leaving this car outside for two weeks, you better move your fucking Dodge out of that garage now."

"Fuck you, you'll park where I tell you to park," Sal says with a smile. He's so happy to see his friend. It's been four years since they've seen each other.

Nolan gets out of the car and he and Sal engage in that "half handshake, half hug" thing that guys do. It usually ends with a couple of big pats on the back, but I guess it works.

"Boy, you look like shit, what have you put on, twenty pounds?" Nolan has never been afraid to call it like he sees it and he's not entirely accurate in this case. Sal has gained almost thirty pounds since he and Nolan last saw each other.

"Sorry, I don't have a personal trainer come and get me out of bed every morning like you, you prick." Sal is right on the money. Nolan has a personal trainer, a chef and a pretty good budget for plastic surgery. Hey, it's not easy keeping up with Sophie, after all she is sixteen years younger than him.

"Alright, alright, I'm just busting your balls, let's go inside."

The two friends walk up the path to Sal's house and Hannah greets them at the door. Hannah was only a year old the last time she saw her Godfather Nolan.

"Hannah, say hello to your Uncle Nolan."

"Hi Uncle Nolan." Nolan picks up Hannah and swings her around the room. She laughs hysterically. Sal misses those days. He used to be able to get Hannah to laugh like that.

"Hi Katie," Nolan says as he places Hannah back down on the ground. "Good to see you." Katie walks over and gives Nolan a peck on the cheek.

"How's your daughter doing, I mean your wife," Katie throws the first punch.

Oh, I forgot to mention that Katie is best friends with Nolan's ex-wife Carrie.

"You know Katie I don't want to get into this. I've been here for five minutes and you're already all over me. If I wanted this type of abuse I would have just stayed with Carrie."

"That's enough," Sal jumps in to halt the conversation. "Nol', let me show you to your room and then we'll grab a beer and relax out back."

"Right there, the second one on the right with the Mercedes in the driveway," Frank directs the driver. Frank hops out of the cab and grabs his enormous suitcase from the driver. He knows that it won't take but two minutes for one of the guys to make fun of him about the huge bag. At least he's being consistent. The guy took up most of the space in the trunk on our trip twenty years ago.

"Daddy, Uncle Frank is here!" Hannah adores her Uncle Frank. He's in Atlanta quite a bit and sometimes stays at Sal's house. He was just there a couple of months ago.

Frank can barely make it up the driveway before Hannah greets him.

"There she is, my little princess," Frank says with a big smile.

"My turn, my turn," Hannah shouts with excitement. It's become a tradition that whenever Frank arrives Hannah gets a ride on top of his rolling suitcase.

Frank rolls Hannah and his suitcase up the front walkway and steps inside.

"Hi Kate, I see your best friend arrived before me, how's that going?" Frank says sarcastically as he knows there is no love lost between Nolan and Katie.

"They're already outside drinking. Nolan is his obnoxious self and Sal is eating it up like usual. I don't know what you guys see in him."

"Hey, he's our friend, good or bad. I'll keep him in line on this trip." Frank and Katie start laughing, as they know that's impossible.

Frank swings open the door to the patio and sees his friends relaxing outside. For some reason he sees this as the perfect opportunity to break into this horrible dance that he's been doing since we were in college. I think it is some kind of pseudo-tribal dance that means it's time to party. We made fun of him back then for it and we still make fun of him now. It involves lots of foot stomping and some type of jig. It's horrible, but very funny.

"Quick Sal, call 911, I think Frank is having a seizure."

"So are you guys ready?" Frank says as he shakes the hands of both of his friends and immediately grabs a beer. "This is going to be great, when does Kevin get here?"

"He called from the road, he's about three hours away," said Sal.

"Good, that gives us some time to finalize his birthday surprise. We're still planning on giving it to him when we are in Phoenix, right?" asks Frank.

"Oh yeah, he's gonna love it", Nolan proclaims.

I decided to drive the ten hours to Atlanta for one reason. I plan on visiting Florida State on my way back home from Atlanta. I've let too much time pass since the last time I was there and I want to make sure I get to walk the campus one more time. It's difficult to think that I'll be doing anything for the last time and I know I'll never get used to that, but the reality is that I don't have too much "healthy" time left. I'm terrified as to how this will all end. I don't want to become a burden on my family and I don't want them to see me suffering. I want everyone to remember me just how I am today, not in pain. Unfortunately, that's not my decision. I'm just along for the ride too.

"Kevin just pulled up," Katie yells out to the guys on the patio.

My relationship with Katie has always been what I would refer to as "neutral". I've never been one to get close with my buddies wives. I don't know, I think that is kind of odd. Frankly, I wouldn't want to be close friends with Katie. She's such a negative person.

"Katie, good to see you, are they out back?" That's about as much small talk with Katie that I can muster up.

"Yep, they're the three immature ones that you'll find out back in a sea of beer bottles. Oh, tell Sal that the grill is not going to turn on by itself."

"Ah, baldy, fat ass and the queer," I boldly state as I walk on to the patio referring to Nolan, Sal and Frank. This is how it will be for two weeks. We are relentless when we get together. No one can slip up for a second, but it's all in fun. I'm thrilled to see these guys.

"OK, so we've left the next two weeks of travel in Sal's hands. Anyone feeling apprehensive about that?" I said with a true sense of disbelief that we let Sal plan the most important part of the trip.

You see, Sal is one of the most unorganized individuals that any of us know. He constantly loses things like keys, phones, wallets and anything else that is a pain in the ass to replace. We used to keep track of all of the money he spent to replace things in college. I don't think he made it through one semester without losing at least one book. He's also a complete slob. We all remember the one time that he actually did his laundry after a couple of months. He had no choice as he literally wore everything he owned twice. Yes, including his underwear. Disgusting, but it gets worse. Instead of taking all of the clean clothes and placing them in his closet and dresser he simply dumped them on his bed and slept on the couch in our apartment for an entire month. He would sift through the clean clothes every day and wear them until the pile disappeared. Then he slept in his bed again. So, as you can imagine, my confidence level in him taking care of the transportation for our trip is very low.

"Look, I promise you that it's covered. You're gonna love our driver!" Sal said with a big smile.

"He'll be here at 7am tomorrow and we'll be pulling the RV out of the driveway no later than 8am, so get your shit together and be ready." We all laughed, as we knew the only person that won't have his shit together is Sal.

Chapter Two

Who needs an alarm clock when a five-year old is around? It was 6am on the nose and Hannah was making her rounds waking everyone up. I thought my days were over sleeping on the floor, but Nolan and Frank scored the spare bedrooms and I wasn't about to risk sleeping on Sal's pullout couch with that damn bar poking into my back all night. So, a pillow, a blanket and the carpet in the family room is where I landed. I hope my accommodations get better as the trip progresses.

"Wow, Katie is that bacon I smell?"

"No, Nolan, I think that's your cologne," Katie started the day with a zinger.

"Whoa, one point Katie!" Frank yells. "Nol', I bet you can't wait to get outta here!"

It sounded like a Mack truck pulled up in front of Sal's house and then the horn blared. It must have pissed off the neighbors at 6:45am on a Saturday morning. This was no RV, this was a condo on wheels. Sal wasn't kidding, he came through on this one. This thing looked just like the cruiser that John Madden drives around in.

"Yes, it's time boys!" Sal shouted. "Anthony has arrived."

"Who's Anthony?" I asked.

"He's my next door neighbor, dumb ass," Sal said sarcastically. "The driver man, who else did you think I was talking about?"

Come to think of it, it was a stupid question.

We all couldn't help ourselves. We needed to take a closer look at this thing. As we made our way down the driveway all of the sudden the hydraulics lowered and the RV's door swung open. What an appropriate introduction for Anthony as we'd find out that he is as full of life as anyone we'd ever meet and even this RV was too small for his personality. This was the perfect way for him to enter our lives.

"Fellas, fellas, fellas, your man Anthony is here and ready for a helluva time!"

"Anthony, this is Nolan, Kevin and Frank," Sal made the introductions.

Not only was his personality big, the man was gigantic. 6'6", at least 300 lbs. He was even heavier when he was playing college ball at Ole Miss. He was drafted by the San Francisco 49ers as an offensive lineman, but his career only lasted one season. He was cut during training camp of the following season and never got picked up by another team and decided to hang them up. His line mate at Ole Miss was a guy you probably heard of, Michael Oher. If that doesn't ring a bell, think of the movie *The Blind Side* with Sandra Bullock. Yep, now you remember who I'm talking about. Well, Anthony's career didn't quite work out like Mr. Oher's, but that's life I guess.

"Ready to take a look inside?" Anthony asked as he laughed at his own silly question.

Anthony led the way into the cruiser. You could tell that he enjoyed the role of tour guide. As we walked up the steps, some, what I believe was friendly pushing and shoving ensued. Yes, four adult men in their forties were pushing and shoving their way into this mammoth vehicle to get the first look.

"OK, so this is the main cabin. You have your couches, dining area, satellite TV's, refrigerator, cook top and of course, we're Wi-Fi equipped," Anthony proclaimed proudly as if he had built this thing.

"Now, check this out." Anthony pushed a button and both sides of the cruiser began to expand. My first apartment after graduation wasn't this big!

"Let the games begin!" Nolan had found his way into the refrigerator and cracked open the first beer of the day. Of course, he didn't need to twist our arms. He passed Sal, Frank and I a cold one and the tour continued.

"Good move, you can bring those along with you on the rest of the tour," Anthony continued to the back of the cruiser.

"Before we show you the sleeping quarters, we need to stop right here and lay down some ground rules." Anthony pointed to the toilet on our left.

"Who's used a chemical toilet before?"

All of us nodded.

"Well, then you know what a pain in the ass it is to empty these things, right?" Frank started to answer, but quickly realized that it was a rhetorical question.

"Here's the rule: #1 only. Don't go taking any shits in here, alright? You need to shit, you tell Anthony and Anthony will pull this bad boy over and find a facility for you to shit in, clear? Good, now let's move on."

"I'm not sure how you fellas decided on whose getting which room, but we've got a few options for you to argue over. Here are the two bunks and the smaller bed."

Anthony pointed out the inferior options before the big reveal.

"Now get ready for your first argument of the trip."

Anthony opened the door to the master suite to reveal the room that we all wanted, but knew only one of us would get. What a palace, nicer than a lot of hotel rooms I've stayed in. Huge bed, sitting area, private bathroom, flat screen TV. Yep, there was going to be a fight.

"Now, ya'll can arm wrestle or something to figure out who's getting this room, but my vote is for the single guy," Anthony high fived Nolan.

"Anthony, let me give you some free advice. The douche bag you just high fived can't be trusted. You'll be much better off staying clear of his bullshit. He's not single, although he probably will be once this trip is over," Sal quickly set the record straight.

"You met the guy five minutes ago and you already had time to lie to him and tell him you're single, you're amazing," Frank laughed at Nolan's uncanny ability.

"If the man tells me he's single, the man is single in my eyes. You can all be single on this trip for all I care. What happens on this cruiser stays on this cruiser. Anthony will be keeping his mouth shut, so have at it fellas and maybe throw some crumbs Anthony's way every now and then." Anthony let out a big belly laugh and headed back to the front of the cruiser and down the stairs chuckling the whole way. It was time to leave.

We all said our goodbyes to Katie and Hannah. The big diesel engine hummed and Anthony pulled away. As we headed west from Atlanta I took in the moment. The four of us just sitting in the cruiser joking, laughing and seeming as though we didn't have a care in the world. It wasn't difficult to figure out that this trip was a much needed break for all of us. We could all feel a calming sense of relief.

I brought up the idea to take this trip five years ago. I figured the twenty-year anniversary of the original trip and our graduation was a good enough excuse to get together and do it again, but I'm shocked that we pulled it off. Considering my circumstances, the timing couldn't be better. These three guys mean the world to me and I'd do anything for them and vice versa. As one could imagine, I look at life a lot different now. I can't help but feel that someone pushed a button and the countdown to my death has now begun. I realize that is very morbid, not to mention depressing, but it is my reality. I suppose as soon as we're born our countdown officially begins, but this is different, knowing that time is expiring at a rapid pace is humbling. I was always very healthy. I took care of myself by exercising, going to the doctor and taking vitamins. I felt like I was invincible which is why I'm struggling with the acceptance of this disease. The emotions that run through me are difficult to manage. At one moment I have a positive attitude feeling like I'm down, but not out. Then I switch to anger and the "this isn't fair and why me?" The most challenging emotion is guilt. Leaving my wife Lisa and my girls is inexcusable. I'll beat myself up over and over on that one. I will have let them down. As a father and a husband I'm supposed to be the rock. Everyone experiences failures throughout their lifetimes, but I can't help but thinking that my actual *life* is a failure itself. Leaving the world at forty-three can't be looked at as a success, can it?

I signed up for facebook, I guess it was about six years ago now. I'd describe myself as a regular viewer, but a rare "poster". I wonder how many people that are on Facebook feel like all of their "friends" are actual friends? I think I have about 300 "friends" on Facebook, but I'd say about five of them are my honest to goodness true friends and three of those five are sitting with me right now.

The rest I would classify as acquaintances. Nice to keep in touch with, but that's about it.

Nolan and I met during our sophomore year at Florida State. He's always been one of those "captivating" guys. What I mean is that he always had a group of people around him listening to every word he was saying and taking it all in. People liked to listen to him whether you agreed with what he was saying or not. His big personality, good looks and his status as a varsity athlete went a long way for him in college. He's always been a player and I can't recall him ever being faithful to one of his girlfriends, or wives for that matter, as long as I've known him. Yes, that is a big fault of his, but as a friend he has been amazing to me and I've managed to overlook that part of his life. Maybe that's wrong, but that's how I've chosen to handle his infidelities. No, it's not me abiding to the "guy code", it's just the feeling that at the end of the day it's none of my business. I've tried to persuade him in the past to go down a different path, but the guy is who he is and won't be changing anytime soon.

I'll never forget the day I met Frank. It was also our sophomore year. At about 9:30am on a Saturday morning a knocking was heard at the front door of the apartment that Sal and I were living in at the time. Now, remember, 9:30am for college students is way too early for someone to be knocking on our door. I stumbled out of bed and opened the door to find Frank standing there with a big grin on his face. He was campaigning for Student Government Vice President. He handed me a flyer and began his campaign pitch. It took about two sentences before I closed the door in his face.

Yep, that's how we met, although an official introduction never took place. Little did I know that Frank and I had a number of mutual friends. Turns out that Frank was "All World" in Tampa where he grew up. A bunch of my fraternity brothers went to high school in Tampa and the next week when Frank showed up to one of our rush parties he was immediately given a pledge pin. Frank ended up winning that election and became "All World" at Florida State too. If they handed out "most popular" or "most likely to succeed" awards at Florida State, he would have been the hands down choice. What's funny is that I never told Frank about our meeting where I slammed the door in his face. Some things are better left unsaid.

Sal was eleven years old when he and his family moved from New Orleans to South Florida. He and I met just a few days after he moved in. We were on the same baseball team and we've been friends ever since. We grew up in what was a small town at the time, Coral Springs. It was a great suburb just outside of Ft. Lauderdale. I keep using the past tense because Coral Springs has changed so much. When we grew up there were only about 20,000 people living there, now there is over 100,000. No longer does it have the small town feel, but it was a great place for Sal and I to grow up. It's astonishing as to how much time Sal and I have spent together. We went to middle school, high school and college together. He's almost like a brother to me, not just a friend. We've shared so much over the years. Like the time we went on a double date together. The double date happened to be the first time that Sal and I actually went on a date with a girl. We still laugh about it to this day.

We were both so nervous. My mom dropped us off at the movie theater and we met the girls, Jodi and Sarah, yes, I still remember their names. I still don't understand the idea of movie dates. What a great way to get to know someone, sit in silence for two hours. Honestly, Sal and I had our sights set on something else at that movie theater. Yes, we were two little pigs. The big question was whether we'd get to first base or even better, how about second base? The reality was that we barely even got up to bat. Sal got the furthest by putting his arm around Sarah and I, quite the Casanova, managed to hold Jodi's hand, but I couldn't even manage that maneuver until the last five minutes of the movie. Nothing like two sweaty palms coming together, now that's love. Sal and I have so many little stories like that. There's nothing that we don't know about each other, well except for one thing, but I'll drop that bombshell on him when the time is right.

The first day of our trip was coming to a close. It was a pretty simple day of traveling, but a fun one nonetheless. We decided to stop in Memphis for the night.

"This is a good stopping point for us, plus I'm starving." Sal gave our Memphis stop his seal of approval.

"I know of an awesome barbeque place that I went to a few years ago," Frank suggested.

"Is it Red's?" Nolan asked.

"Yep, that's it, you've been there?" Frank replied.

"No, but I've heard about it from a few guys I do business with in this area, they said it is an institution, been around for almost a hundred years I think," Nolan said with enthusiasm as he's always been a big fan of barbeque.

Red's has been around for ninety-eight years and has only had two owners. Red, the original owner, passed away in the 60's and unfortunately, his children didn't want to take over the business and it changed hands. The "new" owner, who has owned the restaurant for just over fifty years, still shows up every day even though he is in his 80's. His kids do most of the work now, but "Big Pete" makes his rounds greeting guests and passing out little "Red's" fire truck toys to the kids. Big Pete isn't "big" by any means, but he comes from a huge family and he is the oldest of twelve. Since he is the big brother to eleven siblings, the name "Big Pete" was born. Eight boys and four girls. Of the eight boys, Pete is the only one that didn't become a firefighter, but he does his part to raise money for local firefighters and he loves passing out those Red's fire trucks to the kids.

"Good evening guys, welcome to Red's, my name is Rick and I'll be helping you out this evening, can I start you off with a drink?" Rick didn't quite fit the bill of the typical server at Red's. He was a young guy, probably working his way through college. The rest of the servers in Red's seemed like they had been around for fifty years. Older ladies that knew the Red's menu and system like the back of their hands. The place operated like a well-oiled machine and boy did they all move fast back in the kitchen. They had to, the place was packed.

"We'll start with a pitcher of beer and that famous cornbread that we've been hearing about." Frank took the lead in ordering since he had been here before.

"I'll get that right out to you and come back for the rest of your order," Rick said.

"OK, thanks Dick," Frank replied.

Rick made his way to the kitchen to retrieve our beer and cornbread.

"Frank, did you just call that dude "Dick"? Sal asked in amazement.

"Yeah, that's his name," Frank said confidently.

"The guy's name is Rick, not Dick, you idiot," Sal said as he laughed.

"He must be in his mid-20's, how many guys in their mid-20's go by "Dick"? I asked Frank.

"The fuck if I know, I thought the guy's name was Dick," Frank was beginning to lose patience with this conversation.

"A guy named Dick in his mid-20's, come on Frank, are you serious?" Sal continued to throw fuel on the fire.

"Let's think about it for a minute. Name the youngest Dick that you know of." I chimed in with what I thought was a legitimate question.

"I don't know, I can't think of anyone named Dick," Frank said, again wishing that this subject would be dropped right away.

"There's Dick Clark," Nolan contributed to the conversation. "And he's almost a hundred years old, right?"

"I thought he was dead, right?" Sal asked.

"Dick Cavet, that's another one and I'm pretty sure he's dead too," I said.

"Alright, alright, I get it, now can we drop it?" Frank was finished with this conversation.

Rick came back to the table with our beer and cornbread to find all of us, except Frank, laughing hysterically.

"Hey, Rick, our friend here owes you an apology," Nolan turned up the heat on Frank with the goal of embarrassing the shit out of him. It was working.

"You did notice that when you were walking away, Frank here called you Dick, not Rick, right?" Sal asked Rick knowing that there was no way he didn't hear his name get butchered by Frank.

"I did, but honestly guys, it's not a big deal," Rick said convincingly.

Laughter erupted at the table all at the expense of Frank.

Rick took it in stride and laughed at Frank with us. He was a good sport.

"Yep, I guess there just aren't any young Dicks anymore," Nolan capped off our little immature regression with a final exclamation point that had the entire table rolling, even Frank.

Chapter Three

Like usual, I woke up earlier than everyone else.
Surprisingly, I didn't have a hangover. I consider
that an accomplishment as I usually over do it on
the first night of any vacation and end up paying for
it for the rest of the trip. I have a feeling the others
won't be so lucky. I stayed away from the tequila
shots, but Frank, Sal and Nolan just couldn't resist.

I could hear Nolan walking around in the master
suite. Yes, he scored the big bedroom. He usually
gets his way. I opened his door slowly as I wasn't
sure if he had any company.

"Just you in there Nol'?" I whispered, as I didn't
want to wake up Frank and Sal.

"Unfortunately, yes." A dejected Nolan replied.
Apparently last night didn't turn out as he had
planned.

"How you feelin'?" I already knew the answer.

"Fucking hung over, five tequila shots, what the
fuck was I thinking?" Nolan grumbled as he
walked over to the sink to throw some water on his
face.

"Well, snap out of it brother, big day for you
today."

I was implying to the next stop on our trip. We
were heading to Oklahoma City today to visit
Nolan's Kids. He hasn't seen Michael and Megan
for about three years. Michael just turned fourteen

and Megan is about to turn twelve. Nolan's ego usually doesn't allow for nervousness to show through, but it was quite clear that he was terrified about this leg of the trip. He's convinced that Carrie has poisoned the kids and he doesn't expect a warm welcome from them. The reality is that he has poisoned the relationship and can only point the finger in his direction.

"I don't know if we should do this," Nolan said as he fiddled with his watch.

"Come on, it'll be fine, you're their father, it will be good." I tried to reassure Nolan, but truthfully, I didn't have a very good feeling.

"Stop bullshitting me, OK?" Nolan raised his voice as he could see right through me.

"Michael and Megan have no reason to even talk to me. I shut them out of my life just because I can't stand their mother. Now it's too late, I really fucked this up." Nolan said what the three of us already knew. It was his fault and now he has to clean up his mess. I was shocked that he finally admitted it.

"It's not too late, you can fix it. You will, if you love them." Again, I tried to be positive about the situation, but Nolan interrupted me before I could finish as I apparently struck a nerve.

"You know what, everything always has a silver lining with you. You don't live in reality. I fucked this up big time and it will not get better, so stop telling me that it will. I'll go there for this visit, but

you watch what happens, you'll see that it's over."
Nolan once again raised his voice, which pissed me
off as I was only trying to help.

"Believe me, you arrogant prick, I live in reality,
more than you'll ever know." Part of me wanted to
put him in his place and tell him what I'm going
through, but I stopped short of divulging my big
secret.

Our loud voices eventually woke up Frank and Sal.
Sal walked into the master suite. It wasn't difficult
to figure out emotions between Nolan and I were
running high. I stormed past Sal and headed to the
front of the cruiser to let Anthony know it was time
to go, even if Nolan wasn't mentally ready.

Pancreatic cancer will destroy a person from the
inside out. It's the fourth leading cause of cancer
related death in the United States, but has the
highest mortality rate of all major cancers. 94% of
pancreatic cancer patients will die within five years
of diagnosis while only 6% will survive more than
five years. 75% of patients die within the first year
of diagnosis. Remember, that's what my doc told
me, "maybe a year". After diagnosis with
metastatic disease, which means that the cancer has
spread to other parts of the body, life expectancy is
only three to six months. We caught mine before it
started to spread, but even with that bit of luck, my
prognosis is still grim. This cancer is so deadly
because there are no ways to detect it during the
early stages. Most patients don't even have a
chance to remove the tumor and have to go the
chemotherapy route instead. That's what I'll have
to look forward to when I return from this trip. I'm

terrified of getting chemo, but it's my only chance to hang around a little longer. Notice I didn't say, my only chance to "recover". I'm not trying to be negative, but this disease is a killer and there are no winners. It will get me in the end, but I'll fight the hard fight. I have a feeling the National Cancer Institute feels it is a lost cause to fight this cancer. In 2013, they spent $101.9 million on pancreatic research. While that may sound like a lot, it isn't. The $101.9 million only represented just over 2% of the $4.79 billion cancer research budget for that year. It would seem to me that the disease with the fourth leading cause of cancer related death and the highest mortality rate should get more than 2% of the research budget, but I'm not the one making those decisions. It appears that they've raised the white flag and have the attitude that, hey, no one can beat pancreatic cancer so let's concentrate on other diseases. Tell that to the families that lose their loved ones year after year to this terrible disease.

We were just about an hour away from Oklahoma City. Our day had been very quiet so far. The four of us kept to ourselves for most of this leg of the trip. The newness and the adrenaline of the trip were starting to wear off. Don't get me wrong, we were all still enjoying ourselves, but I think we needed a break from each other. Nolan had been a mess all day and Sal was growing tired of Frank and me playing therapist to him.

"Why are we even stopping in Oklahoma City?" Sal broke about a four-hour silence with a question that he knew would create a stir.

"What?" Nolan said in an angry tone.

"Yeah, why are we doing this? This trip is supposed to be a good time, not some fucking crusade to make everyone feel better about their lives." Sal crossed the line.

Nolan stood up and walked over to Sal. Frank and I popped up out of our seats as it looked as though Nolan was going to get physical with Sal.

"You mother fucker, who do you think you are?" Nolan shouted in Sal's face as the two of them bumped chests.

"What are you gonna do Nol'? You gonna swing on me? What a fucking surprise, go ahead I'm not afraid of you. Your money can't back you up on this one." Sal was always jealous of the success that Nolan has achieved throughout the years, so the money reference didn't surprise us at all.

All of the sudden the cruiser came to a screeching halt on the side of the highway. It startled us and Frank even fell down. As I helped Frank back to his feet Anthony barreled his way back to where the confrontation was taking place in the cruiser. The look on his face combined with the sheer size of this man scared the shit out of all of us. Anthony was determined to take charge of this situation before it escalated into a full out fight between two best friends. He grabbed Sal by the front of his shirt with his right hand and then grabbed Nolan by the same place on his shirt with his left hand. He lifted, yes lifted, both of them off of their feet and set them straight.

"You wanna fight, do ya?" Anthony shouted at both Sal and Nolan while he held them in the air.

"How about this, swing on me mother fuckers! We'll see how that ends up." Anthony dropped both of them onto the couches on each side of the cruiser.

I'd pay a lot of money for a video of that scene. We were all in shock. First of all, to witness one man pick up two men that weigh over 250 pounds each was stunning. Then, what the hell was our bus driver doing? This is a guy we hired and he was threatening to beat us up? No one said it right then, but we were grateful that Anthony stepped in. Yes, he may have overstepped his bounds, but we were headed for a disaster. Nolan and Sal were going to come to blows and Frank and I never would have stopped it from happening.

Anthony started up the cruiser and we were back on the road. A quiet, uneventful day had just turned into a tense one and we weren't out of the woods yet. I'm afraid this stop in Oklahoma City may be the tipping point for Nolan.

When Carrie learned of Nolan's infidelities Michael was just six years old and Megan was four. Nolan was on a flight back to Nashville from New York. When he arrived home he found a note taped to his personal laptop that he had mistakenly left at home. Carrie had always been suspicious and what she found on the laptop confirmed everything. The note she left for Nolan was pretty simple: "Have a nice life and thanks for ruining ours". To top it off,

Carrie had just picked up the family photos they had taken a couple of weeks ago. She left a photo for Nolan. They all looked perfect. A beautiful family, but Nolan had destroyed it. Nolan still carries that photo with him. The edges are a little worn now, kind of like Nolan.

Chapter Four

There was no rhyme or reason as to why Carrie ended up in Oklahoma City. She didn't choose to live there because she had family or friends there. She was so distraught when she found out about the affair that she just grabbed the kids, jumped in the car and headed west. She aspired to make it further than Oklahoma City, but it never happened and they've been there ever since. Carrie has bounced around from admin job to admin job. Nolan has robbed her of her self-esteem and she has become a very bitter woman. She makes waves at every company that hires her and eventually they just let her go. She's held her current job for about five months. AWS & Sons Electrical is where she goes every morning to serve as their admin/receptionist. She makes about $35,000 a year (if she can make it a full year). Raising two kids on that salary is almost impossible and the only help Nolan has offered has been the court ordered child support payment, which is minimal. Carrie regrets not pushing for more, but she did not want Nolan to get custody of the kids, so she settled for the smaller child support payment in return for full custody. She knew Nolan could have dragged the battle through the courts forever if he wanted to and that would have only hurt the kids more. Michael and Megan are what keep her going every day. She'll do anything for them and to her credit, she's raised a couple of great kids.

"Kevin, help me out and grab a couple of these." Nolan motioned over to the closet in his room where I found three gift-wrapped boxes.

I grabbed two of the boxes and had to chuckle a little bit as it was obvious that Nolan had wrapped them himself. There was tape everywhere, what a mess.

"Alright, I got 'em. Wrap these yourself, did ya Nol'?" I couldn't resist.

As we piled out of the cruiser Nolan had one last thing to say to us.

"If this isn't going well, be ready to leave."

Carrie rented a small two-bedroom house in a decent neighborhood. I'd say it was a little over 1,000 square feet. Nolan's closet in Nashville was about 900 square feet and no, I'm not kidding. Sophie loved to mention how big their closet is when talking about their palace and she actually knew the square footage.

Nolan led the way as the four of us walked up the driveway to the front door. No one said a word as Nolan rang the doorbell.

"Hi guys," Carrie looked straight through Nolan and gave Sal, Frank and I a big smile.

"Nolan," Carrie then acknowledged that Nolan was there with a small head nod.

It had been at least eight years since Frank and I had seen Carrie. She looked better than I thought she would look. I know how stressful this situation has been for her and my expectations weren't very high, but I'll give her credit, she's kept herself looking pretty darn good. Sal had seen her a couple of years ago when he was in Oklahoma City on business. At that time, he said she looked great, but I assumed he was just being friendly in saying that. I guess my assumption was wrong.

"So, how's the boys' trip been so far, you're not ready to kill each other already are you?" Carrie knew us well enough to understand that there would be a few arguments along the way and of course, she was right.

"Not yet, give us a couple more days," Frank replied as convincingly as he could. Little did Carrie know that this stop of the trip had been the source of all of our angst.

"Have a seat," Carrie motioned to the family room. The family room served as her bedroom as well. She's been sleeping on the pullout couch for a couple of years now. She didn't think it was right for Michael and Megan to continue sharing a room anymore. Michael is about to become a teenager and sharing a room with his sister wasn't appropriate.

"Where are the kids Carrie?" Nolan said in a demanding tone of voice.

Carrie glared at him as she thought to herself, "oh, now he cares where they are, unlike the last three years".

"Megan is in her bedroom and Michael will be home for dinner."

"Michael isn't here?" Nolan stated the obvious as Carrie just told him that he'd be home for dinner, but that wasn't the point.

"He'll be home for dinner," Carrie emphasized.

Nolan looked over to me shaking his head and mumbled under his breath, "he'll be home for dinner, bullshit."

Things were just about to get heated between Carrie and Nolan and then Megan appeared from the hallway.

"Hi Dad," she said as she walked over to Nolan. No longer was Nolan "Daddy", just "Dad" now. That was the first time Megan had ever called him "Dad" instead of "Daddy", it hurt.

"Hi Sweetie!" Nolan beamed as he saw his little girl, rushed over and gave her a big hug.

"Oh, I've missed you so much," Nolan said as he continued his bear hug on Megan and lifted her in the air.

"Come on Dad, put me down." It was clear that Megan was a little overwhelmed with Nolan's affection. It's hard to blame her. She hadn't seen Nolan in three years and it was awkward to have him try to pick up where he left off like nothing was wrong, but I guess that was all Nolan could do right now.

Megan said hello to the rest of us and took a seat on the floor in the family room. Over the next couple of hours we sat and talked about old times. We had some fun reminiscing about our college days and Megan insisted that we share a few stories about her mom and dad.

Carrie and Nolan met while we were all at Florida State. Sal introduced the two of them during our junior year. Nolan, who had never committed himself to one girl in college, fell hard for Carrie right away. It was out of character for Nolan, but he recognized the connection he had with Carrie and went with it. Carrie fell equally as hard for Nolan and the two were inseparable for the remainder of our college days. They were the first couple to get married out of all of our college friends. I remember that wedding like it was yesterday. What a blast. So many marriages end up in divorce, but I never thought it would happen to Nolan and Carrie. They seemed like the perfect fit for one another. Everything was running along so smoothly for them. After their wedding they moved to New York where Nolan began his promising financial career and Carrie landed a job with a public relations firm. They were two young professionals living in New York City and soaking up every minute of the excitement that the city has to offer. Nolan worked long hours as he was establishing himself in the industry, but with all of that work, the play definitely followed. Living in the city can be intoxicating. It's a different way of life that doesn't work for everyone, but Nolan and Carrie embraced it. Michael was born about six years later and they decided it was time to move out of the city. Nolan landed a job in Nashville and that's where they started their family. Megan came along two years later.

Unfortunately, the great life that they had established would begin to unravel. As Nolan's career took off arrogance came along with it. I remember visiting him and Carrie in Nashville just after Megan was born. It was clear that Nolan had changed. He was slowly turning into one of those pompous assholes that make sure they put everyone in their place by bragging about their successes, money and material items. It was difficult to even have a meaningful conversation with him. If he wasn't gloating about his work, he was showing me the newest toy he had purchased for himself. If I recall correctly, his new toy at that time was the Bentley he had just picked up. He's probably been through at least fifty cars since. The most shocking change in Nolan had to do with his infidelities. No, Sophie wasn't in the picture back then, but Nolan was in the middle of another fling or flings. He traveled to New York so much that he kept an apartment there. It made it so easy for him to establish a separate life and he proceeded to do so. He never wore his wedding ring while he was there and acted like a single guy. While he was in New York he carried on as though his family in Nashville didn't exist. He had girlfriends, yes plural. He'd go out on dates, bring different girls back to the apartment and spend lavishly on these women. Sometimes he would reveal that he was married and sometimes he wouldn't. Some of the girls cared and others didn't as they were just along for the ride. Hanging around "New York Nolan" was a blast for them. It was like he had an alter ego, but unfortunately "New York Nolan" was destroying everything "Nashville Nolan" had built and it was only a matter of time before his life with Carrie and the kids imploded.

I still feel guilty to this day that I never said anything to Carrie about what Nolan had revealed to me regarding his playboy status in New York. I struggled with it often and Lisa and I got into multiple arguments about it. She felt that I should tell Carrie how Nolan was behaving while in New York. I was torn and I eventually chose to keep my mouth shut. I knew Nolan would slip up and sure enough he did. When Carrie found the evidence about Sophie on Nolan's laptop her heart sunk. Not necessarily because of the relationship she uncovered between her husband and Sophie, but all of the sudden everything fell into place. She began to think about a few odd occurrences over the years and realized at that moment that Nolan had been playing her for a fool. It was an instant, irreparable shot to Carrie's self-esteem. She had been nothing but a great wife and mother to their children. She worked so hard to make sure everyone was happy and Nolan simply took it for granted. So many emotions went through her head the moment she put all of the pieces together. Embarrassment, anger and then just pure sadness. All of those emotions led to irrational thoughts. Carrie didn't know what to do, therefore she ran. She grabbed as much as she could from the house, placed the kids in the SUV and got on the highway and started heading west. She was a complete mess, but held it together as best as she could in front of the kids. There were many times during the drive that she thought about turning around, but she knew she had nothing to go back to. The kids were with her and that's all she cared about. That's how she landed in Oklahoma

City. It was about as far as she could mentally and physically make it. She was drained and figured that Oklahoma City was as good as any other place to start a new life. Now, eight years later, the man that caused her so much pain was sitting on her couch trying to be "Daddy" again. It infuriated her.

The front door opened and Michael walked in. Michael was at that awkward age where his voice was starting to change, a bit of acne was developing and he had that funny peach fuzz, flavor-saver mustache going. His hair was just about shoulder length, which drove Nolan crazy, but not as much as the earrings that Carrie let him get a few weeks ago.

Nolan got up and made his way over to Michael. As he was going in for a hug, Michael's hand came forward. A handshake was all Nolan would be receiving. Nolan obliged, as he felt a little awkward as well. Michael wasn't a little kid anymore, he was a teenager that could look Nolan right in the eye. The height differential between the two was no longer. It wouldn't be long until Michael shot past Nolan and would be looking down on him, although it had been a long time since he had looked up to him at all anyway.

"Hey Dad, nice bus," Michael couldn't miss the cruiser out front that was about the same size of his house.

"Yep, thank your Uncle Sal for that one." Nolan acknowledged Sal's good deed for the trip.

"You own that Uncle Sal?" Michael said in disbelief.

"No, Michael, we just rented it for the trip. We'll show you around later tonight, it's very cool, you'll like it," Sal threw out the invite to take a tour of the cruiser.

"Alright, time to eat," Carrie called out from the kitchen. She had prepared a huge tray of lasagna and some sausage and peppers. The feast reminded us of the ones she used to serve in college, no doubt it was going to be fantastic.

During dinner the awkwardness that existed amongst Nolan, Carrie, Michael and Megan began to subside. There was a sense of relief around the table, for everyone. It ended up being a very enjoyable and relaxing dinner, not the verbal slugfest that we all anticipated.

On school nights the kids usually go to bed at 9:30pm, but Carrie gave the OK to allow them to stay up a little later tonight since their dad was in town.

"Michael, Megan, come on, let's go take a look at the cruiser," Nolan motioned to his kids to follow him out the front door. Sal got up and started walking with them and Nolan gave him a look indicating that he would be touring the kids around on his own. Sal got the point and did an about-face.

It had been a long time since Nolan had spent "alone time" with Michael and Megan. Of course, a fifteen-minute tour of the cruiser doesn't scream quality time, but at this point Nolan would take anything.

Nolan popped open the door to the cruiser. In preparation for the tour he had asked Anthony to "disappear" and he went for a walk to give Nolan a few private moments with the kids.

"Wow, this thing is awesome," Michael proclaimed as he took the liberty of the "self-guided" tour route.

"Here, check this out," Nolan pushed the magic button and the walls of the cruiser began to expand.

"Can you drive like this?" Megan asked.

"No sweetie, it will only work when you're parked like we are now," Nolan explained.

The two kids bounced around the cruiser with excitement, opening every door, cabinet and drawer. Megan even made her way to the driver's seat and acted like she was driving the mammoth vehicle. She even laid down on the horn for a couple of long honks.

Now, while Nolan was enjoying the time he was spending with his kids alone, his motive for getting them out of the house wasn't to show them the cruiser. He felt that he needed to speak to them privately and explain the circumstances that led their once happy family down this path.

"Check out your dad's room," Nolan led the way to his master suite.

Michael and Megan looked around for a bit and then jumped on the bed. Nolan pulled up a chair. This moment had gone through his mind for weeks now. He wondered what he would say, how the kids would take it and if he could hold it together during the conversation.

"I'm so happy we're together right now," Nolan started off.

"Uh oh, are you getting serious on us now Dad?" Michael asked as the atmosphere in the room quickly changed from light and fun to downright serious.

"Just give me a few minutes, this is important," Nolan pleaded for some time to share his thoughts.

"I know I haven't been a good father and I'm disappointed in myself more than you'll ever know," Nolan said as Michael and Megan started to squirm, as they knew this wouldn't be a comfortable situation.

"I love the two of you so much and unfortunately, I haven't shown it over the years. I allowed differences between your mom and me to get in the way of us, but truthfully, I'm the one responsible, not your mom. I've failed you as a father and I failed your mom as a husband. All I can do now is try to make amends with the three of you to the best of my ability," Nolan's eyes began to tear up, but he fought them back.

Megan sat there quietly, but Michael couldn't resist the opportunity to ask his father a simple, but complex question.

"Why, Dad, why?" Michael looked into his father's eyes as he also tried to hold back tears.

"I wish I had a great answer to that question, but I don't," Nolan wiped away a tear that had managed to escape down his cheek.

"Well, it hurt us and will always hurt. You have your new family and you completely forgot about us," Michael's voice cracked as the conversation hit a new level of tension.

Nolan looked at both of his kids. Megan was still silent, but her face was covered in tears. It was clear that mentally and emotionally Michael was well beyond his years. He sat up straight and didn't let a tear fall as he awaited a response from Nolan.

"All I can tell you is that people make mistakes in life. I'm not proud of how I've handled this and you both deserve better," Nolan responded by simply telling the truth.

"I never meant to hurt either of you or your mom and I'm sorry for any pain that I have caused. There is not a day that goes by that I don't think about the two of you. If I could go back and fix it, I would, but all I can do now is try to repair what I've broken," Nolan began pacing back and forth.

"I'm in no position to ask for favors from either of you, but I'm going to do it anyway. Please listen to your mom and do everything she tells you. She knows what she's doing and will guide you through everything that you will face in life. I owe her so much for raising the two of you as well as she has. I'm sure you don't think she's perfect all of the time, but let me tell you that she is as close to perfect as any person will get. She'll always put you guys first and will be there for you. I know you'll give her the respect she deserves, don't do what I did. I love you both, thanks for listening to me go on and on. Let's get back inside." Nolan pulled Michael and Megan up from the bed and to his surprise they both clutched him tightly and gave him a big hug. No, things were far from being back to "normal", but right now, he felt better than he had in years.

Sal, Frank and I were in the family room enjoying some wine with Carrie when Nolan and the kids came in from outside. While the three of them had smiles on their faces, it was clear that some crying had taken place.

"So, what did you think, pretty cool, right?" Sal asked the kids.

"Awesome, Uncle Sal, awesome," Michael beamed.

"How come Daddy got the big room?" Megan asked innocently enough.

The four us got a kick out of the question and laughed about it and then Frank provided an answer for Megan.

"Your dad snores too loud, so we made him sleep in there," Frank wasn't going to share the true reason as to why her father commandeered the big bedroom.

It was about 10:30pm, an hour past the kids' bedtime. Of course, the kids wanted to stay up later, but Carrie put her foot down and they finally gave in. Nolan volunteered to put each of them to bed, as he hadn't done it in years. After about ten minutes he strolled back into the family room with a very satisfied look on his face. He felt pretty good about the visit so far. He had feared disaster, but so far he had avoided any big meltdowns.

"Great kids Carrie, great kids," Nolan said as he rejoined the group in the family room.

"I'm proud of them and I know you are too," Carrie's response indicated that she was letting her guard down a little bit with Nolan or maybe it was just the wine talking.

Frank gave me a nudge and I got the hint.

"We've killed three bottles of wine and that's all I can handle, don't open up another one, I'm calling it a night," I said as I made my way over to Carrie to give her a kiss good night.

Frank and Sal followed suit and we headed out to the cruiser.

"You have some great friends there Nol'," Carrie said as she made her way back into the family room after locking the front door.

"I know, I'm surrounded by a lot of great people," Nolan's emotional night was about to continue.

"Nolan, there are times that I want to ring your neck, but for some reason I can't let go of the old Nolan that I loved before your life got way too complicated," Carrie knew the wine had gotten the best of her, but she felt she had to get this off her chest.

"You don't know how often I wish I could go back and do it all over again. Most of my life has been filled with regrets," Nolan slumped back into the couch.

"Me too, we had it pretty good back then, didn't we?" Carrie leaned forward and placed her hand on Nolan's knee.

"I'm so sorry, I'm so sorry." Nolan finally broke down. His emotions had been running at an all-time high and he couldn't take it anymore. He grabbed Carrie's hand, pulled her in and clutched her tightly.

Carrie was right and Nolan had known it for years. He's never loved anyone like he loved Carrie. He had a wonderful woman and a beautiful family. His ego and greed ruined it.

I woke up around 5am the next morning. I'd like to say I was up because of my usual early bird tendencies, but unfortunately that wasn't the case. I felt ill and as much as I was hoping it was due to the wine, it wasn't. Recently, I've been having a hard time keeping my food down which has led to one of two scenarios: I either throw up or I simply don't eat. Of course, I couldn't resist Carrie's lasagna last night, therefore, I'm hugging the toilet this morning. So far, this disease is playing out exactly the way my doctor told me it would. I'm feeling very weak, sick to my stomach and not as mentally sharp as I should be. Now, should I have gone on this trip? Absolutely not, but this trip was planned way before my diagnosis and there wasn't a chance I was going to cancel it. It means more to me now to be a part of this than ever. I know what's waiting for me when I return. Doctor's offices, chemo and the part I fear the most, I need to sit down with Lisa and the girls and share this terrible news with them. Our family is about to go through something that I wouldn't wish on my worst enemy. I still can't wrap my head around that part of it. My illness is going to change their lives in a way that just isn't fair. I know I need to be strong when I share the news with them, but I just don't know if I can do it. I've played the conversation out in my head over and over again. As I've gone through these "mental dress rehearsals", two outcomes are certain: My face is covered in tears and the cancer continues to destroy my insides. I'm afraid that the dress rehearsals are indicative of what the live performance will look like and that breaks my heart.

"Whoa, we have the first yakking of the trip!" Sal screams out as he sees me on the floor in the bathroom.

"Yep, a little too much wine for me last night," I lied.

"Who?" Frank yells out from his bunk.

"Kevin is a light weight. Apparently he had a little too much vino last night," Sal relayed the information back to Frank.

"Pussy!" Frank said with a chuckle.

I wouldn't have expected a different response from either of them. That's how it always was. If you puked, you heard about it for the entire next day or until the next person lost their lunch. That will happen soon enough, it always does. I'll be off the hook sooner or later.

"Why are you two up so early?" I asked with amazement as both of these guys can sleep until noon when they don't have kids or wives around to bother them.

"I really wanted to see the sunrise this morning," Sal sarcastically replied.

"Kevin, I think your puking may have woken up the entire neighborhood. Jesus Christ, it sounded like you were giving birth out of your mouth. Are you the proud father of a little lasagna baby?" Frank provided a little bit more detail than was necessary.

"OK, I get it, why don't you two just go back to bed," I was finished with this conversation.

Sure enough, they both went back to bed. I tried to, but wasn't able to. Nolan usually rises early, so I went to his door and nudged it open slightly to see if he was awake. To my surprise, no one was in the room. The first thought that went through my head

was, uh oh, did he sleep with Carrie last night?
This visit was going so well and it would be just
like Nolan to go and screw it up by doing something
like that.

10am rolled around and I was bored out of my
mind. When were these guys going to wake up?
The door to the cruiser began to open slowly. It
was Nolan who appeared to be sneaking back in.

"Hey, where the hell were you last night?" I
whispered as Nolan shut the door behind him.

"I fell asleep on the couch," Nolan stated in an
obvious tone.

I wasn't buying that and I followed Nolan into his
room to get the true story.

"Come on, give me the real scoop, what happened?"
I knew it wasn't any of my business, but my
nosiness took over.

"I told you, I fell asleep on the couch. You know
how much wine we drank. I guess you could define
it as passing out, not falling asleep, but that was it,"
Nolan actually sounded convincing.

"I saw the way the two of you were getting along.
Your ass would have been in here with us if you
weren't up to something," I continued to press for
more information.

"OK, OK, close the door. I'll tell you, but I don't
want the two of them to know anything. Got it?"
Nolan was prepared to spill the beans."

"Of course," I would have said anything at that point to have him continue.

"Like you said, we were getting along great. We really had a good conversation about the past and I feel like I was able to make amends for a lot of what I've done. Of course, one conversation doesn't fix everything, but it went really well." The expression on Nolan's face told the whole story, he was very content.

"OK, then what?" I prodded him to continue, as I knew this was just the beginning of the story.

"We spent a lot time talking about the kids and their future. I assured Carrie that I'd do a better job moving forward, you know, keeping in touch, sending money, and visiting, all of that kind of stuff."

Nolan sounded like a new man, but I knew better. I've known him for way too long and when he is up to something, I can sniff it out from a mile away. Then the other shoe dropped.

Nolan headed toward the door of his room to go wake up the others and turned to me with a big smile and said, "Then we had sex on the couch, man she's still got it, dirty, nasty sex. I'm surprised you guys didn't hear us, or the kids for that matter".

My jaw hit the floor. On one hand I wanted to laugh, but on the other I was disgusted. He almost sucked me in. For a minute there, I thought I was seeing the new and improved Nolan, but he's just the same douche bag that he's been for a long time. What a dick.

The four of us walked back into Carrie's house to find a breakfast feast waiting for us. Pancakes, omelets, sausage, bacon, hash browns and grits, you name it, it was on the table. We also found Carrie with a non-stop grin on her face. She was beaming. Yes, the look of a satisfied woman that probably hadn't been with a man in awhile, but also a woman that was probably played. Who knows what else Nolan told her last night. Knowing him, he said whatever it took including telling her that he would leave Sophie and start over with her and the kids.

"Good morning Carrie," Nolan said as he walked over and gave her a peck on the lips which everyone saw and immediately looked at one another with "what the hell was that" expressions on their faces.

To our surprise, Michael and Megan were sitting on the couch watching TV.

"Playing hooky today, are we?" Frank asked the two kids whose eyes were glued to the television.

Carrie answered for them, "Yep, I figured they could have the day off since their dad was in town."

"Dad, when do we get to open our presents?" Megan asked.

"Not yet, you can open them later today," Nolan motioned to Carrie for approval.

The morning quickly turned into the afternoon. Everyone, except for me, was full thanks to Carrie's phenomenal feast. I decided to sit this one out and surprisingly enough no one noticed that I didn't eat anything for breakfast. They all probably figured I still wasn't feeling well from last night.

It was time for us to get back on the road. Our next stop was Breckenridge, where Nolan has a house. Sal, Frank and I said our goodbyes to Carrie and the kids and headed back out to the cruiser. We left Nolan inside to have a last bit of private time with his "family".

"Oh, I'm going to miss you so much," Nolan grabbed Michael and Megan and combined the group into one big bear hug.

"Daddy, when will you be back?" Megan asked as a tear rolled down her cute little face.

"Soon, baby, soon," Nolan fought back tears himself and also just realized that he was "Daddy" again which brought a huge grin to his face.

The visit had gone much better than he imagined, although, he definitely left the door open with Carrie for some future heartbreak. It was pretty obvious that she believes something more will come out of this visit. I never understood how she continually falls back into her old ways with Nolan. He's treated her like a doormat for such a long time, but she continues to come back to him. It's a shame, as I believe it all comes back to her low self-esteem issues. She's such a strong, talented, beautiful woman, but lacks the confidence to break free from a guy like Nolan that treats her so poorly.

"Carrie, come here," Nolan motioned Carrie over to the family room as the kids stepped into the kitchen.

"I love you and we'll talk more soon," Nolan whispered.

"I'll miss you baby, love you so much," Carrie whispered back as her eyes began to water.

"Open those gifts later on tonight, you'll like what you see, I promise," Nolan said as he made his way to the door.

Carrie, Michael and Megan walked outside with Nolan and watched as he made his way into the cruiser. We didn't say a word as he came inside, but a simple gesture from Sal was all we needed. He gave Nolan a pat on the shoulder and grabbed his arm. Nolan gave Sal eye contact and received a big smile in return. The visit, by all accounts, was a success. Emotional, but successful. Anthony started up the cruiser and the massive engine roared. We rolled away and the big horn blared as we headed for Colorado.

We were about four hours into the trip and not much conversation had ensued, as we all needed a little break from the drama. We were happy that the Oklahoma City visit went well for Nolan, but so far, this wasn't how we had envisioned our vacation. Spending some time at Nolan's place in Colorado should help us feel like we're having some fun.

"Nolan, here, your phone is ringing," Frank handed Nolan his phone.

"Voicemail," Nolan said as he looked at the screen and saw that it was Carrie calling.

"Guys, do me a favor, if Carrie calls any of you, just let it go to voicemail, OK?"

"Why?" Sal asked.

"Because I asked you to, that's why," Nolan shot back.

We all thought that was an odd request and then it became even more strange.

"She's calling me right now." Frank looked at his phone and sent the call to voicemail as requested. "Maybe it's an emergency."

"Look, I know why she is calling and trust me, it's not an emergency," Nolan said.

Just a few minutes later my phone began to ring and sure enough it was Carrie.

"I know, I know, voicemail." I hit the button and Carrie was sent to my voicemail.

"Ah, looks like she's trying another route," Sal's phone vibrated with a text message alert.

"Please tell Nolan to call me right away." Sal read the text out loud.

"Alright, she made her rounds, now can we get back to our trip?" Nolan asked his rhetorical question.

"Sure thing, I'll send her text to voicemail." Sal chuckled, as he knew all he could do is ignore Carrie at this point.

Chapter Five

As the cruiser barreled its way through the open terrain of Kansas, the mood seemed to lighten up with the guys. Our conversation was much more interesting than the scenery. Just open fields to look at as far as the eye could see. The sun was starting to set and it was about time to find a place to eat dinner. We came upon a little town called Colby and decided to give "Peggy's" a try, not that we had much of a choice.

Peggy's was your classic diner. The sign on the front said "Since 1907". The four of us walked in along with Anthony. It was obvious that we weren't from around here, but we were still greeted with a big smile at the counter.

"Five tonight fellas?" A lady with long brown hair in a ponytail wearing a uniform with a big "P" on it asked with a smile.

"That'll do it," Sal responded.

"So where you guys from?" Belinda asked as she sat us down at a table and handed us each a menu.

"Let's see, we have Texas, Florida, Georgia, Tennessee and Mississippi all represented here," Frank gave Belinda the details of where we all came from.

"Wow, I guess that's your big bus out there then, right? When we saw that pull up we thought you were some type of country band on tour or something," Belinda smiled.

"Well, sorry to disappoint, Kenny Chesney won't be joining us for dinner," Frank laughed.

"I'll give you guys a few minutes to look at the menu," Belinda said as she headed back behind the counter.

"Man, if you're gonna blow your nose like that can't you just go to the bathroom?" Sal said to Frank as he slid his chair away from the table.

"Yeah Frank, that's disgusting," I chimed in, as Frank was busy wiping the snot away from his nose.

"What the hell is that you're using?" Nolan asked in disbelief.

"What are you talking about, it's a handkerchief," Frank said.

"A handkerchief?" Sal asked. "What are you, seventy years old?"

"Right, who the hell uses handkerchiefs anymore?" I asked.

"When I need to blow my nose I use a handkerchief, what's wrong with that?" Frank defended himself.

"I'll tell you what's wrong with it. Let's see, you blow your snot into that thing and then you put it back in your pocket, correct?" Sal proceeded to lead us through "handkerchief 101".

"But I," Frank tried to chime in, but Sal kept going.

"Then, when you have to blow your nose again, you pull that disgusting thing out of your pocket, try to find a spot on it that's not filled with snot and then you blow your nose again, right?" Sal said in a question format, but he wasn't looking for an answer from Frank.

"So, when do you actually wash that thing? Do you wait until it is just full of boogers or is there some type of rule, like three blows, then wash or is it four?" Sal was on a roll here and we just let him keep going, as this was amusing to all of us, except Frank.

"Look, people use handkerchiefs all of the time, it's not uncommon," Frank once again defended his use of these nasty little hankies.

"Yeah, I'm sure the handkerchief sales business is just busting through the roof," I said.

"Fuck you all," Frank shot back at us. "Not you Anthony, just these three idiots."

"Speaking of Anthony, let's ask him," Frank was hoping Anthony might back him up on this one.

Anthony paused for a second, made eye contact with each of us around the table and then revealed his thoughts on the situation.

"That mother fuckin thing in your hand is disgusting man. As far as I'm concerned, you may as well be going in to the toilet and wiping your ass with that thing too and shoving it right back in your pocket. I don't have the words man, just plain disgusting. How 'bout doin us all a favor and tossing that thing in the trash right now?"

"And there we have it, a sound response from a sound mind. Atta boy Anthony!" Sal erupted into laughter as his point was made.

We all got a kick out of that little side bar and that's the last we saw of Frank's handkerchief too!

Nolan has owned his house in Breckenridge for about four years. He's used it about four times. It's just another item on a long list of excess for him. The cruiser maneuvered well through the winding roads leading to Nolan's place. Modest for Nolan, only about 5,000 square feet with a four-car garage, which was full and a hot tub along with a heated pool.

"Let's go boys, we're here," Nolan said as he tapped a sleeping Sal on the knee.

It was dark out, but it was easy to tell what a beautiful setting we were in. The tall trees blocked the moon, but the light peeked through the branches and guided us up the walkway to the front door.

As we reached the front porch, Nolan stopped us and said, "Now, check this out".

He guided us around the corner of the wrap-around porch and he didn't have to say another word. As we turned the corner we were greeted by one of the most spectacular views. A break in the trees revealed a moon that was almost full and more stars than any of us had seen in years. The silhouette of the mountains provided the backdrop for this amazing scene. If this was a preview of what the next two days were going to be like then we were all in for a treat.

Nolan led the way into the house through a side door that opened to the kitchen. This gourmet kitchen had it all including granite countertops, oak cabinetry, an old farmhouse sink and all stainless steel, top of the line appliances. Nolan's favorite appliance was the monstrous gas range. He considered himself an executive chef in training and made sure all of the homes he owned had professional appliances. To his credit, he is a pretty good cook.

"Beer, wine, scotch, what'll it be fellas?" Nolan's left hand was pointing to the refrigerator and his right hand to the hallway that led to the bar.

"Why don't we open up a nice bottle of wine," I suggested knowing that Nolan's wine choices would be out of this world.

"Works for me, the cellar is down the hall on the right and then down the stairs. Grab anything you want," Nolan gave me the green light.

"Man, why don't you come here more often?" Sal said as he melted into the leather couch in the family room.

"Seriously, this place is like heaven," Frank agreed with Sal's comment.

"I don't know, time I guess. It always seems like I'm too busy to enjoy this kind of stuff, but you're right, I should come here more often," Nolan responded as if the thought never occurred to him before.

I emerged from the wine cellar with three bottles of wine. Now, I'm not a wine novice, but I have never seen a collection of wine like Nolan's. The cellar was littered with bottles from the 60's and 70's.

"OK, you said 'anything you want', so I grabbed a few bottles," I said as I presented my three choices to the group.

"Let me take a look," Nolan came over to the kitchen counter and reviewed my selections.

"Nice work, this is the one we should open first," Nolan grabbed the bottle in the middle, set it aside and left the room to grab four glasses.

"Frank, you're the wine snob, what do you think?" Sal asked.

Frank walked over and his eyes almost popped out of his head.

"Holy shit, that's a '61 Chateau Petrus!" He proclaimed.

"I thought it might be a good one, but I was only judging by the year," I said.

"That bottle is worth at least $5,000, probably over $10,000," Frank was flabbergasted.

"I know," Nolan said as he came back in the room. "Actually, $13,000. A client gave it to me, pretty cool huh?"

"Now let's see how it tastes," Frank said as he removed the cork and poured four glasses.

We all swirled our wine around, took a nice whiff and proceeded to take a sip. We should have let a wine like that breath a bit, but we were too anxious to taste this wine that was our senior by about ten years.

"Worth every penny," Frank gave it his seal of approval.

"Cheers guys," I said as our glasses chimed in unison. Finally we were at a point of the trip that wasn't so tense. This is what we all were hoping for when we planned this trip five years ago. Good friends, good stories and just plain old fun. Three more bottles of wine met their demise before we decided we were saturated and needed to hit the sack. The best night of the trip was in the books.

It was about 3am when we all called it quits. My head hit the pillow and I fell asleep, but unfortunately, I couldn't stay asleep. I'd like to point to the wine as the culprit, but around 4:15am I woke up writhing in pain. I knew why I was hurting and of course, the wine doesn't help my situation, but it wasn't the primary cause of my discomfort.

I literally rolled out of my bed onto the floor. It felt like someone had pushed a dagger into my side and began to twist it. Many thoughts went through my head while I was in a fetal position clutching my knees wondering when this pain would subside. Perhaps I was going to die right now? It felt like it was a possible outcome.

I pulled myself out of the fetal position I was in and the most horrible pain shot through my body. I needed to scream. I grabbed whatever I could find on the floor to place in my mouth to muffle the noise. I happened to find the socks I was wearing that night and shoved them in my mouth. It was a disgusting option, but at the time I didn't care. I let out a groan that was muffled by the socks, but was still very loud. Tears began to roll down my face from the pain and I began to sweat profusely.

The room I was staying in had a bathroom attached to it. I began to crawl, pushing myself forward with my elbows. The bathroom door was slightly open and I pushed my way through. A couple more pushes with my elbows had me lying on the cool tile floor. My temperature had skyrocketed and the floor felt amazing on my body. The pain was starting to subside and then the feeling that I would begin to know so well came over me. First, my mouth starts salivating to the point where I need to spit. The saliva serves as a warning to get to the toilet immediately. Next, the gag reflex starts. I place my head over the toilet. Finally, the vomiting begins. Throwing up is never pretty, but this episode happened to be one of the most disgusting I've ever witnessed. We drank so much red wine that everything that came up was red. It looked like something out of The Exorcist, except my head wasn't spinning around.

The pain was now gone, along with everything I ate and drank that day. I collapsed to the floor and laid there for a couple of hours just staring at the ceiling. I couldn't sleep and frankly, I was terrified. The pain I just experienced was by far the worst I've felt in my life. I thought it might be the end for me. This was going to be it. They'd find me lying on the floor of the bathroom in boxer shorts with a pair of dirty socks stuck in my mouth. What a classy way to go.

Being as stubborn as I am, I refused to believe that my health would be declining so quickly. That's why I did two things. One, I decided to proceed with taking this trip and two, I haven't shared my diagnosis with my family yet. Both of those decisions may turn out to be mistakes. So far, I've been able to hide my sickness from my friends. They don't know any better. They just think I can't handle my liquor and I'm a lightweight. I so desperately want to continue with this trip and I'll do my best to make sure I don't ruin it for the guys. My intention is to share my news with them at some point on our journey, but I don't know when. The mood may strike me at a certain point, but I also wonder if I should even tell them at all. I don't want to depress everyone at a time when we are starting to enjoy each other's company. Selfishly, I'd like to tell my friends, as I need some advice on how I should break the news to Lisa and the kids.

No offense to my pals, but when it is all said and done Lisa and the kids are my number one priority.

Lisa and I were introduced to each other at a mutual friend's engagement party. Neither one of us was out there "looking" at the time. Quite frankly, Lisa was enjoying her single life after a relatively long relationship and I was in the process of finalizing my divorce. Needless to say, the start up of our relationship took us both by surprise.

Both of us had been prepped by our friends prior to their engagement party. While they didn't go as far as setting us up on a date, they did make both of us aware that the other would be attending the party and nudged us in the right direction for an introduction. We met that night and immediately hit it off. Neither one of us expected things to move so fast, especially considering our present situations, but we just went with it.

Our courtship was a bit awkward as I was in the process of trying to expedite my divorce procedures. Technically, I was still married while we were dating. Looking back on it, I'm surprised Lisa didn't run for the hills. I can just imagine how our friends described me. Nice, successful guy, handsome and oh by the way, he's married, but is in the process of getting a divorce, so don't worry about that. Talk about a red flag. Not to say that Lisa didn't have a red flag of her own at the time. Of course, it wasn't as bad as my situation, but I was warned that she had four cats. My immediate reaction was to think that I was being set up with some crazy cat lady.

We dated for about a year and a half and then I popped the question. I hit a homerun with my proposal. With a little hard work and planning I managed to surprise Lisa with a trip to the Bahamas for the weekend. After she said yes and I placed the ring on her finger I had a limo pick us up and take us straight to the airport. It was one of the best days of our lives. It would only get better from there.

Our wedding wasn't huge, but it was perfect in our minds. We both have large extended families and all of the relatives had a great time. It was a special way to officially start our lives together.

Like any marriage, we were faced with challenges. Our biggest challenge revolved around our desire to start a family. We waited about a year after we got married to start trying to have a baby. Unfortunately, the process wasn't simple. We had no luck getting pregnant until about a year after trying and then our bad luck got even worse. Lisa had two miscarriages along the way. After the second one we decided to take a break from trying. It was too emotional for both of us and was draining on Lisa mentally and physically. It took us about a year to start trying again and our persistence paid off as we were blessed with our little girl Lynnie. Her first name is actually Linda. We named her after my mother-in-law.

Life for Lisa and me after Lynnie was born changed dramatically. I'd say 95% of the change was good, while about 5% was challenging. In other words, our life was pretty good. The day Lynnie was born was the best day I've ever experienced in my life. Everything changed for me that day. I was no longer worried about myself. My focus was on doing everything in my power to make a good life for Lynnie and Lisa. My two angels deserved a perfect life. Now, I know that no one has a perfect life, but I was determined to try and get as close as possible.

The euphoria of having one child immediately made Lisa and I want to have another and provide Lynnie with a sibling. About two years after Lynnie was born we were blessed with another little miracle. Reilly came into our life with a bit of drama attached. I guess she was eager to meet her parents and her big sister. She surprised us about four weeks early. Everything turned out fine, but of course, the whole process was a bit stressful for our growing family. Lisa and Reilly had to spend about nine days in the hospital for monitoring purposes. They were given the green light and sent home and our family of four was moving along quite nicely.

Lisa is an amazing mom. The balancing act she goes through each day not only with the kids, but she manages to continue her successful career as an executive for a large chemical distributor. I don't know how she does it. I'm pretty sure she has super powers.

Our life has been pretty darn good. Of course, we have our moments, but when it is all said and done we are a happy family. The one constant in our marriage is the simple fact that we enjoy spending time with one another and we always, I mean always, make each other smile. I've always believed that being able to place a smile on someone else's face is one of the most powerful gifts a person can provide to another. Lisa and I have that unique ability to make each other smile no matter what the circumstances.

I've had a lot of time on this trip to think about how my conversation with Lisa will go when I sit down with her upon my return. The time I've had hasn't helped me come up with a solution or a plan. I'm at a loss. How do you tell someone that you love so much that you'll be leaving her soon? The guilt I feel about leaving my family behind continues to weigh on me. I don't care about myself. I care about them. When Lynnie was born I made a promise to Lisa that from that day forward I would be there for her and Lynnie no matter what happened. I'll be breaking that promise and it cuts me deeply. The pain of this disease can't match the emotional pain I'm feeling right now. When I pass on I will have failed them miserably. As much as I want to be with my family right now as opposed to being on this trip, I'm happy I'm here. I'm so scared to tell them what is happening to me. I realize delaying it doesn't help the situation, but I don't know how I'll make it through that conversation. Much like when we originally took this trip twenty years ago, when that trip ended, the real world began for each of us. Now, twenty years later, I'll come home from this trip and I'll be back in the real world, but not for the beginning of my life. I'll be preparing for the end.

The Colorado sun started peeking through the window in my room. I was lying on my stomach and thought I heard someone in my room. I rolled over to find Nolan and Sal standing next to my bed. At first, I thought something was wrong, but was relieved to find out it was just Nol' and Sal up to no good, as usual.

"Frank is still sleeping like a baby and we need your help," Sal said with a look in his eyes that confirmed my thought that the two of them were up to something.

"Yep, ol' Frankie is begging to be slid," Nolan said as a big grin emerged.

As I heard about their plan, I was happy for two reasons. One, I wasn't the person being slid and two, we were about to have a blast sliding Frank.

Now, a bit of clarification on exactly what being "slid" means. Back in college it was always a bad idea to go to bed before the party ended or worse, to pass out before everyone else. In other words, try to be the last man standing or have a very strong lock installed on your bedroom door. For those that went to bed too early by either their own choice or due to passing out, they were risking being "slid". To perform the perfect slide, it takes about three guys, plus one unwilling and unknowing participant. The idea is to enter the room of the passed out or sleeping individual quietly. Then, position yourselves at the side of the bed. Place your hands under the mattress and on the count of three, lift up! The person in the bed slides off the other side of the mattress, preferably into a wall. As you can imagine, it is quite startling to wake up like that. If the three guys performing the slide get ambitious they cannot only slide the individual off the bed, but they can take it a step further and perform the "pancake". As it may sound, the pancake is when you flip the person off the mattress and then flip the mattress on top of them. A "pile on" usually ensues after. Again, not a fun way to wake up, especially with a hangover. So, Frank was the target and we were determined to slide him good.

"Are you sure he's still asleep?" I asked.

"Yes, I just checked, he's snoring away in there," Sal whispered.

"Come on, let's go," Nolan led the way to the room Frank was staying in.

This scene was very amusing. Three grown men tip-toeing down the hallway trying not to bust out laughing. We reached the door, which had already been cracked open slightly by Sal. Sure enough, Frank was sawing logs in there. He'll never know what hit him.

Sal ever so lightly pushed the door open. It creaked a little bit and then came to a rest against the doorstop. Frank was lying on his back. Suddenly he flinched and we thought we may need to abort, but luckily he made a couple of grunts and got right back into his snoring routine. I made my way to the front portion of the bed, I was about ten inches from Frank's face. Sal positioned himself in the middle and Nolan got ready at the bottom of the mattress. Sal and I placed both of our hands under the mattress. Nolan had his left hand underneath the mattress and held his right hand in the air. Sal and I focused our eyes on Nolan's right hand. The signals started from Nolan. His index finger was raised, then his middle finger and finally his ring finger. We lifted the mattress in unison. First we heard a yell from Frank and then a nice loud thump that sounded like either a knee or a head hitting the wall. The slide was complete. All that was left was the pancake. Frank wasn't making it easy. He wriggled around and tried to free himself from being pinned against the wall. It was a valiant effort, but the three of us were too much for him. It was kind of like that scene in the Titanic when the last remaining portion of the ship kind of bobbed up and down before it sunk. The mattress made it to an upright position, perpendicular with the box spring and hung there for a few seconds as Frank fought back. Then, one final push from the three of us sent it over and the pancake was complete. We piled on the top of the mattress while we erupted with laughter. Definitely one of the better slides we've pulled off. It was just like riding a bike. It had been twenty years since the last slide, but we pulled this one off perfectly. The three of us left the room, still laughing. Frank remained under the mattress, defeated.

By the time we all showered and got dressed it was about noon. Nolan was anxious to show off his culinary skills and make use of his professional kitchen. Sal, Frank and I left him to do his thing and made ourselves comfortable on the back deck.

"Now this is what I'm talking about," Sal said as he grabbed a cold beer from the cooler and plopped himself down on a lounge chair.

"Yep, total relaxation," Frank agreed with Sal's assessment.

They were right. I don't think I've ever been in a place so tranquil. We could hear a small stream flowing while a number of different birds chirped. This was a happy time for all of us. We all had our own stressful situations that we were currently battling, but for a few moments we were able to forget about everything and just enjoy each other's company. Nolan came through with an amazing feast. My culinary skills consist of cooking up a pretty good steak on the grill from time to time. When Nolan sets his mind to it a gourmet feast is the end result. He started us off with a choice of bacon wrapped scallops or smoked salmon with some type of jelly glaze. We all enjoyed both, as it was too difficult to choose one. For our main course he prepared a dish that included grilled duck, asparagus and twice baked potatoes. I don't order duck often, if ever, but this was amazing. It melted in your mouth. The meal didn't stop there. He finished us off with a crème brulee that was amazing. It was official, Nolan wasn't lying when he said he could cook and we were officially spoiled for the rest of the trip. I'm not sure any meals moving forward would beat this one. The food, the atmosphere, everything was perfect. After dessert we finished everything off with a nice glass of 18-year old scotch. If our trip had ended right there, I would have been satisfied.

The great meal and the glass of scotch led to nap time for all of us. As each of us dozed off, the thought of being slid crept into our minds, but it was a risk we were all willing to take, as we knew the day wasn't over.

Later that night we made our way to a cool little bar that Nolan knew about. We enjoyed a light dinner and listened to some pretty good music. The local band, called "Swag", was cranking out all of their original music. I'd say they were a mix of Jack Johnson and Warren Haynes. Not a bad sound to emulate. The band wrapped up around midnight and that was our cue to call it a night.

We were all a bit groggy when we made it up the steps into Nolan's house. An agreement to not slide anyone was made and we headed to our separate rooms for the night. I could already tell that I was going to be in for another rough episode. I woke up around 3:30am in pain. Luckily, it was somewhat dull this time. I decided to walk it off. I quietly went out to the kitchen. As I was about to turn the light on I could see a silhouette of someone sitting at the kitchen table.

"Who's that?" I whispered.

The person sitting at the table didn't answer.

"Who is that?" I asked again, but didn't whisper this time.

Again, nothing from the silhouette. I walked over to the light switch and flipped it on. My eyes needed to adjust as the brightness from the kitchen lights hit them. When I was able to finally focus I was startled to find Nolan sitting at the kitchen table. Not because he was sitting there, as I knew it had to be him, Sal or Frank in that chair, but I was shocked to see what he was holding.

In his left hand, he was clutching the same bottle of 18-year old scotch that we were drinking earlier that day. It was almost empty. It had been over half full when we placed it back in the bar earlier. In his right hand, he held a 9mm handgun with his index finger placed on the trigger.

"Get the fuck outta here Kevin," Nolan barked in a voice that was not quite a yell, but very loud nonetheless.

"Nolan, just calm down, what's going on," I said as I took two steps toward the kitchen table.

"Stop right there," now Nolan was yelling.

I didn't listen and took another couple steps forward.

"Get away, not one more fucking step Kevin," Nolan started to shake. He brought the scotch bottle up to his lips and took a gulp. The shaking stopped.

"I don't think you know what you are doing Nolan," I raised my hands up about waist high, palms down with a gesture as if to say, ease up buddy.

"I know what I'm doing, now stay there," Nolan took the gun and pointed it in my direction.

I froze. I've never had a gun pointed at me, but then again, who has? It's not a common occurrence. To my surprise, Frank walked into the kitchen through the entrance that was to Nolan's left. He stopped dead in his tracks once he saw that Nolan had a gun and was pointing it at someone.

Frank didn't know that Nolan was pointing the gun at me.

"Who's over there?" Frank yelled around the corner requesting that the person Nolan had sized up with the gun reveal himself.

"It's me Frank," I said.

"What the fuck is going on?" Frank began to panic.

"Shut up, shut up, shut up, both of you!" Nolan kept the gun pointed at me, but gave Frank a wild-eyed look.

"You don't want to do this Nol'," I calmly said as I stared at the gun shaking in his hand.

Frank was silent. He and I couldn't see each other. I had no idea what he was doing, but was hoping that he would help me bring Nolan back from this dark place that he has arrived at. I was scared, but remained calm. I knew I was not the target for Nolan. After all, what had I done to deserve having a gun pointed at me? Right now, I was convinced I was just in the wrong place at the wrong time.

"I can't do it, I can't," Nolan began to cry, but still pointed the gun in my direction.

"You can't do what?" I had no idea as to what he was referring to.

"It's over," Nolan put his head down into his chest and brought the gun down to the table. He was silent for about five seconds and then his head popped back up to reveal a crazed look on his face.

"My fucking life, that's what's over," he screeched as his arm rose with the gun.

Nolan's arm circled around, paused briefly, once again pointing the gun in my direction. Then he turned it on himself. He was pushing the gun into his right temple, so hard that blood began to drip down the side of his face.

Then, in what was a blur, I saw Nolan's body slam into the kitchen table. The table slid into the refrigerator. I ran over thinking the worst had happened. I had lost sight of Nolan as the table slid forward. He was underneath it. To my surprise, I found Anthony lying on top of Nolan. The gun had flown out of Nolan's hand as Anthony tackled him. It slid across the floor leaving a spatter of blood along the way. Sal entered the room behind Anthony. He had quietly seen what was going on and decided to wake Anthony to see if he could help out. Once again, Anthony had brought peace to a situation that was spiraling out of control. It made me start wondering if he had been sent on this trip for a reason. He was like a guardian angel.

Now that the gun had been pried from Nolan's hand it was time to get to the bottom of this. Why would a guy like Nolan even think of taking his own life? We stayed up for hours listening to the amazing story that Nolan unwound and realized his life wasn't that wonderful.

It turns out that Nolan was a fraud. Everything he owned was paid for using unsuspecting investors' funds. In essence, Nolan was running a ponzi scheme that amounted to over a billion dollars. While the market was thriving, he was living the high life wooing investor after investor with returns that seemed like they were too good to be true. Nolan used his solid reputation to ease investors' minds. They continued to fork over millions of dollars to Nolan and hadn't been interested in cashing out until the market started to spiral downward. About eight months ago the first few investors started to request that their money be returned. Nolan, being the smooth talker that he is, was able to convince most of them to hold out stating that it was just a blip in the market and everything would be fine. His assurances worked with most and for the ones that he wasn't able to convince he made arrangements to return their money. He had enough money in reserve to handle a few investors, but he knew his funds were limited and began to recruit others aggressively to replenish his funds. He hit pay dirt when he and a Japanese businessman crossed paths on a trip to Las Vegas during the Super Bowl. He was able to secure enough money to keep his scam alive, at least until other investors got antsy.

The market continued to crash and so did Nolan's scam. The Japanese funds turned out to buy Nolan another two months and then everything unraveled. Investors came calling for their money and Nolan ignored them. He was finished sweet-talking everyone. He chose instead to avoid them entirely. Phone calls, texts, emails and even in person visits to his office in Nashville went unanswered. He thought about fleeing the country, but decided to seek counsel from his stable of attorneys. The advice he received was pretty simple, come clean. Nolan, whose ego is monster-sized, resisted that idea at first. His arrogance kept him believing that he could somehow find a way to right the ship, but his ship had already sunk.

It turns out that right before he left for our trip he raised the white flag and told his attorneys that he was ready to come clean. The plan was to come back from the trip and turn himself in to authorities. His attorneys advised him that similar cases result in jail time that would exceed any years that he had left. He would die in prison.

The thought of dying in prison led us to where we were tonight, Nolan holding a gun to his head choosing to end his life rather than face life in prison. He explained that he couldn't handle the embarrassment that was about to result from his scam. We weren't too surprised that he focused the attention on himself. We can't help but think about his family and how this will affect them, but also all of the other families that will be affected. He single handedly wiped people out and destroyed lives. As we sat there, all of those people had no idea as to what was going to take place as soon as we returned. They'll soon find out that all of the money that they worked so hard to accumulate over the years is gone in a blink of an eye.

We had always wondered why Nolan had resisted allowing us to invest with him. We just figured that we didn't have the kind of funds that he requires for investing, but we now know that he had some kind of moral compass. He wasn't going to scam his friends. That's the only redeeming quality he possesses at this time.

Unfortunately, the judgment he used in not getting his friends involved did not apply to his employees. They too would be going down with the ship and Nolan didn't care. His CFO and his top investment strategist were loyal to a fault and now they would also pay for getting involved in this tangled web of deceit that would soon unravel. As a matter of fact, authorities had quietly visited Nolan's corporate headquarters in Nashville yesterday and seized documents, hard drives and anything else that could be used to build their case against Nolan and any others that had been involved. That list of "others" was long, but luckily didn't include any of us. That we were appreciative for, but as I continued to listen to Nolan tell his story I had a hard time feeling sorry for him. I was visibly shaken and mentally exhausted. Having a gun pointed at me was an experience that I wouldn't wish on my worst enemy.

Hours went by as we listened to how Nolan concocted his fraudulent investment portfolio by creating fake websites, bogus holding companies and even had people pose as bankers and meet in-person with unsuspecting investors. He told us how he had hired a hitman to take care of a certain investor that threatened to go to authorities as he began to doubt the validity of Nolan's investments. The hit never occurred, but the fact that he was willing to even have a conversation about taking another man's life was shocking. Nolan explained that much like a drug addict needs their next fix, that's how he felt, but his fix was money. He had to keep the scam alive, not only to appease his investors, but also to satisfy his own craving.

The sun was up, but not one of us was able to go to sleep. We were all still on edge.

"So, now what?" Frank asked the group.

"I'd say its time to turn this thing around guys," Sal offered his thoughts.

"Is there really any other option at this point?" I asked.

Nolan removed the ice pack that he was holding against his right temple and placed it on the kitchen counter.

"Guys, I understand why you want to end this trip and I don't blame you, but I'm hoping you'll reconsider," Nolan surprised us with this statement as we all thought for sure he would be the biggest supporter of our idea to end the trip.

"This is it for me. Once I get back to Nashville my life is over. I'll never see you guys again and I'll never see the outside of a jail cell. I need these next few days." Nolan was now begging us to continue the trip.

I had enough of this nonsense and couldn't take it anymore. Of course, I wanted to continue with the trip. These guys had no idea as to how much this trip meant to me, but I was still upset at Nolan.

"I don't really give a shit about what you want Nol'!" I got up from my chair and starting pacing back and forth in the kitchen.

"You pointed a fucking gun at me and you want me to just continue hanging out with you like nothing happened?" I said as I pointed in Nolan's face.

"Kevin, please believe me, I never had any intention of hurting you or any of you guys," Nolan explained.

"I was in a dark place. Talking to you guys about everything has been exactly what I needed. I'm relieved now that I was able to speak to someone other than my attorney about this mess." The words "I'm sorry" still hadn't come out of Nolan's mouth.

I walked out of the room. Nolan hopped out of his seat and grabbed my arm and swung me around.

"Kevin, I'm so sorry. It wasn't you. You were just in the wrong place at the wrong time. I would never hurt you. You're my best friend." Nolan's eyes began to tear up.

"Come here Nol'." I walked over to the living room to get some privacy with Nolan.

"I don't like what you did to me and I don't like what I've heard tonight about what you've done to others, but I'm not going to judge you right now. There will be a time and a place for that." Nolan didn't know how important this trip was to me. I knew we wouldn't be turning around, as I wouldn't let that happen. I just needed to set things straight with my friend.

"Get things under control for the rest of us. Stop thinking about yourself for a minute and think about the three other guys that are on this trip. We need this trip too." I didn't mean to sound like a parent speaking to a child, but sometimes Nolan has to be handled like he is a child.

"Fair enough," Nolan said as I began to walk back to the kitchen.

He grabbed my arm once again. "I'm sorry buddy, I really am." He seemed to mean it this time. That was a big step for a guy like him.

"Alright, let's go tell the guys that we're not going home," I said as I put my arm around Nolan. Yes, I was still upset with him, but I don't have time to hold grudges. He has his own demons that he's battling, he doesn't need his friend to battle him as well.

Chapter Six

The itinerary for our trip, that was very loosely put together, told us that we should have been on the road heading for San Francisco hours ago. Opinions varied as to what we should do next. Stay one more day in Breckenridge or should we get on the road and leave this crazy part of the trip behind us? Ultimately, we decided to hop on the cruiser and get out of Colorado.

We finally got on the road around 2pm. The four of us hadn't slept yet. A strange vibe filled the air in the cruiser. Unfortunately, these moments of awkward silence were becoming common on our trip. I think we were all still in shock. Nolan had shocked us with his story and of course, the whole "gun to the head" thing didn't help either. It didn't take long for all of us to fall asleep. I was the last one to nod off and we had only been on the road for about 45 minutes. Anthony drove through the night as we all slept off what had been a crazy 24 hours. It was about 6am when I woke up and I was surprised to find Sal awake.

"What's up Sal, figured you'd still be sleeping," I said in a whisper as I sat down next to him.

Sal was fiddling on his iphone.

"Man, they grow up so fast," he turned the iphone in my direction and showed me a picture of Hannah when she was just a baby.

"You ain't kidding pal, seems like just yesterday that Lisa was pregnant with Lynnie."

"Yep, I remember how excited I was when Katie and I found out we were having a little girl. I don't know why, but I always wanted a girl. Probably because of the relationship my dad and my sister have. It was always different than the relationship I had with my dad."

"I know, it's just different. I love my girls in a way that's different than the father-son relationship, but how would I know?" Sal knew that I was referring to the strained relationship that I've had with my dad. Strained is not the right word. Non-existent is more appropriate.

"When's the last time you saw your parents?" Sal asked.

"Just about a year ago. I was in Phoenix for a meeting and I stayed a few extra days."

"How are they doing?"

"Oh, you'll get to find out for yourself buddy. We're going to make a pit stop at their place on our way back home," I said with a chuckle.

I got up to hit the head and Sal continued to scroll through his photos on his phone. He had a lot on his mind these days. He and Katie's marriage was on thin ice and his company was going through a massive restructuring. Sal wasn't sure if he would have a job much longer.

Sal and Katie used to have a great thing going. A model marriage in the sense that they enjoyed each other's company and put family first. Neither one of them was too wrapped up in their careers which made life pretty good for Hannah. She was their primary focus. Everything revolved around her. Of course, that's how most families should function, but in this day and age careers and other distractions seem to take center stage. I've been guilty of that.

The odds were stacked against Sal and Katie when they first met. Sal was graduating and Katie had just started at Florida State. Sal managed to find work in Tallahassee and that allowed their relationship to continue. Sal knew that was the only way, as a long distance thing would never work. He gave up a few job opportunities to stay in Tallahassee. At the time, he didn't have any regrets, but now, as their marriage is crumbling it's hard for him not to look back at what he may have passed up. You see, Sal has never truly had a career. The old saying, love what you do and you'll never have to work a day in your life, never applied to Sal. His motivation was a paycheck. Do as little as possible and get paid. It wasn't necessarily because he's not a hard worker. It's because he doesn't enjoy his job, which has made it challenging to get motivated. In my opinion, he's part of the majority, not the minority. Most people wake up each day in search of a paycheck and spend hours at jobs that don't motivate them. I have plenty of other friends that wish they had a true "career", but instead they have a paycheck. Get in at 9am and get out at 5pm. Live for the weekends and dread Sunday evenings knowing they have to go back in the morning. It's sad if you think about it. We spend more time working than we do with our families. Being at a job that you despise must be a miserable existence. I've been lucky to have jobs that I've enjoyed. Yes, I had a difficult time learning how to balance my career with my home life, but I've learned a lot since the girls came into my life. Things are better now.

Sal, on the other hand, is fighting an uphill battle. He's made it clear to all of us that he and Katie are on the brink of divorce. At this point, it's a matter of when, not if. I'll give both of them credit though. They tried to save their marriage. They've sat through hours of counseling, sought out advice from their minister, read books, but nothing has seemed to work. About a year ago they stopped trying and Sal derailed. He's always been a partier, but he's taken it to a new level lately. Frank and I have seen him in action as he's visited each of us on work related trips. He's become a regular at strip clubs and has taken up "friendships" with some of the girls. His lifestyle change has also led to a few new habits. Sal has always smoked weed, but he kept his drug use in check. Not anymore. Frank and I have seen him snort coke and we know he's messed around with heroin a couple of times. Both of those drugs scare the hell out of me, but the heroin thing was shocking. Sal's no dummy. He understands how addictive heroin can be, but the group he's running with now are a bunch of addicts and he's not making wise decisions. We haven't seen him use on this trip and hopefully he sticks to the booze around us. Lord knows we don't need any more drama on this trip.

Anthony pulled the cruiser into a parking lot as Frank and Nolan woke up.

"Where are we?" Frank asked as he cleared his eyes.

"Hold on a second, for Christ sake would you put something on!" Sal yelled at Frank.

Frank was standing in front of us in nothing but his boxers, but that wasn't the issue.

Nolan, still tired and not very attentive, finally looked over at Frank and understood why Sal was suggesting that Frank cover himself.

"Yeah, Frankie, help us out before someone loses an eye," Nolan said laughing.

"What the fuck is up with you guys, you've never seen morning wood?" Frank began to walk over to Sal.

"You old fucks probably haven't seen your dicks hard without the help of viagra in years!" Frank said jokingly as he knew we all weren't at that point, yet.

"Get the fuck away from me Frank and put some God damn clothes on," Sal said as he jumped up and moved away from Frank and his "friend".

"Alright, alright, calm down you pussy," Frank said as he walked over and grabbed a pair of shorts.

Nolan was looking out the window and knew exactly where we were.

"Reno, nice work Anthony!" Nolan commended Anthony for his choice of stops, but also for his driving skills. The guy is an animal. He drove while we slept. We were on the road for about 16 hours. He must be exhausted.

"Anthony, come back here," I waived him back to have a seat.

"What's up fellas?" Anthony said as his big body grabbed a portion of the couch.

"Do you like to gamble?" Nolan asked.

"I'll occasionally roll the dice or play a few hands of blackjack, sure," Anthony said with a smile.

"Well, we figured that you've earned some time to enjoy yourself on this trip. Lord knows you've put up with enough shit from me," we all agreed with Nolan's statement.

"That's why, Reno will be your time to have a little fun, on us," I said as I motioned over to Nolan.

Frank and Sal were in the dark on this one, but Nolan and I had a conversation right before we left Breckenridge and agreed that it was time to let Anthony enjoy himself a little bit. Now, we didn't know we would end up stopping in Reno, but that worked out perfectly. Anthony had saved the day a couple of times for us and it made sense to let the guy have some fun too.

"That's right big fella, Reno is on us," Nolan said as he reached into his bag.

"I like it, I like it," Sal popped up and started clapping. "You the man Anthony!"

"Here you go buddy," Nolan threw an envelope over to Anthony.

Anthony snatched it in the air and took a look inside.

"Mother fucker, there must be like 10 G's in here," Anthony said as he flipped through the bills in the envelope.

"Very good, right on, 10 grand," Nolan said. "You spend that anyway you'd like, gamble, hookers, drinks, it's yours."

Now, no one made mention of it, but after everything Nolan shared with us about his checkered financial past, it was hard for us not to think that the money he gave Anthony was secured illegally. The cat was out of the bag and there was no turning back now. Anthony had the money in hand. He was fired up and ready to go.

"Let's park this thing and check-in," I said.

"Where are we staying," Frank asked as he had no idea that this plan even existed.

"Harrah's, just up the road from here," I said.

"Let's go fellas!" Anthony made his way back to the front of the cruiser. He had been up all night driving and was ready to get some sleep, but this news gave him the second wind he needed.

"Oh boy, this is gonna be ugly," Sal said with a big grin.

None of us had said it, but I think we were all feeling that our trip had been too planned out so far and this little diversion was something we all needed. After all, when we set out on this trip twenty years ago we simply got in the car and drove west. We stopped when we wanted to stop, slept in the car most of the time and most importantly, created memories that will last a lifetime.

We've created some new memories on this trip. Of course, there are a few things that we'd all like to forget, but twenty years later our lives are much more complicated, therefore, this trip has had its fair share of complications. When it's all said and done though, this trip will go down as something we'll remember fondly. I love these guys and I'm going to miss them dearly. I'm focused on taking it all in and creating those memories that I referred to. Memories that will last a lifetime, even if my lifetime might be coming to an end soon.

Our rooms weren't ready yet, so we hit the breakfast buffet. Our meals were accompanied by bloody Mary's and screwdrivers. It was clear that this stop in Reno was going to be a complete mess. We hadn't hung out with Anthony on the trip yet. When we'd go out and eat or drink, he stayed in the cruiser or went to a Starbucks to kill the time. It seemed a little odd that he was now hanging as part of our crew, but it's hard to argue that the guy doesn't deserve some type of R & R.

"Alright Ant, so what's it gonna be?" Nolan asked as he polished off his first bloody mary.

"What was I going to do? I was going to sleep for about 12 hours while you fellas got silly in Reno, but plans have changed!" Anthony said with a big smile as he pulled out the envelope with the 10 G's.

"You can sleep when you're dead buddy," Sal said.

I had gone over to the front desk to get a better idea as to when our rooms would be ready.

"Looks like our rooms will be ready around two o'clock," I said as I grabbed my seat at the table.

"Why don't we kill some time at the pool? They have a pool side blackjack table," Nolan suggested.

"Hold on a second, isn't this Anthony's day?" Frank asked the group.

"True, true. So, what do you want to do Anthony?" Nolan asked.

"I'm up for the pool as long as you boys don't get jealous. When Anthony takes his shirt off all of the female attention will be coming my way!" Anthony finished that remark up with that big belly laugh that we've all grown to love.

After breakfast, we made a lap around the casino to check it out. It was about 10am when we made our way out to the pool. We situated ourselves in the middle of the pool area and grabbed five lounge chairs. It was still early, but we expected the poolside crowd to gather soon. The four of us removed our shirts and plopped down into our lounge chairs. It was clear that twenty years had passed. Sal took the prize for being the most out of shape. Not to mention that he probably hadn't seen the sun in awhile. Boy was he white. Frank, while he wasn't overweight, had no shape to him at all. He could benefit from a few push ups every now and then. I had my usual look. Not tan, but not pasty white. Not fat, but probably about ten pounds overweight. Let's face it, I looked like a guy in his early forties. Last, but not least, was Nolan. Of course, he had the benefit of multiple cosmetic surgeries and his at-home tanning salon.

"Bald, yes, but am I beautiful or what?" Nolan said as he threw his shirt to the ground.

"Just sit your ass down dude," Sal said with a laugh.

I have to admit, the guy looked pretty damn good.

"Yeah, sit yo' ass down, this is Big Anthony's pool today," Anthony pulled his shirt off.

He still looked like he could play. What a beast this guy was. To say that he stood out at the pool was an understatement.

Now that we all made a spectacle of the simple task of taking our shirts off, it was time to become familiar with our server for the day. She was in for an interesting afternoon, but a well compensated afternoon as well.

"Hello Gentlemen, welcome to Harrah's. My name is Kayla, I'll be helping you out today. Can I place a drink order for you?"

We all had to do a double take as we weren't sure whether we were poolside at a casino or in a strip club. Kayla was a hottie, in that sort of stripper way. Hawaiian, dark tan, about 5'4", 105 to 110 lbs. and a huge rack. It took all of five seconds for Nolan to start making an ass out of all of us.

"So, Kayla, how old are you?" Nolan asked. We weren't sure where he was going with this, but it was likely that it would embarrass someone.

"I'm twenty-five, why do you ask?" Kayla replied. It was obvious that she knew how to play the game. This wasn't her first rodeo. She saw all of us as guys with fat wallets and she knew if she played her cards right a big tip would follow.

"Perfect. Now take a look at this fine group of gentlemen here," Nolan waived his hand back and forth as he was sitting in the middle of our group.

"Oh, but forget about the big guy at the end. He doesn't count for this conversation," Nolan excluded Anthony from whatever point he was trying to make.

"Got it," Kayla said as she continued to play along.

"Here's the question. We're all in our early forties. Would a beautiful young lady like you ever consider a guy like us?" Yep, Nolan was on his way to embarrassing us.

"If you're asking if I've dated older guys, the answer is yes," Kayla smiled.

"Alright, now we're getting somewhere," Nolan smiled back.

Nolan loved this kind of shit. I think, actually, I know he loves it because it helps to feed his massive ego. He always needs to know that he still has "it". Although, determining whether he has "it" or not is always a little blurry, as we know that if he didn't have the cash, it's doubtful that he'd get the girl.

Kayla is an old pro at this kind of banter. She managed to answer Nolan's questions without providing definitive answers. She gave enough information to keep us all engaged and to give Nolan the hard-on that he was hoping for.

"I'll be right back with your drinks guys. Oh boy, this is gonna be a fun group today", Kayla flipped her hair back and strutted over to the bar to fill our drink order. It was pathetic as all five of us drooled as we stared at her ass while she walked away.

"Man, now that is hot. I wonder if she has any friends that may want to join us tonight?" Nolan said to himself out loud.

"I'll give it to you, you certainly don't lack confidence. I think she likes you buddy", Frank said as he patted Nolan's bald head.

We know Frank was joking, but I think all of us had this sneaking suspicion that Nolan may work his magic and we just might be seeing a little more of Kayla later on tonight.

As the morning turned into afternoon the drinks continued to flow and we all caught a few hands of blackjack at the poolside table. Nolan's banter with Kayla continued throughout the day and the level of risqué rose as Nolan's saturation level rose. Most of it was harmless, but Nolan has no self control and crossed the line a few times. It turns out that Kayla has a boyfriend and Nolan took hold of that nugget and wouldn't let it go.

"So, how long have you been with what's his name?" Nolan asked Kayla as he sucked down some more rum punch.

"First of all, his name is Brad and it's been about seven months," Kayla continued to smile even though Nolan was becoming belligerent.

"Seven months? That's no boyfriend, you're just dating," Nolan was apparently a relationship therapist now.

"Kayla, I apologize for Nolan's inquisitive nature. He is an only child and constantly needs attention. If you don't mind, order us up one more round and bring us the check. We need to check in to our rooms now." Frank took control of the situation that was about to derail.

Kayla made her way back to the bar. Nolan stared Frank down with a "what the fuck" expression on his face.

"What was that?" Nolan asked Frank.

"Come on, it's time to get our rooms, we've been down here for almost five hours," Frank replied.

"Listen Frank," Nolan raised his voice to a level that could be heard across the pool area.

"You don't tell me when to stay or go, got it?" Nolan threw his empty cup down.

"Settle down Nolan, can't you ever just have a good time without becoming a giant prick," I said.

"A good time? If it weren't for me you boring fucks would be sitting around in your rooms with your thumbs up your asses. At least I bring something to the table," Nolan did his best to insult us.

I've grown tired of his bullshit on this trip. It seems like every time we get to a place where everyone is enjoying themselves he tries to tear it down. What I said next was not my finest moment, but I couldn't resist.

"That's right Nolan, forgive me, you'll have plenty of time to sit around with your thumb up your ass, you fucking felon."

It was cold and I knew it. I also knew it cut him down to the bone. He didn't say a word and neither did anyone else. Kayla arrived with our last round of drinks and the check. When she left to retrieve our drinks the mood was much different than it was now. Sal grabbed the check and signed it, making sure to provide Kayla with a generous gratuity. We all got up and started to make our way to the front desk. Kayla couldn't help but think she had done something wrong. We had gone from a jovial group to a very somber group in a matter of minutes.

"Are you guys OK?" Kayla said as we all walked away. "Thank you guys, enjoy the rest of your stay."

It was about 4pm when we all got settled in our rooms. Before we went out to the pool we had made a reservation for 8pm in the hotel's steakhouse. It was kind of nice being alone in my room. We've been on top of each other since the trip began and a break was long overdue. I used my time to check in with Lisa and the kids. Although I was anxious to get home to them, I wasn't ready for it. As soon as I get back I'll need to sit down with Lisa and tell her the news. I haven't even told my friends yet and I'm hoping that I can use them as sort of a practice run. I know it may seem odd to tell my friends before my wife, but I need some advice from these guys. I'm not even sure when I'll be sharing the news with them, but as one day turns into the next it is clear that this trip will be over before we know it. I'll have to figure out a time to pull the trigger soon.

I made my way downstairs around 7pm to grab a drink in the bar. I didn't call the other guys. I was still enjoying the break. The bar was crowded with the pre-dinner and show crowd. I found a single seat right smack in the middle of the bar. It was the access spot that everyone that wasn't sitting at the bar was using to order their drinks, but I politely made my way past the group ordering drinks and slid into my seat.

"What can I get you?" The bartender's name was Jack and he had one of those handle bar mustaches. I can't recall ever seeing one of those in person.

"I'll have a Macallan 12 on the rocks with a splash of water," I love a good scotch. Although, a true scotch drinker would prefer to take it neat, but that's where I draw the line.

"Good choice," the lady next to me commended my selection. She raised her glass to show me she had ordered the same thing, minus the splash.

She was a striking woman, very well put together. I'd say she was in her late thirties or possibly early forties. Piercing blue eyes, blond hair, the right amount of make up, manicured nails and jewelry that complemented her sea blue dress perfectly. Her chest was modest and she appeared to have an athletic body, but it was hard to tell while she was seated.

"So, where are you from?" She went with that line as opposed to the "come here often" route, although I didn't think she was trying to pick me up. This was just harmless small talk.

"South Florida, how about yourself?" I know, I'm such the conversationalist.

"Boston, well, at least that's where I'm living now, originally from Baltimore." My thoughts of her being a working girl went away with that statement or maybe I'm just naïve.

"What brings you to lovely Reno?" I asked.

"Work, a convention," she replied.

"Oh yeah, what do you do?"

"I'm a sex therapist."

"Really?" I replied

"No, just kidding, but that's more exciting than my actual job. Medical devices, I sell them." She said with a smile.

"Sorry, but you're right, sex therapist is a bit more interesting," I smiled back.

"We have another boring reception and dinner in about an hour. I'm just killing some time away from the group until then", she needed a break as well.

"Me too. Had to get away for a bit," I took another sip of my Macallan.

"Are you here for work?"

"No, on a trip with a few of my buddies. They'll be down here soon." Although, I was hoping they'd take their time. I was enjoying my talk with the lady from Boston. All I need is Nolan butting in with his bullshit.

"By the way, my name is Kevin, what's yours?"

"Janet, nice to meet you. Hey, Jack, can you grab us another round. This guy likes a splash though." Janet took it upon herself to get me a refill even though I had about a half glass left. She also took a shot at my "splash", which I got a kick out of.

"Very nice Janet, we'll get along famously," I laughed and then took a big swig of my drink, as I knew another was right behind it.

I don't know why, but for some reason I felt a connection to Janet. Maybe it was because I'd only been around the guys for the last few days and it was just nice to speak to a woman. The fact that she was very attractive didn't hurt either, but she also seemed like a good soul.

I could see her ring finger was occupied with a big rock and she could also see that mine had a band on it.

"How long have you been married? Any kids?" Janet asked.

"Ten years, two little girls," I replied. "How about you?"

"Two years, but it's my second time around. I have a boy and a girl from my previous marriage," Janet grabbed her iphone and scrolled to a picture of her kids.

"What are they, twelve and fifteen?" I took an educated guess.

"Close, eleven and fifteen," Janet corrected me slightly.

"Did you bring anyone along for the ride," I asked.

"No, my husband couldn't make it, busy with work and these conventions aren't exactly kid friendly, neither is Reno."

"Makes sense." The drinks were beginning to disappear quicker and quicker. I kept looking at my watch and over my shoulder. I knew eight o'clock was approaching rapidly and I didn't want my time with Janet to end.

"Janet, don't take this the wrong way, but I have to tell you, you have a unique way about you. Such kind eyes, but very striking. You're an attractive woman." I wasn't sure where I was going with this, but I just blurted it out.

"Well, thank you Kevin. No, I'm not going to take that the wrong way, a woman enjoys being complimented," she laughed and placed her hand on my wrist in a playful way and then removed it.

I guess we were full out flirting now. I hadn't flirted with a woman in a long time. It felt good, although I did feel like I was doing something wrong.

"Janet, I have to tell you, it's been a pleasure meeting you and I'm sorry that I can't enjoy another Macallan with you, but my friends are probably waiting for me at the restaurant." It was about ten after eight. I stretched my time with Janet out as long as possible.

"Maybe I'll see you around later. Our company is hosting an event at Vault, it's a nightclub in the Legacy hotel. It's supposed to be the top spot around here. Bring your friends over, it'll be fun."

We both got up from our barstools and decided that the last 70 minutes warranted a hug and a kiss on the cheek. Granted, that was a little odd, but there was something about this woman that drew me to her. I know that I shouldn't even think about going to Vault as nothing good will come of it, but I couldn't help myself.

"That sounds like a plan. I know the guys will be up for it. Give me your number and I'll text you later when we are headed that way." We exchanged numbers and I knew I shouldn't have, but I did it anyway.

"There he is," Frank said as I strolled up to the table.

The guys had already sat down and each had a drink in hand when I arrived. Pete's Steakhouse had a great ambiance. It had only been open about four years, but it was designed to look like an old school

steakhouse. It had an early 60's feel to it and made
you feel like you were in a scene from Mad Men.
Other than the hostess that greeted the guys and
showed them to the table, there wasn't another
female employee in the place. Every waiter was a
guy and they were dressed in tuxedo shirts with a
vest and black bow tie. Pete's was famous, or as
famous as a four-year old restaurant can be, for their
bone-in filet. They also had this ridiculous list of
martinis, sixty-two different kinds. Seemed a bit
overkill to me, but every restaurant has their own
little thing that makes them unique. Let's hope that
the uniqueness isn't isolated to some lame martini
list.

"Ah, your fourth finally made it. What can I bring
you to drink sir?" Michael the waiter asked me as I
took my seat next to Frank and across from Sal and
Nolan.

"Vodka martini, up, olives, olive juice on the side,
goose," I replied. Yes, just the right drink after
three scotches. Boy, this night is going to be
trouble.

"You got it, I'll be right back," Michael headed
over to the bar to retrieve my drink. It was apparent
that Michael didn't quite fit in with the 60's theme
as I'm pretty sure being as openly gay as he is
wasn't prominent back then.

"Where were you?" Nolan asked as if I was doing
something wrong.

"I went down to the bar around 7 for a couple of
drinks," I replied.

"Oh yeah, why didn't you call us?" Nolan asked.

"Frankly Nolan, I needed just a little bit of time to chill out. No offense to any of you guys, but we've been on top of each other the entire trip," I said politely.

"Still would have been nice to let us know. We were waiting for you and almost lost our reservation because they didn't want to seat us without the whole group," Nolan kept going on with this trivial detail.

"Seriously? Are you kidding me, come on man, just drop it. Let's enjoy our cocktails and figure out what we're going to eat," I was beginning to lose my cool.

"Michael!" Nolan yelled across the room. Of course, the guests around us looked over wondering why someone was yelling in this nice restaurant.

"Yes, sir, what can I do for you?" Michael had hustled over to our table from across the room.

"How about a wine list," Nolan asked.

"I will be right back with the wine and martini list," Michael placed my martini in front of me and scurried away.

Fresh off of my conversation with Janet, it was hard not to be thinking about her while I sipped my martini. I was just about to tell the guys about Janet, but at the last minute decided it wasn't worth it. I was already buzzing pretty well, but still had some type of wits about me, so I kept it to myself for the time being. Little did I know the cat would be out of the bag shortly.

Michael returned to the table without the wine list. Instead, he was holding a bottle of wine. I could see the label and was already pleased. It was a bottle of my favorite wine, Caymus. I couldn't quite make out the year, but Caymus is Caymus, doesn't matter what year.

"So, which one of you is Kevin? Let me guess, was it our late arrival?" Michael asked and was correct in his assumption.

"Right on Michael," Sal confirmed.

"Well Kevin, this bottle of 1995 Caymus is compliments of your friend Janet," Michael showed me the label and sure enough, it said 1995.

I knew this wine well and it wasn't the cost that impressed me so much about Janet's choice, after all the bottle was probably a couple hundred dollars and didn't break the bank. What impressed me was that she acknowledged not only my favorite winery, but she also chose 1995. During our conversation I had mentioned how much I enjoyed Caymus, but also shared with her the details of our trip. She knew it was the 20th anniversary of the trip we had taken back in 1995.

Michael removed the cork and poured the wine into my glass. I swirled it around a bit and took a big whiff. Of course, it smelled great. I brought the glass up to my lips and took a taste.

"Fantastic Michael, fantastic," I gave him the nod to fill all four glasses.

Each of the guys grabbed their glasses and took a sip and then all eyes were on me. The table was silent for a few awkward seconds.

"OK, OK, now who the fuck is Janet?" Sal finally asked the question.

"I can't believe you guys actually waited that long to ask," I laughed as I took another gulp.

"Yeah, spill it man, who's Janet?" Frank pried.

I was having fun with this now. There was something exhilarating about this whole Janet thing.

"You heard the man, a friend, just a friend," I chose not to divulge too much.

"Married men don't have female friends, which is an undeniable fact, trust me," Nolan chimed in with a statement that was spot on.

"Did you turn the table on a hooker? She's buying you shit?" Sal took a guess as to who Janet was, although it wasn't a very educated guess.

"She's not a hooker, give me some credit here," I replied with a half-smile.

"Are you bangin' this chick?" Sal couldn't handle it and was jumping to conclusions.

"Man, you guys are a bunch of school girls. I met her at the bar. We had a few drinks together and frankly, we kind of hit it off," I finally set the record straight on Janet.

"Alright, now we're getting somewhere. What's her story?" Nolan asked.

"She sells medical devices, in town for a convention of some sort," I answered.

"Married?" Frank jumped in.

"Yep, second time around, couple of kids from the first one," I shared a bit more about Janet.

All of the sudden my phone vibrated. I grabbed it and took a look. Sure enough it was Janet with a question: "How's dinner?" I guess she was anxious to find out if the wine had arrived. She beat me to it, as I was about to send her a text to thank her.

"Is that your girl?" Nolan asked.

"It's Janet, yes, if that's what you mean," I said as I took a picture of the bottle of Caymus.

"You exchanged numbers, oh shit, look out. You're an adulterer now, just like me dude!" Nolan was proud to have me in his "club", although I hadn't done anything to qualify for membership.

I sent Janet a picture of the Caymus bottle with a note: "You didn't have to, but thank you so much…very thoughtful!"

"Look at you Kevin, we leave you alone for an hour and you're out prowling on the town," Nolan was getting such a kick out of this.

I couldn't help but smile. I have to admit, it was kind of fun. So far, it was just playful banter with Janet and it was nice to be noticed by another woman. I'm not sure if I still have "it", but it's nice to know that I've got some game left in me.

My phone vibrated again to the joy of my friends and I liked seeing that I had another message from Janet as well.

"You're blowin' up. She wants you dude!" Sal expressed his excitement as the texting continued between Janet and me.

This time her text said: "Anytime, enjoy. See you later?"

"What's it say?" Frank asked while practically grabbing my phone out of my hand.

"Calm down, keep your hands to yourself. She just said enjoy the wine." I didn't quite divulge the entire text.

I purposely left out the "see you later?" portion of the text. That question mark at the end of that text message is more than just a question mark. I know what will happen if I "see her later". On one hand, it excites me, but on the other, it scares me to death. I've never so much as kissed another woman since Lisa and I have been married. I'm not sure why I'm not putting the breaks on this situation with Janet. I'm smart enough to know that when I'm sober in the morning I'll have regrets and feel guilty, if I follow through on it. Right now I'm staring at that question mark. I have the choice to see her later or delete her number from my phone and move on. No one is forcing me to head over to Vault later. It would be easy to blame my bad decisions on the trip, the guys, the booze, Reno or anything else I can come up with, but in all reality, they are just excuses. People too often point the finger and shift the blame for their own mistakes on others, but the accountability usually lies within. Even in my present three-scotch, one martini and Caymus state, I still know that the accountability will lie squarely on my shoulders if I do anything stupid tonight. I grabbed my phone and answered her question: "Of course".

Dinner wrapped up around 10:15. Pete's was as good as advertised. Four bone-in filets later and we were stuffed, but the night was just getting ready to begin. It reminded me of our days at Florida State, minus the expensive steak dinner. We didn't get to the bars until at least 10:30. Here we go again.

As we filed out of Pete's to get a cab over to Vault Nolan was on the phone.

"OK baby, see you in a few," Nolan hung up the phone.

"Who's that?" Sal asked.

"Oh, you'll see soon enough, get ready for a good time boys," Nolan laughed.

"Let's just take two cabs over there. No need to wait for the van," Frank suggested.

"Good by me, let's go Frank," I walked over to the first cab and opened the door.

Sal and Nolan hopped in the cab behind us. Vault was about four miles away.

"So, what's your name?" Frank asked the cab driver. For some reason, Frank always needed to engage in conversation with the cab driver. His favorite question was: "What's the craziest thing that's ever happened in your cab?"

"My name is Karim," the cab driver responded.

I could see his license up front and it looked like his full name was "Abdikarim".

"Where you from Karim?" Frank asked.

"Somalia," Karim replied.

"Oh yeah, Mogadishu?" Frank asked.

"When I was little boy, my family live in Mogadishu. We had to leave, too dangerous," Karim responded.

"Alright Karim, now give us your best cab story, but make it a quick one, we're almost there," Frank had to get his cab story.

"Cab story?" Karim looked in his rearview mirror at Frank with a confused look.

"Yeah, you know, something crazy that's happened in your cab, you must have a good one for us," Frank kept searching for his story.

"OK, I see, I see, yes, I have good one, just a few weeks ago," Karim had a story for us.

"In morning, I pick up a queen at hotel," Karim started to tell his story.

"A queen, like a drag queen?" I asked.

"Yes, drag queen. She tell me to go to another address. I pick up a little Asian man there," Karim continued.

"Little man, like a midget?" Frank asked.

Karim started laughing. "No, just little man, no midget."

"The little man gets in cab and tells me another address. We pick up another queen." Karim was right, this is a crazy cab story and we haven't even heard the end of it.

"You know, I get a little bit nerve now, wondering why so many stops."

"So, let me see if I have it straight. Two drag queens and a little Asian guy are in the cab, right? I asked.

"Yes, yes. Then it get crazy," Karim had a big smile on his face.

"Little man sitting in middle with arms around two queens, very big queens. Little man places sunglasses on. Then two queens disappear into his lap. I hear belt buckle and zipper. Little man with big smile then turn into moaning and you know, he finish," Karim had us laughing just picturing this odd group.

"Then what happened?" Frank asked.

"Then little man give me same address where I pick up first queen. I drop her off there, then drop him at same place where I pick him up and last queen at her same place. Only 9:30 in morning!" Karim once again was laughing as he finished his crazy story.

"You are the man Karim. I've asked that same question to so many cab drivers over the years and you win, that is the strangest story I've ever heard!" Frank was ecstatic.

"They each give big tip, especially little man. He happy," Karim said with a smile.

"I bet he was! Here you go Karim and thanks for the story," I gave Karim a healthy tip and we stepped out of the cab to continue our night at Vault.

Frank and I quickly recognized that Vault was not exactly our "speed". There was a pretty big line outside that we were perusing as we waited for Sal and Nolan to arrive. I'd say that we had about 10 to 15 years on the rest of the crowd. We kind of looked like the old creepy guys that I remember seeing hanging out at clubs when I was younger. I took a closer look at Frank and determined that he *was* the old creepy guy that I remembered. Frank has a bit of a hairy chest and he wears a gold chain. Tonight he had too many buttons unbuttoned and looked like some kind of cheesy guido.

"Frank, come on, button up. Give me at least one man," I grabbed Frank's shirt and pushed the button and the buttonhole together hoping he would follow my lead.

"Seriously?" Frank looked at me like I was crazy.

"Yes, just one buddy. Look around, we're already out of place as it is," I motioned over to the line of beautiful people in their twenties.

"Fine, fine, are you happy now?" Frank gave me one button and yes, I was happy.

To our surprise and embarrassment, as Frank buttoned his shirt we heard a cackle of laughter coming from the line. It appears that a hot group of young girls was watching and listening to our entire conversation. I think one of them was recording it on their phone. They got a big kick out of my prodding Frank to button his shirt and I had to laugh too. We were out of our league at this place.

We had been waiting outside of Vault for about 15 minutes and there was still no sign of Sal and Nolan. They were right behind us as both cabs pulled out of Pete's. It made no sense that the same four-mile trip would take them so long. I decided to give Sal a call.

"Where the hell are you guys?" I asked Sal.

"Hold on, hold on," Sal replied and then he started yelling at the cab driver along with Nolan.

"Where the fuck are you going?" Sal yelled as he was past the point of being patient.

"You said Vault, I taking you to Vault, right," the cab driver responded.

"Four fucking miles man, our friends have been there for twenty minutes already and we left at the same time," I could hear Nolan yelling now.

"See, Vault, right up here," the cab driver motioned ahead on the right, they were finally there.

The cab pulled up and of course, it was a big scene.

"We're not paying you, you fucking crook. Who the fuck do you think we are, some dumb tourists?" Nolan continued to shout while still in the cab.

All of the sudden the doors locked in the cab.

"You pay me, I drive, you pay," the cab driver turned around and was screaming at Sal and Nolan.

"Fuck you," Sal punched the back of the cab driver's seat.

Frank and I were now standing outside the cab watching this whole thing unfold.

"Open the door mother fucker, open it," Nolan began to tug at the door handle and broke it off.

"I call police," the cab driver yelled and then opened his window.

"Police, police, help!"

He was waiving his arms wildly outside the cab. I could see in the distance that a cop was making his way over to see what was going on.

"How much, how much do they owe?" I yelled at the cab driver.

"Twenty-five," he replied.

I threw thirty dollars into the cab. He unlocked the doors and Sal and Nolan got out. They both had to exit the driver's side as Nolan had broken the handle on the passenger side door.

"You break my door," the cab driver yelled while still seated.

"Fuck you, you're a crook," we held Nolan back as he tried to escalate the confrontation into a physical one.

"Here, fix your door man," I gave the cabbie another fifty bucks.

"Fuckin' crook!" Sal yelled as the cabbie was getting ready to pull away.

As the yellow cab began to move away, he left us with one last thought. "Who cares, I never see you again!" He laughed and sped off.

The entire line of guests outside of Vault witnessed the whole scene. We had only been there for a half hour, but had given them a couple of laughs already. Guido Frank and the cab confrontation weren't the way we had envisioned starting off the night, but things were about to improve dramatically.

Frank, Sal and I started heading over to get in line.

"Hold on for just a couple of minutes guys. Oh, there they are," Nolan started walking in the opposite direction.

We could see a group of three girls walking over to him and then after a closer inspection we realized Nolan had done it again. One of the girls was Kayla. Yes, that Kayla. Our waitress at the pool this morning.

Now, I recall thinking how hot Kayla was when she was wearing her Harrah's issued waitress uniform at the pool. Seeing her in her "going out" attire was astonishing. This girl should not be waiting on tables poolside, she should be on the cover of magazines. Her legs were a mile long and her skirt was borderline illegal it was so short. She was wearing a tight shirt that showed off her cleavage. Her blue eyes against her dark, tanned skin shot right through you and she topped it all off with a beautiful smile and flowing long dark hair. It turns out that Kayla had slipped Nolan her number as we were leaving the pool. Of course, Nolan not only convinced her to meet us out, he had her bring a couple of friends.

Over time, we've all learned a few things about women, but one absolute consistency is that the attractive ones run in packs. This line of thinking was right on the money as we all took a closer look at Kayla's two friends.

Monica and Elizabeth were both right up there with Kayla in the looks department. Monica appeared to be Brazilian. She was wearing a pair of tight jeans that accentuated her ass with a glittery tank top. Her chest wasn't as big as Kayla's, but her body overall may have been slightly better. It was clear that Monica worked out constantly. Her biceps were toned and her stomach appeared to be rock hard. I'm pretty sure that she could curl more than Frank. Elizabeth had an interesting look to her. My bet is that she was once the ugly duckling, but not anymore. She had Auburn-reddish hair and a very light complexion with faint signs of freckles on her nose and cheeks. She was the tallest of the three girls, about six feet with her heels on. She had a very lanky body. Long arms and legs, not much of a chest. Frankly, she looked like a lot of the runway models that you see on the catwalks. Maybe she is one?

"Gentlemen, you know Kayla, but let me introduce you to the beautiful Monica and the lovely Elizabeth," Nolan stated proudly as he put each arm around the girls and brought them over to say hello.

Frank, Sal and I said our hellos, after we wiped the drool off of our faces.

"Alright, now that we've exchanged pleasantries, are we actually going to check this place out?" Sal was anxious to keep his buzz going and he started to walk over to the back of the line.

"Sal, have fun buddy, we're going this way," Nolan motioned over to a door about thirty feet away and began to head that way with the girls.

This place didn't even have a VIP entrance, but Nolan figured out a way to get us in the side door. Yes, it cost him a few bucks, but we all knew Nolan was on a mission since his next stop was prison. He was going out with a bang. We all walked by the long "non-VIP" line and smiled at all of the suckers waiting. We would be the comic relief no more. The group of girls that had such a good time laughing at us earlier watched as Nolan worked his magic again.

The "side" door happened to be the delivery entrance. As we winded our way through the back of the club it reminded us of that scene in Goodfellas where Henry gets the special treatment and tips everyone along the way. Nolan was our Henry tonight. Hundred dollar bills were flying out of his pocket. What did he care? It wasn't his money anyway.

The gentleman that was leading us through the maze that would eventually end up in the club stopped before what appeared to be the entrance into the club. We could certainly hear, but now we could feel the house music pumping through the walls and floors.

"Ladies and gentlemen, welcome to Vault. My name is Steve, it's a pleasure to have you here tonight. I'm speaking to you now because as soon as we walk through this door, you won't be able to hear a word I'm saying," Steve smiled.

"We have two tables set up for you in our VIP area. As you're probably aware, this building used to be a bank. Our VIP area is in the old vault, hence the name of the club. You'll love it. Follow me and I'll get you there safe and sound," Steve opened the door and led the way.

The place was packed. It had three levels with a main dance floor on the first floor, which happened to be directly across from our VIP tables. The second and third floors overlooked the dance floor below and had their own bars that stretched from one end to the other. Both floors had private suites with balconies on each end that hung over the dance floor. I had never seen a place like this, even when I lived in New York.

We arrived at the VIP tables and were introduced to our host for the night, Madeline. Calling these VIP "tables" was a bit of an injustice. We had our own private suite with a refrigerator, wet bar, leather chairs and a couch along with a flat screen television.

"Madeline!" Nolan had to shout as the music was deafening. "This is great, but can you bring a bunch of Red Bull for us?" Apparently the girls' preferred drink was Red Bull and Goose. We had plenty of Goose, but no Red Bull. After all, we're a bunch of forty-plus year olds, not exactly Red Bull speed.

"No Problem!" Madeline shook her head up and down and darted off to retrieve the Red Bull.

Sal decided to get things going with a Jack and Coke. I poured myself a Goose and club soda while Frank went with Goose and tonic. Nolan was enjoying the company of Kayla and Co. and failed to recognize that we were all imbibing again. We knew what he was doing though. He needs to fit in with the youngsters. He'll be joining them with the Red Bull and Goose as soon as Madeline returns.

"Let's take a lap," I said to Frank and Sal while waiving my hand in a circular motion. Sign language may be our primary form of communication tonight.

Frank and Sal nodded their heads and followed me out into the massive crowd.

Maneuvering through the crowd without spilling our drinks quickly became a challenge. We made it to the other end of the dance floor and found a stopping point that was two steps up from the main floor. It gave us a nice bird's eye view of the place. The people watching was amazing. None of us had been in a place like this for years, probably ever. The dance floor was littered with multiple types of people. Of course, there were the groups of girls that are all dancing with each other acting bitchy when a guy tries to infiltrate their little circle, but we all know that one will eventually peel off from the group and give it up to some "lucky" guy. Then you have the "hook-ups" out there grinding on each other ready to take their one night-stand to the next level. There's no doubt a few unwanted pregnancies will result from this night.

Frank, Sal and I were enjoying our people watching time when I felt my phone vibrate. The text was from Janet. It said, "look up". I looked directly above where we were standing to no avail. I didn't see her. Then I looked all the way across the dance floor to the third floor and there she was leaning on the balcony railing. It turns out her company rented out the entire third floor. I waived in her direction, which of course, caught the attention of Frank and Sal.

"Is that her? Janet?" Sal yelled as he pointed up to the third floor balcony.

"Stop pointing asshole," I yelled back at Sal.

"What, what, I can't hear you," Sal mocked me as he kept pointing at Janet.

"She's a hottie dude!" Sal confirmed what I already knew. "Bring her down to our VIP area man".

I motioned to Janet to have her come downstairs. She shook her head side-to-side and motioned for me to come up there.

"I'm going up there, wanna go with me," I motioned to Sal while pointing to the third floor.

"You go, I'm going to work my magic with Monica, or Elizabeth, either or," Sal laughed and grabbed Frank by the arm to make their way through the sea of people.

As I pushed my way through the crowd I couldn't help but think I was going down the wrong road. I have to admit, I enjoyed the flirting, but I was well aware that I was playing with fire.

I made it over to the spiral staircase that wound up to the third floor. Since this was a private party I wasn't sure how I was going to get in, but I pressed on. I made it to the third floor landing and other than the same music playing on the first and second floors, the atmosphere was completely different here. I looked around and then it dawned on me. This is where all of the old people were hanging out. I fit right in with this demo and that's why I simply walked right in without anyone saying a word. As a matter of fact, a guy in his early twenties was stopped right behind me and turned away when he couldn't produce proof that he was part of the medical device convention group. I believe that proof was a simple lanyard, but it was obvious, this guy was a douche that didn't belong.

All of the sudden I felt someone grab my elbow. That was it, I was being kicked out. I turned around to find that I wasn't being ejected, it was Janet.

"Hey there!" I said with a big smile and went in for the peck on the cheek. I realize that was a bit odd as I just met her, but it felt appropriate.

"So glad you're here," Janet smiled back at me and grabbed my hand to take me deeper into the party.

"Aren't you worried?" It was so challenging to carry on a conversation, but she heard me loud and clear on this one. These are people that she works with. They know she is married. I realize she is only holding my hand, but still.

"I'm only holding your hand, no worries here, maybe later," Janet winked at me and kept moving along.

Frank and Sal arrived back at the VIP area, which happened to be empty.

"There he is, what an idiot," Frank pointed out to the dance floor. Nolan was dancing, well, if you want to call it that.

Don't get me wrong, I won't be on Dancing with the Stars anytime soon, but Nolan is just God awful. He's so bad that it is embarrassing to look at.

"I'm gonna waive him over. He's going to ruin any chance that he had with those girls if he keeps that up," Frank made a beeline onto the dance floor leaving Sal to tend to the VIP area, as if it needed tending.

Janet and I made our way into her suite. It was similar to ours, but the balcony overlooking the dance floor was perfect.

"Look at that guy, oh my goodness, that is simply terrific," Janet began laughing uncontrollably.

I took a closer look and sure enough, it was Nolan.

"Watch this, it will get better," I said as I could see Frank busting through the crowd. He was either going to dance, which is also a treat or pull Nolan out of there.

Janet finally figured out that the goofy guy on the dance floor was Nolan. "Oh, that's him, that's him, your buddy!" She continued to laugh hysterically.

"Just keep watching," I said.

Frank, in his most stealth move yet, decided that he wasn't going to simply bust out onto the dance floor and pull Nolan off. He decided that he was going to dance his way onto the dance floor to grab his friend. I'm not sure what he was doing, but it was some sort of half-dance, stroll, but it was too much for Janet and I.

"Frank!" I yelled knowing that there was no way he could hear me two floors down. "Woo hoo, you go Frankie!" Man, was this a riot.

As our laughter subsided, I noticed that we were all alone in the suite. Before I knew it, Janet decided to be the aggressor. She grabbed me and kissed me passionately to the point that we fell onto the couch. I have to admit, I reciprocated immediately and began to grope her body starting up her thigh all the way to her breasts. Her dress was pulled up above her right thigh. She pulled me on top of her and I placed my hand on her panties. She thrust her hips into my hand. Of course, I was aroused. Janet grabbed my dick outside of my pants. I began to think that we were going to have sex right here on the couch in the suite. Suddenly, someone walked in and Janet jumped up from the couch. It reminded me of when I was a teenager at my girlfriend's house and her parents would walk in. We'd jump up and act like nothing was going on, but we knew we were caught red handed. This was the same situation except we were adults and the person that walked in happened to be one of Janet's best friends, not only at work, but as far back as high school.

"Jesus Christ Janet, what the fuck are you doing? I didn't see this, no don't put this on me, I won't be able to look Michael in the eyes the next time I see him," Paula yelled in disgust.

Janet ran out the door after Paula. I sat on the couch with my head in my hands wondering how I let this situation evolve to this. Lisa would kill me if she knew about this. I'm an asshole, plain and simple. No excuses.

I gathered my composure, tucked my shirt back in and headed out of the suite. I was met at the door by Janet.

"Can I talk to you?" She asked.

"Janet, this is a bad idea, right?" I knew I was right, but something inside me was secretly hoping that she would disagree.

"Kevin, we knew this was a bad idea from the moment we starting flirting at the bar, but I just can't help it. Don't worry about Paula. She'll cool down soon enough," Janet grabbed my hand moved behind me and put her other hand on my back directing me out of the suite. "Let's go find your friends."

We made our way over to the staircase. Paula watched us as we started down and what I expected to be a punishing glare, actually was a look of disappointment and a headshake from side-to-side. Much worse than a glare. As I looked at Paula I couldn't help but see Lisa's face with the same expression. What the hell was I doing?

We came upon the boys and the party had heightened to the next level. Nolan was on the couch with Kayla making out like their plane was going down. Sal even got into the action with Monica. He had her pressed up against the wall with his tongue down her throat. I have to admit, nice get for Sal. I didn't know he had it in him, well, with "non-working" girls. After all, Monica is not a stripper, well at least I don't believe she is?

"Frank, you remember Janet," Frank was sitting with Elizabeth sipping a cocktail. It didn't appear either one was into the other, but the night was still young.

"Janet, this is Elizabeth," I introduced the two ladies.

I directed Janet to the couch and sat her down next to Elizabeth.

"Frankie, come over here for a second," I motioned to Frank to follow me over to an area that was out of the ladies' hearing range.

"So what's your story? Any sparks between you and Elizabeth?" I pressed him for details.

"Come on, that's not happening. No interest on her part and no interest on my part," Frank replied.

"She's hot Frankie, why aren't you giving it a try?" I sounded like Nolan now.

"Kevin, I'm not sure what you are up to you right now and it's really none of my business, but I'm not going to take a page out of that book. It's just not worth it. Sorry to rain on your parade, but hooking up with this girl has no positives attached to it. Why risk my marriage like that? Not going to happen," Frank laid to rest any thoughts that he and Elizabeth would be following in the footsteps of the rest of our group.

Before I could get a response out I felt hands rubbing my shoulders. I turned around and Janet was with us.

"Everything OK, you guys look like you were in a deep conversation?" Janet asked as she could see the serious look on Frank's face.

"Nope, we're good, so what's up?" I grabbed Janet's hand.

"I think your friends are ready to go," Janet motioned to Nolan and Sal as they headed our way.

"Let's do it, we're outta here, back to the hotel," Nolan proclaimed as he and Kayla stumbled over to us. "I have an SUV waiting outside, let's go".

I was relieved to hear Nolan say that we were leaving. Separating from Janet would save me from doing something stupid.

"Alright, I guess we're going," I said to Janet as we started to make our way out of the VIP area.

"Come on, let's go," a drunken Nolan put one arm around me and his other arm around Janet ushering us out. Janet looked over at me and gave me a look as if to say "when in Rome". She was coming back with us.

We made our way through the crowd. Nolan was with Kayla, making out the whole way. Sal was with Monica, doing the same. Janet and I were simply holding each other's hands and Frank and

Elizabeth, thrown together not by choice, weren't even walking next to each other.

We piled into the SUV that only sat seven, but Nolan was happy to place Kayla on his lap for the ride back to the hotel. Janet and I didn't say much to each other during the short trip back to the hotel. I was nervous and I could sense that her free-spirited ways were beginning to diminish a little bit as well. Reality was setting in for us. We both knew what the next step was. We're both adults, it's late and we're heading back to our hotel rooms. Surely, it's not to have a nightcap and a handshake. Other than Frank and Elizabeth, the writing was on the wall for all of the couples in the SUV.

The SUV pulled up to Harrah's. I'm pretty sure that Nolan and Kayla made out the entire way back to the hotel. They were both hammered, but having a good time nonetheless. The drunken group stumbled into the lobby and headed toward the elevators.

"Whose room are we going to?" Frank asked as he was under the impression the eight of us would continue partying in someone's room.

"You're going to your room pal, that's where," Sal joined in the conversation as he and Monica almost fell over.

Elizabeth looked at both of her friends with disgust. Frank being the gentleman that he his took her aside and offered to pay for a cab to get her home. They walked back outside as the elevator door popped open and enveloped Sal, Monica, Nolan and Kayla.

Janet and I were left alone. Neither one of us had pushed the "up" button to call the elevator yet. Janet pulled me in and gave me a kiss and a smile. She leaned over and pushed the button. My heart was racing. I heard the "bing" of the elevator and the doors opened. Janet grabbed my hand and I took a step toward the open elevator.

"Janet, I need to say good night now," I pulled her back from the elevator doors. The doors shut and she replied, "I know, I know".

She hit the button again and the doors opened. She gave me a peck on the cheek and squeezed my hand and walked into the waiting elevator. She hit floor number 17 and looked at me as the doors closed and just like that she was gone. I have to admit, part of me wanted to hop in the next elevator and go after her, but I couldn't do that to Lisa. What I had done already was bad enough and going upstairs with Janet would cross the line even more. A sense of relief came over me.

"Good job Kevin," I didn't realize that Frank had come up behind me. He had witnessed the goodbye with Janet.

"I'm still an asshole, but I could have made it a lot worse," I replied to Frank's complimentary gesture.

"You could have, but you didn't, so just leave it at that. Now, the other two idiots upstairs, that's a whole other ballgame," Frank laughed and we entered the elevator.

It was a long, interesting night, but one that I'll never forget. As I walked down the hallway to my room I felt my phone vibrate. Sure enough, it was Janet texting me.

"Good night, stay in touch"

I replied: "Good night Janet" and then deleted her number from my phone.

It was about 10am when I woke up the next morning. I probably would have slept longer, but I awoke to a sharp pain in my stomach. I had been doing pretty well and I knew I was due for an issue sooner or later. I hurried over to the toilet and unfortunately, that wonderful steak dinner that I had last night ended up coming out the wrong end. Luckily, this puking session put an end to the pain that I was feeling. I was anxious to see the guys this morning and hear their stories from last night. I was also looking forward to connecting with Anthony, as I'm sure he had a spectacular night filled with a bunch of good stories as well.

I grabbed my phone and noticed that I had three new text messages. Oh boy, I assumed these were from Janet, but I was wrong. All three were from Lisa. I had forgotten to text her last night before I went to bed and she was worried. Now, a lot of wives would be worried that their husbands were out cheating on them, but that's not Lisa. She was simply concerned for my safety. It's ironic that in this instance, she should have been concerned about the cheating. I couldn't imagine if Janet was in my room right now and I had to look at the text messages from Lisa. The guilt would have been enormous. A naked woman lying in my bed, while my wife is worried at home. I dodged a bullet on this one. A huge sense of relief came over me.

I had just gotten out of the shower when I heard a knock at the door. I looked through the peephole to find Frank and Sal waiting outside.

"Come on, get some clothes on, we're starving," Sal said as he barged into my room.

"OK, OK, I'll be ready in about ten minutes," I replied. "Where's Nolan?"

"I spoke to him. He said he was going to hit it one more time and then he'll be ready," Sal laughed.

"Speaking of hitting it, how'd it go last night with Monica?" I asked with a somewhat clear conscience, as I know how I could answer the same question about Janet.

"I was telling Frankie that I think my dick is broken and my balls are empty, what a freak she was, holy shit!" Sal smiled as he popped open a diet Coke from the mini-bar.

"So where is she, still in your room?" Frank asked.

"Hell no, get this, she's not only a freak in the sack, but she's also a complete nut job," Sal continued with his story.

"You know what they say, crazy in the head, crazy in the bed," I yelled out from the bathroom, as I was finishing up getting ready.

"Exactly." "So we wake up this morning and I decide to get a quickie in before I send her on her way. She obliges and then it gets strange", Sal is enjoying telling us this story pacing back and forth with his arms flailing around.

"She rolls over and says 'what now?'"

"I look at her and tell her that we're getting back on the cruiser and moving on to the next stop, but it was clear that's not what she was asking. She says, 'no, what now between us?' I'm thinking to myself, what the fuck is she talking about? I'm pretty sure what took place between us was clearly a one nightstand, but apparently she has a different idea," Sal continued.

"She knows you're married, right?" Frank asked.

"No, she doesn't, but that's beside the point Frankie, just let me finish," Sal was irritated with Frank's "mother hen" question.

"Then she says this, and I'm not kidding, 'I love you Nolan and I want to see you again'!" "Yes, yes, she said Nolan, it was fucking great. You don't know what I had to do to hold back the laughter. Seriously, I had to turn over and face the other way. I think I bit a hole through the side of my mouth trying not to laugh," Sal was laughing hysterically now.

"That's fucking great man, holy shit, then what?" I asked as I laughed as well.

"I told her about my impending prison sentence and that she has no future with me!" Sal started rolling on the floor after he let that one out.

Frank and I joined him, as although Nolan's situation isn't funny, the fact that Sal was quick enough to throw that one out there to Monica was hysterical.

"It gets better, I gave her Nolan's cell!" Sal had done it. This was the funniest story of the trip so far, hands down.

It took us a few minutes to gather our composure after that story. It was time to get out of Reno. We hadn't heard from Nolan and the other unknown was Anthony. None of us had seen or heard from him since we left the pool yesterday. All we knew was that he was drunk and had $10k to blow. Hopefully we still have a driver for this trip and the cruiser for that matter. I'm sure he'll have a few stories for us when we catch up with him. It'll be hard to top Sal's though.

"Yeah, meet us downstairs in ten minutes. I'm not sure, no one has seen him since the pool," Sal hung up from Nolan.

"Nope, he hasn't seen him either, but he hasn't called him yet. I'll try him now." Sal grabbed his phone in an attempt to reach Anthony.

"It's going straight to voicemail," Sal said as he began to leave a message. "Ant, where are you buddy, we're going to be in the lobby in ten minutes. Time to get outta Dodge."

"That's not a good sign," a concerned Frank said.

"He's probably passed out in his room. Anyone know what room he was in?" I asked.

"I have no idea and I don't even know what his last name is, do you Sal?" Frank replied.

"Yeah, it's Patterson, call the front desk," Sal pointed to the phone.

"Yes, can you connect me to Anthony Patterson's room," Frank asked the attendant at the front desk.

"She put me on hold. No, I'm still here. He what? Do you know why? Seriously, he's a friend of ours and we don't know where he is. Come on, that's ridiculous." Frank hung up.

"Well, that's not good. She said he was 'removed from the premises' at 1am last night," Frank relayed the bad news to us.

"We better get downstairs and find the cruiser. It's gotta be down there. He was too drunk to drive that thing anywhere and towing that thing has got to be a bitch," I threw the last of my things in my suitcase and we headed downstairs.

The elevator couldn't move fast enough. We got off in the lobby and saw Nolan sending Kayla on her way. Surprisingly enough she didn't seem too concerned to be doing the walk of shame in her own place of business. I have a feeling that it wasn't the first time that's happened.

"Nolan!" Sal yelled and waived him over to us.

"Have you seen or heard from Anthony?" Sal asked.

"No, I thought you guys knew where he was," Nolan replied.

"Nope, the front desk told us that he was "removed" from the hotel at 1am last night," Frank shared the details with Nolan.

"Seriously, that's a good night man," Nolan laughed.

"Yeah, a good night, but who knows where that dude is. He could be in jail, dead, who the fuck knows," Sal began walking to the back entrance of the hotel, as that is where the cruiser had been parked yesterday.

Sal opened the door and luckily, the cruiser was still there. We didn't have the keys, but at least it was still there.

"He's gotta be in there," Frank said.

"Oh, I think someone is in there alright!" I said as we approached the cruiser.

We stepped closer and closer to the cruiser and we could see it ever so slightly rocking back and forth. Yes, Anthony was in there getting busy or at least we think it was Anthony.

Frank approached the door and tried the handle, but it was locked.

"Hold on man, let him at least finish up in there," Nolan requested with a laugh.

Now, here was the scene. The four of us standing outside the cruiser that we rented while our driver was in there banging some chick. I looked around at our group and it was clear that we weren't the young pups we were back when we took this trip twenty years ago. Back then, rebounding from a night like last night would have been easy. Hell, we would have already started drinking by this time in the day back then. Believe it or not, this brief moment was one of the best times of the trip so far. The vibe amongst the four of us hadn't been better. We had a fantastic time last night and everyone was smiling and laughing. Times like these are what we all remember from the last trip. These little moments in time that left a memory that will make us all smile in five, ten, even twenty years from now. I'm gonna miss these guys terribly. These are my guys. The good, the bad, the ugly, whatever comes along with them, I love them. I didn't say much as we waited outside the cruiser. I just listened and observed. I knew this was one of those moments and I wanted to make sure it was securely deposited into my memory bank. There was no need to snap a picture, as this was a time that I'll never forget. I smiled and took it all in. Hopefully, Anthony could last a little longer!

About seven minutes later the rocking stopped. Frank was very anxious to get on the road.

"Can I knock now?" A frustrated Frank asked permission, although he was going to knock no matter what we said.

Frank walked over to the cruiser door and before he could knock he heard the door start to open. Anthony popped the door open and to our surprise, he decided that boxers or a towel were too difficult to find to cover himself in. As a matter of fact, he didn't even take the condom off!

"Fellas, where you been? It's time to get the fuck outta Reno boys," Anthony said with a big smile as his condom-covered dick stared us in the face.

The laughter was outrageous and there's no way the woman, whoever she was, in the cruiser didn't hear us.

"Let's go, time to get outta here now. Come on baby, we're late," Anthony yelled back to his woman friend.

We could all faintly see through the windows a woman making her way to the front of the cruiser. Anthony was now standing outside the cruiser, naked, unless of course you count the condom that he had on still.

"Alright baby, cabs are at the front of the hotel," Anthony ushered his one nightstand along.

"Hello, how are you?" Frank tried to be as polite as possible.

Anthony's woman looked at Frank in disgust. She was disheveled, humiliated and let's just say, Anthony likes them big. She was holding her heels in one hand and her purse in the other. Her skirt was way too small for her and was hiked way up as we could almost see the merchandise. I'd say she was just a drop over two bills. She had a pretty face, even after a night like she just had she was able to hold her own, but boy was she big. Her tits must have been triple D's or maybe larger, if there is such a thing. An ass that would have made Sir Mix A Lot proud. We all stared at her as she made her way to the front of the hotel to catch a cab. It was like a train wreck, you so badly want to look away, but you just can't stop staring. Anthony snapped us out of it.

"You like that boys, yep, Anthony hit that all night," Anthony's huge belly laugh followed. "Now, let's get going."

"That's cool Ant, but how about throwing some clothes on first," Sal motioned to the big condom wrapped cock that was hanging there in front of us still.

It was a little after noon by the time the cruiser pulled away from Harrah's. Reno proved to be a stop on the trip that will be hard to top. Many a story came out of Reno, but probably only a couple that we can actually share with others. Most of our escapades will live and die with the four of us, well, the five of us as Anthony has some dirt on all of us now. Then again, we have some dirt on him, although it doesn't matter since he has no one to answer to, unlike the four of us.

"Where to fellas?" A fully dressed Anthony asked the group.

"We're heading to Napa Ant," Sal replied. "I think it's about four hours away."

"Sounds about right, that's a piece of cake. I was hoping you weren't going to ask me to drive ten hours!" A relieved and tired Anthony revealed.

Chapter Seven

All four of us were exhausted after last night, but the adrenalin rush from such a fun night kept us all awake. We were all in need of showers and some Listerine desperately, but for now we were content with sitting around bullshitting and laughing about the details of last night. Now that I was sober, I felt a little guilt for what I had done, but the relief was more overwhelming because I knew what I hadn't done. For Sal and Nolan, I don't believe guilt was one of the emotions that they were feeling right now. It was just like college. Their emotions were all about pride and satisfaction of a night that went well. They got laid. After all, in college that was often the goal of each night for both of them. This morning wasn't much different than sitting around the lounge in our fraternity house and swapping stories like we used to do twenty years ago. Of course, that's an exaggeration as everything is different now. Kids, marriages, mortgages and prison terms of all things now litter the landscapes of our lives.

While we were all sitting there laughing and sharing our own version of last night's events I think it hit us, that this is it. This trip won't happen again. It was a miracle that we were able to get it together this time. The odds of it happening again are minimal, after all Nolan is going to prison and of course, the guys still don't know about my situation. The reality is, it will not be repeated, not a chance. We know it, but not one of us is going to say it. We're determined to live in the moment because this is a special time for us that will never, ever happen again.

We were on the road for about an hour and a half and it was just Nolan and me that were still awake. Sal and Frank were wiped out and passed out almost in mid-sentence as the stories continued to flow from the night before. I was wired and was very surprised that I didn't want to sleep as well, but for some reason I wasn't tired. I had a slight headache, but was more dehydrated than anything else. These weren't symptoms that would be able to hold me back. The easiest thing to do is just grab another drink.

"Nol', want one?" I was holding two cans of beer in my hand. We bought Natural Light cans for the trip just for fun, as that was our beer of choice back in school. More of a forced choice since it was the cheapest.

"You're an animal, sure I'll have one."

I tossed over the cold can and Nolan snagged it with one hand. We simultaneously popped open the beers. Nolan's foamed over a bit, as it was a little shaken up with my toss.

"Cheers buddy," Nolan raised his can and we tapped together the two beers.

"How you feelin' man?" I asked as we both took big swigs.

"A bit of a headache, but I'm good," Nolan replied.

"No, that's not what I'm talking about. How are you holding up?" I made it clear that I was referring to his situation, not his hangover.

"Oh, I gotcha. Yep, to tell you the truth this trip has been such a great distraction I haven't really thought about it, well ever since the episode in Colorado."

I can't remember the last time Nolan and I had a "heart-to-heart", but it seemed like we were heading in that direction. He's not the easiest nut to crack. He never likes to appear vulnerable, therefore, he keeps a lot of his feelings bottled up inside.

"It's OK to be scared you know. I sure as hell would be," I continued the conversation hoping to prompt Nolan into letting his guard down a bit.

"It's the finality of the whole thing that depresses me the most. I mean, I don't really have a chance to beat this thing. I did it and the paper trail is all there, leads right back to me," Nolan sighed and then took another swig from the Natural Light can.

I was careful not to chime in with any "I told you so" type of comments. This wasn't the time for that kind of dialogue. At this point, what's done is done.

"So, what's next?" I asked.

"When we get back I'll drive to Nashville and I'm turning myself in. I'll go straight to a federal prison, not sure where, but that's where I'll go to await trial. There will be a ton of depositions to follow as others will fall before this is all over," Nolan provided me with details for the first time.

"I'm surprised that you were even able to go on this trip," I wondered how he pulled this off.

"Yeah, call it a last request. I had to beg my attorney, who then begged the judge to allow me to wonder the country for a couple of weeks. I guess I proved to them that I'm not a flight risk. I'm not, but the star of the DA's show almost blew his brains out in Colorado. That I'm sure would have surprised everyone," Nolan smiled and shook his head back and forth.

"Would have ruined our trip for sure," I tried to make light of the crazy series of events that took place in Colorado.

"You know, I wouldn't have done it, pulled the trigger," Nolan suddenly got serious. "I wouldn't go out that way. That's how everyone would like for it to end, but that won't happen. I know what people think of me. I take the path of least resistance, right?"

I didn't answer Nolan's rhetorical question.

"Not this time. I'll take my medicine. It will absolutely suck, but I'll take it and see where I end up. I know it's likely that I'll die in prison. That hurts, it really does. I got greedy. I had plenty of money that I earned legitimately, but it just wasn't enough. Once I got in too deep I spent most of my time trying to stay afloat. The stress was killing me."

Nolan finished his can of beer and crushed it in his hand. He walked over to the refrigerator and grabbed two more cans. This time he flung one over to me, which I grabbed with two hands, opened it and quickly sucked the foam before it overflowed.

"This is the most relaxed I've been in years. Believe it or not, it's a relief to be going to prison. Not that going to prison is something I want, but it signals an end to all of the cover-up, lies and plain old deception that my life has become," Nolan leaned back and looked beyond my shoulder to the scenic drive that we were on as we inched closer to Napa.

Nolan's phone began to vibrate. He grabbed it and took a quick look.

"Yep, her again. She won't stop," Nolan placed the phone down next to him, as he had no plans to respond.

"Was that Carrie?" I asked.

"Of course," Nolan replied.

"Have you spoken to her since we saw her?"

"No, don't want to. I know what she's calling about."

"Well, you did sleep with her and just hauled ass, right?" I figured answering her call might be appropriate.

"I wish that's why she was calling, but it's not," Nolan said confidently.

"So why the hell is she calling then?" Now I was curious.

"I'm surprised that not one of you guys asked me what was inside the boxes that I left for her and the kids."

"Why are you surprised? We've all given our wives and kids gifts before, what was so special about these?" I wasn't sure what could be so important about these gifts.

"It's probably better that you don't know. I don't want to get you involved," Nolan replied.

"Come on now, you can't leave me hanging like that," I pleaded with Nolan to reveal what was in the boxes.

"If I tell you, you'll have to commit perjury if you're called to testify, so drop it," Nolan said trying to protect me, but I wasn't having any of it.

"I'll deal with that, plus, what the hell would I be called to testify for?" I felt strongly about that statement. I've never had anything to do with Nolan beyond our friendship.

"Fine, each box had $50k in cash inside. I needed to help them out with something before all of my assets were frozen. I grabbed a bunch of cash from the house and packed it up for them. $150k obviously won't set them up for life, but I figure it will go a long way to help with college tuition and a few other things. After all, I owe them something, that's my family." Nolan had a defiant look on his face as to say, "screw you" to the authorities.

"Do me a favor Kevin, keep that to yourself. I don't want the guys to know. I really shouldn't have told you, but what's done is done, just do me that favor and go to your grave with it, thanks," Nolan wasn't looking for a response and one wasn't required. I knew what to do with the information and he didn't know that "taking it to my grave" was a shorter timeframe than he understood at the time. Soon he'll know.

When we embarked on this trip the last person I thought I'd have a heart-to-heart with was Nolan, but sure enough it happened. It made me feel great inside. Almost like I accomplished something no one else could. Maybe I just caught him at the right time. I'm sure if I fell asleep and Sal or Frank were awake they would have shared this special moment with Nolan, but I'd like to believe it was me that made him feel comfortable enough to share his thoughts in what must be a ridiculously challenging time for him. Maybe I'll tell him sometime how much this conversation meant to me, but for now we'll move on and chalk it up to good timing. Thanks Nolan, my friend.

"You guys been boozin' this whole time?" A groggy Frank asked as he stretched, reaching the ceiling of the cruiser, twisting his torso side-to-side.

"Want a Natty Frankie?" I asked as there were a few left even though Nolan and I put a nice dent into the supply during our talk.

"Why not, fire one over for Sal too," Frank volunteered Sal for a beer, which was a safe bet.

"Where are we Ant?" Sal yelled to the front of the cruiser.

"About 45 minutes out. St. Helena, right?" Anthony yelled back.

"Napa boys, Napa, good times await!" Sal stated what should have been obvious for all of us.

Anthony was guiding the cruiser through the winding roads as the picturesque scenery flew by mile after mile. The four of us were staring out the windows of the cruiser taking it all in. A little bit closer and our noses would have been pressed against the windows. We had all been to Napa in the past, but the sights are always pleasing no matter how many times you've had the opportunity to take them in. Whipping past the rows and rows of vineyards thinking of how meticulous farming them must be to get the grapes just right to blend the perfect bottle of wine. It's a labor of love for a lot of the vineyard owners and we're just here for a short time to sample some of their hard work.

This part of our trip will be tamer than the train wreck that took place in Reno. Yes, we'll drink plenty, but it's a bit more challenging to get in trouble in Napa, although I wouldn't put it past this group.

"Coming up on the left Ant, Heritage Inn," I said as we approached our destination.

I booked this place quite a while ago, as a client recommended it to me. Granted, he recommended it as a perfect place to take Lisa for a romantic getaway, but I'm hoping the atmosphere will be right for us to not over do it. In other words, show some class.

The cruiser pulled into the long driveway, which was lined with enormous oak trees. Anthony drove slowly as some of the branches hung so low that they ever so slightly scraped the top of the cruiser. In addition to the oaks, wide-open fields with manicured lawns that appeared to have just been mowed flanked the driveway. Anthony took us as far as he could go, as the clearance in front of the lobby was too low for the cruiser. We filed out of the cruiser, I'm sure still reeking of booze, but showers were on the way. Yep, the lawn was just mowed. I took in a big whiff. I love the smell of freshly cut grass.

As we approached the entrance two gentlemen greeted us and politely opened the heavy wooden doors for us, each grabbing one. They directed us to the front desk. The front portion of the lobby was equipped with luxurious marble floors that turned into a red carpet with a gold trim that contained a sitting area, tasting bar and a fireplace. We each roamed around the lobby taking in the framed photos that lined the walls. They served as a historical timeline of the property and the property owners that dated back to the mid-1800's. Just as my client had indicated, this place was a gem.

"Hello gentlemen, welcome to The Heritage Inn," Holly greeted us from behind the front desk. "I'll be happy to assist you with check-in. Would you mind sharing the name in which the reservation was booked?"

I made my way over to Holly and provided her with the necessary information.

"OK, here it is. We have four cottages reserved for tonight and they happen to be ready right now." Holly said with a smile. She was very cute, we'll have to keep Nolan away from her, this isn't Reno.

We gathered our room keys from Holly and instructed the bellman to the cruiser to grab our luggage. As we walked from the lobby towards our cottages we enjoyed taking in the scenery. The property opened up to a small vineyard, well, small for Napa anyway. It was so peaceful as the vines stretched out and crept up the side of a hill that we could see in the distance. A gazebo was strategically placed on the edge of the vineyard that was perfect for partaking in a bottle of wine or two with friends. I'm sure we'll be back to this spot shortly to kick off the night.

"It's almost five o'clock now, how about we meet down here at 6pm. We can knock back a couple of bottles right here and then head to downtown Napa for our dinner. Sound good?" Frank took the lead on the night's events.

All four of our cottages were side-by-side in a somewhat secluded area of the property. We passed through a small gate and made our way along the brick path. One-by-one each of us peeled off the path as our cottage appeared. My cottage was the last one down the path.

Being back in Napa brought back great memories of my first time here. It was with Lisa and it was our first anniversary. The accommodations weren't this nice on our trip, but it didn't matter. We had a fabulous time enjoying each other's company, taking in the sights and of course, tasting plenty of wine. That was nine years ago. We had planned on making it back here for our ten-year anniversary, but like so many things in life we felt like we could put it off and figure out a way to squeeze it in later. We had booked the trip, but ended up canceling as work and everyday life just got in the way. I'm regretting that decision immensely now. I haven't had a lot of time to accept my sickness and where it will eventually lead me, but I'm quickly understanding that I've made some big mistakes in my life. Most of which have to do with the fact that I've placed work ahead of my personal life. I've been so driven to succeed professionally and I've climbed the ladder successfully, but I'm realizing that there is a lot more to life than fancy titles and money. Don't get me wrong, I love my career and all of the exciting things I've been able to do because of it, but I don't know how to balance anything. It's full speed ahead or nothing with me when it comes to my professional life. While it has paid off for us financially, I feel like I've failed as a husband and father. I have plenty of friends that have struggled finding a career. They've bounced around from industry to industry, from job to job and I know they look at me sometimes and say 'wow, that guy is living the dream'. What they don't know is that I'm looking at them and realizing that they are the ones living the dream. There's nothing more important in life than family and friends. All of the money and professional success a person can accumulate and achieve doesn't mean much without having someone to share it with. Yes, I have a fabulous wife and two adorable little girls, but am I a part of their lives? Not the way I should be. Lisa has said to me many times that it's all about work with me and she and the kids come second. I, of course, vehemently denied that statement and my anger didn't hide it. I know I was angry and denying it not because I was right, but because Lisa has always been right. My number one fault is that she's been telling me that for years and I just didn't want to listen. Now I'm sitting here with the clock ticking down to the final seconds of my life and I'm just full of regrets. I've already started pleading with God to help me make things right. I've even resorted to the old bargaining technique. 'Please God, if you cure me from this illness I'll be the best husband and father ever, please God, give me a chance'. I'm going to fight this and I'm going to fight hard, but what if I don't make it? That's what scares me. I've been thinking a lot about the saying, "How can you die if you've never really lived?" That's the way I feel. I haven't lived, I've just worked. I desperately need another chance and I'll be doing whatever I can to beat the odds.

The water coming out of the showerhead cascading over my body felt fantastic. It was like I was finally getting rid of the sin from Reno. It was about 5:45pm when I got out of the shower. I quickly ironed a shirt and a pair of pants and made my way over to the gazebo.

"Sally, what's up buddy?" Sal was the first one there, which was odd as he's usually the last one to do anything.

"We're all set, I have four bottles ready to go. Three cabs and a pinot," Sal directed my attention to the group of bottles lined up on the small table in the back portion of the gazebo.

"Wow, you've been busy. Let's pop one of those open and get this started. You pick."

The view from the gazebo was incredible. The sun was just about ready to dip down into the hills and was producing long shadows. The wine bottles were lined up in a perfect position and the light was careening off the glass and provided a little sparkle. Sal walked over to open a bottle and his long shadow followed him along.

"You better be pouring four glasses Sal," Nolan yelled over as he and Frank made their way up the path to the gazebo.

"One step ahead of you," Sal had already starting pouring the third and fourth glasses.

"Look at this boys, look at this," Nolan proclaimed as he walked up the steps into the gazebo.

"Cheers guys," Sal raised his glass and we all met in the middle of the gazebo to clink ours together.

A bottle of wine doesn't last long when it's split amongst four people. We polished off the first bottle and we were a couple sips into number two when a young couple came walking up the path with a bottle of wine and two glasses.

Both were quite tall. I'd say the guy was about 6'4". He was lanky with a shaved head. The kind of shaved head by design, not because he was bald like Nolan. He had one of those funky little soul patches. His plaid, short-sleeve button down was unbuttoned low enough to reveal his tank top undershirt. His jeans were a bit worn and he was wearing sandals.

The woman, who appeared to be either the guy's wife or at least his fiancé, was about 5'10". She had curly auburn hair that flowed down to the mid-point of her back. She was wearing a tank top with a long flowing patterned dress. She was also wearing sandals. They both had that "granola" type look.

"Good evening guys, mind if we join you?" The guy politely asked with a smile while holding the bottle up in one hand and the glasses in the other.

"As long as you don't mind the four of us intruding on what was probably going to be a nice romantic sunset for the two of you," Frank replied.

The couple smiled and continued up the steps to find a seat in the gazebo.

"Well, let me make the introductions. That's Frank, this guy over here is Kevin, there's Nolan and I'm Sal. We're from South Florida, Atlanta, Nashville and Houston. OK, now your turn."

"Wow, OK, I'm Matt and this is my wife Brooke. We're just over here from Santa Cruz."

"We're on our honeymoon," Brooke chimed in.

"Alright, congratulations. Hold on, give me those glasses," Frank grabbed the glasses and walked over to our bottles of wine.

"Cheers and congratulations," Frank gave Matt and Brooke full glasses of one of our cabs.

"May it be your only honeymoon," Nolan raised his glass and laughed at his own toast.

Matt and Brooke looked to be about twenty-five or twenty-six. Kind of young to get married if you ask me, but to each his own. They looked happy, but hell who wasn't happy on their honeymoon?

Our reservation wasn't until 9pm and it became clear that the four bottles that Sal bought weren't going to last that long. Nolan, in a typical Nolan move, dialed the front desk from his cell phone and requested that four more bottles be delivered to the gazebo. After all, the front desk was about 100 yards away and who would want to walk that far?

The "kids" were having a good time with us and we were enjoying their company as well. Both were very sharp and well cultured. For such young people, they've traveled quite a bit. Being so young, they didn't have a big budget, but they made their travels work by staying in youth hostiles or just camping out along the way. They were getting as much of it in before the grind of real life set in, although, just by speaking to them for a little bit it was clear that they weren't going to fall victim to the grind anytime soon. They had everything in front of them now. It was a very exciting time for them and the nice part about is that they recognized that. Boy, they must have special parents. These kids had it all together.

"So, how old are the two of you?" Sal asked.

"I'm twenty-seven and Brooke is twenty-five," Matt replied. I was only a year off in my guess.

"Are you gonna have kids right away?" Sal continued getting even more personal.

"Well, not right away. Maybe in a few years," Brooke responded as she took another sip of wine.

"Good move, no need to rush it. Don't make the same mistake I made, make sure you really like each other first," Sal said referring to the obvious rough patch that he and Katie had been going through.

"Don't get me wrong, I love my daughter, but she'd be much better off if the wife and I weren't getting a divorce," Sal clarified his earlier statement and got our attention.

The confirmation that Sal was getting divorced was news to all of us. Granted it didn't come as a huge surprise, but to have him nonchalantly throw that big piece of news into a conversation with strangers was a bit odd.

"See Matt and Brooke, check out the faces on these guys over here," Sal pointed to each of us.

"Look at them, they're shocked. Yep, we're getting divorced, finally. We can't stand each other. It's either divorce or prison for me, no offense Nolan. If we stay together any longer one of us is going to kill the other, guaranteed," Sal spoke with a sense of defiance almost as if Katie were sitting here with us in the gazebo.

Nolan looked up from his glass of wine with a smirk. For some reason he seemed to take pleasure in the fact that other people's relationships weren't bullet proof.

"Sal, me and you buddy, we can sure fuck up a marriage," Nolan laughed and patted Sal on the shoulder as I went for a fill up.

Sal's calm demeanor changed quickly.

"Oh yeah Nol', you think that was it, huh?" Sal stood up and walked over to Nolan.

"That's where you're wrong. I'm not like you, so don't throw me in that shitty category," Sal glared at Nolan as his voice rose to a level making Matt and Brooke a bit uncomfortable.

"Explain that one Sal, go ahead. I'm sure you got caught sticking your dick in one of those sluts that you hang around with, right?"

Those comments were enough to send Matt and Brooke away quickly.

"It was nice meeting you all. Enjoy the rest of your trip," Matt said as he grabbed Brooke's hand and walked down the steps of the gazebo.

Frank popped up from his seat and caught up with them.

"Sorry about this, we didn't mean to ruin what should have been a nice romantic evening for you. You forgot your wine and glasses, here you go."

We could always count on Frank to do the nice thing. He made his way back up the steps to the gazebo to an uncomfortable silence, but at least it was silent. Unfortunately, the silence didn't last too long. Sal and Nolan were already buzzing and they weren't going to drop this conversation so easily.

"Tell that asshole over there that he has the entire thing wrong," Sal requested that I relay what he said over to Nolan. Now we were getting immature.

"I think he heard you, right Nol'," I said sarcastically.

"I fucking heard him alright. Yep, he's a saint. Married men are supposed to hang out in strip clubs and fuck strippers, that's normal. Well, I guess normal for me," an arrogant Nolan laughed.

Sal was losing his patience with Nolan. Frank and I would have chimed in, but we weren't sure what to say. We knew Sal had been hanging with the stripper crowd and doing all sorts of things with them. We'd be happy to defend him, but we weren't sure how we could do it.

"Fine, fine. I'll come clean," Sal said softly, but loud enough for us to hear. He sounded defeated.

"Katie and I got divorced about six weeks ago. I begged her to put on an act and allow you guys to meet at the house before we left. She reluctantly said yes," Sal began to spill the beans about his charade.

"Seriously, why the hell would you need to hide it from us?" I asked.

"Because it's fucking embarrassing, that's why!" Sal fired back.

"And you know why it's embarrassing? Because as much as you would like to think Nol', and probably you two as well, I wasn't the one who did the cheating. It was Katie."

"She was having an affair for at least a year. It was happening right under my nose and I was too naïve or stupid for that matter to figure it out. I thought everything was great. She hid it really well," Sal started to get emotional as he poured his guts out to us.

He continued to go through detail after detail. It turns out that about a year and half after Hannah was born Katie began to have an affair. The guy she was having the affair with was married as well. They knew each other back at Florida State and Sal was to find out that they actually hooked up once there while Sal and Katie were dating.

"Remember those fucking twin Sig Eps, Mike and Jason Westbrook?"

We all remembered those guys. They were in a rival fraternity, but seemed to be pretty cool guys to hang out with when we'd see them out from time to time.

"It was Mike. That's who she was banging. Right under my fucking nose. We even went out with him and his wife while the affair was going on. I'm an idiot." Sal shook his head from side to side in disgust.

"He finally decided to end it once his wife figured it out. The guy actually came to me without telling Katie first and apologized. Part of me wanted to kick his ass, but the other part of me was impressed that he took the high road and confessed to it. My anger was
then directed at Katie. I baited her into a conversation and then accused her of having an affair with Mike. Of course, she denied the whole thing, making me feel like a bigger idiot. I called her out on it and told her that Mike and I met and he confessed to the whole thing. Boy, was she floored. Instead of consoling me, she grabbed her phone and called Mike. She was screaming like a lunatic at

him, 'you ruined my life, you ruined my life you son of a bitch'".

"I insisted that we try to repair our marriage, but things continued to spiral downward. That's when I gave up and started hanging with the wrong crowd. I'm out of that circle now. I'm too old and it's it way too dangerous. Jesus Christ I almost go hooked on heroin. I'm actually surprised you guys didn't pick up on it at the house. I haven't lived there for almost a year. Yep, Frankie, even when you visited a couple of months ago the charade was on. I have an apartment in Buckhead."

"No, we didn't pick up on it. We just thought Katie was being her nasty self," I tried to lighten the mood the best way I knew how at that moment, by taking a jab at Katie.

It worked. Sal started laughing. "I can't believe I've been living this farce for so long. You know what? It feels good to get it off my chest. It's still fucking embarrassing, but look who I'm talking to, you guys are the biggest embarrassments I know!"

"Finish that last bit and let's get outta here. I'm afraid what else we might learn," Frank indicated that it was time for dinner. We could see our cab sitting out front of the hotel.

Our cab ride to the restaurant was only about fifteen minutes, and luckily, it was uneventful. We didn't have a repeat of our experience in Reno. Our night, in fact, was the exact opposite of Reno. Everyone enjoyed great wine, nice cuts of steak and a scotch to cap the night off. Napa didn't lend itself to a night of carousing. It was just what we needed after Reno, a tame night. Honestly, this night was exactly what I was looking for when we planned this trip.

Chapter Eight

Life is about learning and growing along the way.
Growing as a person, a husband, a father, a boss or
whatever it might be. Some lessons you learn the
easy way and some you have to learn the hard way.
Usually, the ones you learn the hard way have the
most impact. As we sat there and sipped on our
scotches, I looked at my three friends. What
lessons have they learned? What have I learned?

I'm sure if Nolan was asked he would say that
money isn't everything. He let the pursuit of it ruin
his life along with others around him that trusted
him with their financial futures. There's probably a
lot more to it though. It can't be quite that simple.
My take on it is insecurity. For such a successful
guy, Nolan has been insecure his whole life. He's
always had to "one-up" everyone to feel good about
himself. When the "one-upping" became too
difficult he resorted to his shady activities, never
thinking about the end result. Now he's going to
die in prison. He'll have plenty of time to reflect on
his past and I'm sure he'll be kicking himself for
going down the path that he chose. Part of me feels
sorry for him, but part of me knows that he's getting
what he deserves. That's tough to swallow. As
much of a pain in the ass Nolan is sometimes, he's
still a great friend. He's the kind of friend that
would drop everything to help me if I needed him.
Friends like that are rare finds in life. I'll do
everything I can do to help him as he navigates
through his complex legal situation. I'm not sure
what I can offer, but sometimes just being there for
a friend is all a person needs to do. When this story
breaks there will be a lot of people that jump ship

and distance themselves from Nolan. I know he can count on the three guys sitting at this table with him. We're not going anywhere. That's what friends are all about.

On the surface it would be easy to say that Sal's lesson was all about trust. More specifically, trusting Katie blindly. We all know that is bullshit. Deep down Sal knows that he made some big mistakes along the way. Irreparable mistakes. When Hannah was born, Katie's role as the girlfriend, then fiancé, then wife ceased to exist. She was now "Mom" in Sal's eyes. As a father should, Sal doted over Hannah. His little girl was the center of his universe. Unfortunately, the attention and more importantly the affection he displayed to Katie became non-existent. This wasn't something that Sal did on purpose and Katie didn't get jealous of her own daughter, but it quickly became a problem. A problem that Sal just couldn't see. He thought everything was great, but little did he know that Katie was suffering inside. She tried to convey her dismay with the direction their relationship was heading. Sometimes through subtle attempts and sometimes directly, but Sal chalked her reaction up to her period or just being moody. The reasons that men cheat vs. the reasons that women cheat are entirely different, well, at least the majority of instances. Men that cheat just can't help themselves and need to stick their dicks in something different. Different is the key word or "strange" as it's sometimes referred to. Typically there isn't any type of mental connection or feelings involved. Usually, it's just another piece of ass to inflate the ego. Nothing more, nothing less. Certainly wrong, but yes, it's that simple. Women on the other hand, that's a different story. It's all about emotions. The worst thing a husband can do to a wife is ignore her. I don't mean ignoring as in not speaking or acknowledging her. I mean ignoring by limiting or eliminating affection. Simple things, which really aren't so simple, like kissing hello or goodbye start to disappear. Saying "I love you" also gets removed from the daily routine. Then, more complex things, like sex become a chore or just disappear altogether. Women can't function properly in a marriage without affection from their spouses. When it disappears and they feel like they've done everything to try and recapture it only to fail time and time again, they either give up or go find it somewhere else. Katie went and found it somewhere else. She doesn't love Mike, but she loves the affection that Mike provided. She'll probably never love someone as much as she loves Sal. They've created so many memories, have a wonderful little girl and made each other smile while they were together. Seeing that derailed is saddening. I never expected it. Now they're past the point of no return and Sal's learned a very hard lesson.

Frankie has lived a pretty good life so far, or at least it appears so from the outside looking in. As we're learning on this trip, no one never knows what's truly happening in another's life. We all may be best friends, but sometimes there are certain pieces of our crazy lives that we keep to ourselves. Maybe Frank has something he's hiding or maybe not. He was always the guy in college that we knew would go on to be very successful. The only surprise is that he never parlayed his law career into a political career. I figured that would have happened by now, but instead Frank has settled into a predictable role within his law firm. When I say predictable, I mean things don't change much for him day-to-day. It appears that he likes it that way, but that also doesn't match up with his DNA. He's wired for something bigger, but it just hasn't happened yet. That has always surprised me and frankly, disappointed me a bit. It's not my role to judge Frank's lot in life, but I feel blessed to have a friend like him and selfishly was hoping he would make a bigger mark on society. He's a special breed, but it seems like he's wasting his talents at the law firm. I can't get inside his head to truly understand what's going on and perhaps I'm making a bigger deal out of it than I should be. Considering the messed up lives that Nolan and Sal have revealed on this trip I should be content with one friend that has all the pieces together rather than create some type of expectations that aren't fair to Frank. After all, I'm his friend, nothing more, nothing less. There's no reason for me to be disappointed in him, but I'll always have something in the back of my mind that wonders where his drive derailed. I guess that happens sometimes, for better or for worse. Maybe he's figured out what matters to him most are Erica and the kids. There's no shame in that. He's learned a lesson that I should have learned a long time ago. There's nothing more important than family and friends.

There will be plenty more. That's how I rationalized it. A dance recital to a six-year old means everything. A six-year old's dance recital should mean everything to a father as well. It was two years ago. Lynnie started taking ballet lessons and Lisa and I were so proud of her. A lot of kids take lessons and go through the motions. Not Lynnie and that's what impressed me so much. Don't get me wrong, she was having a lot of fun, but for a six-year old, she was very serious about these lessons. She only had lessons two times a week, but she practiced the other five days. She didn't practice because we made her practice. She did it on her own. She was showing a work ethic that an adult would be envious of. Lisa and I embraced her passion and helped her as much as we could. Lisa, of course, was much more helpful than I was for a couple of reasons. One, she took dancing lessons all the way through high school and two, she was home more often than I was. The program we enrolled Lynnie in was six weeks. It culminated with a recital that included all age groups starting with Lynnie's group and all the way up to the teenagers. Lynnie counted down the days on her Hello Kitty calendar marking each day that passed with a red X. Lisa and I were well aware of the date as Lynnie seemed to remind us a couple of times each day. The day was Thursday, June 17th. I'll never forget that day, but for all of the wrong reasons. That was the last day Lynnie danced and unfortunately, it's because of me. It was June 8th when we had a conference call with a prospective client. My boss was on the call with me and a few others from our marketing department. We were very close to closing this deal, which would be a major coup for our company, a real game-changer for us as we continued to increase our market share. I still remember the exact words that came out of my boss's mouth, "OK, we'll see you on the 17th". My heart sank. I knew I wouldn't be able to get out of this trip to LA and I also knew that rescheduling it was not an option. My boss wouldn't allow it, not for my daughter's dance recital. I thought, maybe I can call in sick and miss the trip? I was scrambling to think of something that would allow me to miss the trip and see Lynnie's recital. I decided to sit tight and hope that something else would happen leading to the rescheduling of the meeting as that happens often. The end of the week came and went, but no such luck, we were still scheduled to leave for LA on the 16th and come back on the 18th. Every day Lynnie would mention the recital date and I'd cringe. I was still waiting and hoping for a miracle, but it wouldn't come. It was Tuesday, the 15th and I decided that I needed to share the news with Lisa and more importantly, Lynnie. I told Lisa first and although she was disappointed, she understood. She was a little upset that I took so long to let her know, but overall, she got it. Lynnie on the other hand didn't take it so well, as expected. Lisa and I sat down with her and I gave her the bad news. Tears started rolling down her little cheeks. It broke my heart. I wanted to cry as well, but I knew I couldn't. I had to put on my happy face and do what I could to make sure Lynnie was OK and that my absence wouldn't hurt her performance. After the tears stopped rolling, Lynnie said something that I'll never forget, "That's OK Daddy, don't be sad, you can see me at my next recital". That floored me. Such a mature statement from a six-year old, it was shocking, but it made me even more proud of her. It also made me even more upset that I couldn't be there. On the 17th, our meetings wrapped up around 6pm West coast time. I called Lisa to see how the recital went. It ended around 8pm East coast time. I had received a text from Lisa earlier saying everything went great, but I

- 173 -

wasn't able to speak to her until my meetings were finished. Indeed, everything did go great. Lynnie was spectacular. Her hard work paid off. Lisa said she stood out from all of the other girls and took well to the live performance setting. She loved it. When I spoke to Lynnie she was beaming. Her bedtime was at 9pm, but she had so much adrenalin flowing Lisa and I knew she wouldn't be able to sleep and we were OK with that, she deserved to stay up a little later. After I said good night to Lynnie and wrapped up a few things with Lisa, I sat on the bed of my hotel room in silence. The only sound coming out of the room was my sobbing. I was so happy for Lynnie, but felt terrible about missing the recital. I broke down and let out a good, long cry. I've never been someone that cries a lot, actually, I rarely cry, but when I do it's a biggie. This was a biggie and it felt good to get it out. I was carrying a lot of stress at the time. Work, of course, contributed, but most of my stress was about the recital. Most importantly, it went well, that was my main focus, but it killed me to miss it. It was one of those "life's not fair" moments and I had to just plain old deal with it. I made this bed and now I'd have to lie in it. Little did I know what kind of affect I would have on Lynnie moving forward. There would be another recital in about eight weeks. I marked my calendar as soon as I found out, but it wouldn't matter. Lynnie continued with her lessons for about two weeks after the recital, but Lisa and I noticed something. Lynnie wasn't showing the passion and effort that she showed previously. At first we thought it might be a case of "been there and done that", as there was so much build up to the first recital. Unfortunately, that wasn't the reason she

wasn't showing much emotion. Lisa and I decided
to sit down with Lynnie to make sure she was OK.
What she revealed was crushing. She said, "Daddy
won't be able to see me on October 23rd, so I don't
want to do it". Lynnie's fear of working hard for
the next eight weeks only to find out that I wouldn't
be able to see her perform deflated her. I robbed
her of the passion, I robbed her of the fun. That was
a tough one to swallow. I'd like to say that I've
spent the last two years changing my ways and
learned how to put family first, but that hasn't
happened. Now that I'm sick, I wish I could go
back and do it all over again, but I know that's
impossible. I'm not sure how many days I have
left, but all I can do is be the best father, husband
and friend during that time. Maybe Lynnie will let
me borrow that Hello Kitty calendar and I can mark
each day off with a red X. I hope I have a lot of red
X's left.

Much like I do when I'm home in Florida, I woke
up just before sunrise. It was the first time on the
trip that I felt good when I got out of bed. Finally, a
hangover free morning. My cottage had a nice
sitting area outside that looked onto the vineyard.
The morning air was a bit crisp, it must have been
in the high 40's or low 50's. The sun was coming
up over the hills providing the vines with their first
taste of sunshine on what was destined to be a
beautiful northern California day, perfect for riding
around from winery to winery tasting the best wines
that Napa has to offer.

Although a few days have passed since I met with
my doctor and received the news that will change
my life drastically, it still hasn't sunk in. This trip

has been a nice distraction, but when I'm alone I feel the stress of what's to come soon. I've been obsessed with how my conversation with Lisa will play out. I mean, how do you tell the love of your life that you're dying?

The reality is that when I do muster up the courage to tell her, it will be our problem, nobody else's. That's how it works with life's big events. Sure, there will be family and friends that express concern and help out where they can, but when it's all said and done it will be Lisa and I fighting this thing. I'm fortunate to have a strong person like Lisa to lean on. She's a rock and that's what I'll need and more importantly that's what the girls will need. God works in mysterious ways, but I can't help but think that this is a challenge that was thrown our way for a reason. I'm fully aware of how this all may end, but I have the best wife, friend and person in the world who will be in my corner every step of the way. Knowing that brings a smile to my face, but also saddens me. Such a great woman and I may not be able to enjoy her company much longer. It's heart breaking, but provides me with the extra motivation that I need. Every day that I battle this thing is another day that that I'm able to spend with her.

A friend of mine lost her mother several years ago to cancer. Her mom was taken way too soon, she was only 57. Over the years she and I have spoken in depth about how everything unfolded from her mom's diagnosis, to her battle and to her ultimate demise. After everything she went through the thing that hurt the most was the time after the dust had settled. When her mom passed away she had plenty of family and friends in town to console her. Slowly but surely all of those people had to get back to their own lives. Pretty soon it was just she and her dad. She wasn't married at the time and wasn't dating anyone. The first night she spent back at her house was a sleepless one. It was the first time she was left alone since her mom had passed and it was just plain awful. She had so much time to think and reflect on everything. Her emotions went from being sad to being angry and back to sad again. The cycle continued and she sometimes felt like she wanted to take her own life. Thank God she didn't, but the loneliness was tough to bear. I know Lisa will experience the same type of loneliness as soon as everyone is gone. She'll have the kids of course, but otherwise, she'll be on her own to pick up the pieces and move on with her life. It's unfair and that's why I'll fight. She doesn't deserve this.

We hired a driver to show us around Napa. The driver would serve two purposes. One, we know we'll all be drunk and shouldn't be on the road and two, hiring a driver that knows his way around provides opportunities to visit private wineries. The private wineries that we'll visit today will most likely have the owners on sight. Wine making for many people is a labor of love and it's great to meet the owners and see the passion that they exude when it comes to wine making.

It was about 9:30am when I began making the rounds going from cottage to cottage rounding the guys up.

"Sally, let's get a move on buddy," I wrapped on his door a few times.

"Hey man, good morning." Sal was buttoning up his shirt and looking around the room for what I'm sure was his wallet.

"Lost your wallet again?" I smiled as I watched him sift through his dirty clothes.

"Nope, just misplaced it. Ha, here it is!" Sal pulled a pair of pants out of the mess that was his suitcase and retrieved his wallet from one of the pockets.

Frank and Nolan appeared at the entrance to Sal's cottage.

"Beautiful day boys. Finally, I didn't have a fucking hangover. I guess there's a first for everything on this trip," much like me, Nolan was pleased with how he woke up this morning.

Sal closed the door to his room and we made our way to the front of the property. There waiting for us was a black Suburban. It would be our transportation for the day, but the driver had yet to reveal him or herself.

"Hello gentleman," a chubby guy dressed in your typical limo driver's uniform exited the lobby and made his way over to the four of us.

"Which one of you is Frank?"

"I'm Frank." Frank made his way over to our driver and shook his hand.

We all introduced ourselves to Alvin. Alvin was about 5'7", heavyset, probably weighing around 240 pounds and appeared to be in his mid-thirties. He was fashioning a goatee much like a lot of fat guys do to cover their double chin. He was wearing his black limo driver hat, but I was pretty sure there was a bald dome hiding under there.

"Frank, I'm not sure if you've shared our destinations with the rest of the guys, but I'd be happy to go through it with the group now," Alvin offered to provide us with the itinerary.

"Go for it Alvin. The only thing I've shared with them is that you are the best in Napa and you're going to take us to a few private wineries, so don't let me down," Frank replied in a bit more serious manner than Alvin seemed to be expecting. Frank always gets tense when he is in charge of planning things. Probably because he knows if it doesn't work out right we'll be busting his balls forever about it. He's 100% accurate in his thinking.

Alvin proceeded to tell us about the six wineries that we'll be visiting throughout the day. Four of the six are private wineries, while the other two aren't mainstream, but they are open to the public without appointments. He seemed like a good sport and that's pretty much a prerequisite when dealing with us as Anthony has found out.

The Suburban pulled away from the Heritage Inn. Simply driving through Napa is one of my favorite things about being here. As the Suburban whizzes down the road the rows of vines zip by, it's a person with OCD's dream. Everything in each vineyard is laid out perfectly, evenly spaced, all of the vines look identical to one another. I'm pretty sure that I could just drive around this area for hours and be content, but I knew there was plenty of great wine tasting ahead of us.

It was clear after visiting the first two wineries on the list that Alvin knew what he was doing. It turns out that Alvin grew up in the area and has been involved in the wine business in some way since he was a kid. Starting with summer jobs and then moving on to full-time gigs after he graduated from high school. He opted not to go to college, something that he figured out was a mistake, and therefore, he's taking on-line courses now with the hope of finishing his degree in about two years. He has no intention of leaving the wine business, but sees himself as more than just a guide and/or driver. Frank had chosen the right guy to guide us through Napa. Our first two stops included meet and greets with the owners of the wineries, who also happened to know Alvin when he was a kid. Alvin was buddies with the owner's kids as well. Our visits seemed more like a trip over to a friend's house to drink a few glasses of wine and shoot the shit on the patio. The day was shaping up to be a fantastic one.

"Alright guys, we're going to wear out our welcome here," Alvin made his way outside to gather the troops and move on to our next stop.

"Plus, we're going to be late for our next appointment and I have a reputation of staying on schedule that I don't want to ruin," Alvin laughed as we were actually a half-hour late to this stop. He winked at his friend.

We thanked the owners, gathered up the bottles of wine that we purchased and made our way back to the Suburban.

"OK guys, we're about ten minutes away from our next stop. We'll be visiting what is my favorite winery around here. Of course, they produce delicious wine, but this winery also happens to be the home of my best friend. A buddy of mine that I've known since I was four years old. He's like a brother to me. Oh, by the way, this is where we'll eat lunch. Not only can they make wine, but they can serve up a mean lunch too," Alvin smiled as we pulled onto the main highway.

Everyone had a pretty good buzz going now. After two wineries and multiple tastings, we were primed up. No, we aren't the type to taste and then spit out the wine. It's there to drink, not spit into a bowl. Leave the spitting to the snooty experts, not us.

"There it is," Alvin slowed the Suburban down and began to turn left down a long driveway. We saw the sign "Kelleher Vineyards" at the front of the driveway.

"I know Mickey is here today and his parents Paul and Sylvia most certainly will be around. Possibly another sibling or two, but we'll see."

We filed out of the Suburban and made our way to the front door. The driveway wasn't paved and the main house was pretty simple. It looked like it wasn't more than 2,500 square feet, maybe three bedrooms, and just one story. It had a beautiful wrap around front porch with a bunch of rocking chairs that had the letter "K" painted on them. The breeze was ever so lightly blowing through the oak trees that engulfed the front yard. I could make a place like this home.

"Alvin, good to see you pal," Paul opened the front door before Alvin had a chance to. Knocking wasn't in his plans as his relationship warranted an open door policy.

"Hi Mr. Kelleher, as always, it's a pleasure," even though Alvin is an adult now it just didn't seem right to say "Paul".

"Gentlemen, welcome to the Kelleher Winery. We're very happy to have you. I understand that you've traveled a good way to join us today, East coast guys, right?" Alvin apparently provided Paul with a few tidbits about us.

The Kelleher's home was very inviting. It had a country type feel to it, but the décor wasn't overwhelming like I've seen many times. The front door opened up to a small foyer that was littered with family photos, a few of which I noticed Alvin's mug in. We continued walking through the family room where the TV was on, some type of cooking show and a fire was crackling in the fireplace. Not quite fireplace weather today, but it looked nice. The wood floors creaked underneath us as we made our way to the kitchen to find Paul's better half, Sylvia.

"Hello boys, welcome. I'm just putting the finishing touches on your lunch," Sylvia was wearing oven mitts placing what appeared to be a quiche in the oven.

"Let me take these off and I'll give you the proper welcome Alvin," Sylvia grabbed her left oven mitt with her teeth and yanked it off and pulled her right one off with her free hand. She gave Alvin a big hug, which he returned with a squeeze.

It was clear that these people were like family to Alvin and vice versa. We were getting the opportunity to come along for the ride as Alvin visited his other "family". We loved every minute of it.

"OK fellas, let's head out back and get to the wine tasting, sound good?" Paul led the way through the sliding glass door.

While the Kelleher's home was on the simple side, the backyard was the complete opposite. It looked like something out of a movie. The plush, green lawn stretched back about one hundred yards. A red brick path shot down the center of the lawn leading up to an Olympic size swimming pool. Multi-colored lounge chairs placed two by two under their accompanying cabanas flanked the pool. The part that caught all of our eyes was the swim up bar at the far end of the pool. Six underwater stools nestled up to the bar that was fully stocked. This place was more like a resort than a winery. Beyond the pool about another thirty yards was a large barn that served as a workplace and the residence of Alvin's buddy Mickey.

As we were gazing at the wonderful surroundings we saw a small door to the barn open. Out of that door came a man in a wheelchair being pushed along by a woman. From a distance, the man appeared to be elderly, but as he got closer we put two and two together quickly. The man was Mickey and the man was battling cancer as we could see how chemotherapy had taken its toll by the presence of his baldhead.

"Mickey, my man!" Alvin jogged over to Mickey and met him about halfway up the path. He grabbed the wheelchair from the woman who was Mickey's nurse.

"Mr. Kelleher, we're all set for today, I'll see you in the morning," Mickey's nurse continued toward the house to close out her day.

"Guys, this is my friend Mickey. Mickey, this is Frank, Sal, Kevin and Nolan. I'm showing them around today and I told them I couldn't miss my favorite spot." Mickey smiled and turned his neck as far as he could to get a glimpse of Alvin behind his chair.

One by one we all made our way over to Mickey to shake his hand. His hand was a bit cold and clammy without much strength in his handshake. He smiled and said hello to each of us welcoming us to his little slice of heaven on earth.

"So, you hired this guy to drive you around," Mickey's voice was weak and scratchy.

"So far he's batting a thousand," Nolan replied.

"If only you get him to shut up for a few minutes, you'd probably have a great day," Mickey chuckled a bit until the laugh turned into a cough.

I felt uneasy looking at Mickey. He was frail, his eyes had dark circles around them and of course, the chemotherapy had taken his hair. I couldn't help but think that it might be me sitting in that chair soon. It was pretty clear that Mickey didn't have a lot of time left. The photos hanging on the walls in the foyer showed an entirely different looking Mickey. He was once a strong, athletic guy that competed in triathlons. Leukemia had changed all that. He and his two siblings were to take over the winery one day, but unfortunately, the end of the road was near and that wouldn't be happening for Mickey.

"Mickey", who was born Michael, picked up the nickname Mickey due to his large ears. When he was a kid the family visited Disneyland and like most kids, he insisted on getting his own pair of Mickey Mouse ears. When the little Mickey hat was placed on his head it was hard to tell whose ears were bigger and thus the name "Mickey" was born and it's stuck ever since.

Paul waived us over to the large tasting table that was placed underneath a beautiful trellis wrapped with vines that were just beginning to bloom with red flowers. The green vines along with the red flowers popped nicely from the white trellis.

The four of us allowed Alvin to wheel Mickey over and we followed along. Paul had three red wines on the table along with two whites.

"We'll start with our Sauvignon Blanc, if that's OK with you gentleman?" Paul showed us the bottle and we nodded up and down indicating that he was the boss here.

Sylvia came strolling over with a few appetizers, some fresh fruit and bread for us to gnaw on. Paul poured a small amount of wine into each of our glasses and proceeded to do the same thing for him and Mickey. I don't know why, but I was a bit surprised to see Mickey drinking. I figured in his condition that it may not be the best thing for him and by the look Paul received from Sylvia as he poured the wine for Mickey I could see that she agreed with my assessment of the situation. Paul knew that Sylvia was glaring at him, but he didn't care. His attitude and belief was to let Mickey enjoy the remaining time he had and that wine wasn't going to make much of a difference at this point. More importantly, Mickey was smiling and enjoying being one of the guys. He had done this so many times before when he was healthy that Paul figured why take it away from him now?

We were all enjoying each other's company. Mickey was telling story after story about his winemaking experiences and it turns out he is quite the world traveler. Nolan, of course, tried to one-up the poor guy, but Mickey was one step ahead of Nolan when it came to traveling the globe. He had done and seen a lot for a guy in his mid-thirties. His family's lot in life allowed for him to lead a different lifestyle than most people his age. It was clear that the Kelleher's were what I would refer to as "good people". They had a lot more money, experienced a lot more than the four of us combined, but they stayed grounded. What you see is what you get with the Kelleher's, just plain old-fashioned good people.

"OK, this next one is Mickey's favorite, it's his baby," Paul poured a red wine into all six glasses that were lined up in front of him.

"It's called 'Mickey #8'. A cab that I really think I've nailed this time. I certainly hope so after trying six times before," Mickey swirled the red wine around in his glass and then took a nice whiff.

"What happen to the seventh try?" Sal asked, as he understood the name was 'Mickey #8', therefore there should have been seven prior, not six as Mickey mentioned.

"Very good Sal, you're sharp," Mickey smiled, as this part of the tasting almost seemed like it was part of he and Paul's dog and pony show.

"Most people don't even question me on that one. Who can guess why there are only seven 'Mickey's', but this one is called #8?" Mickey took another sip and sat back in his wheelchair awaiting a response.

"I think I know Mickey and I believe it has something to do with the New York Yankees, right?" I asked with confidence.

"Go on Kevin," Mickey hinted that I was on the right track.

"You see, Mickey Mantle, of course, wore number seven and I'm betting that there are some type of copyright infringement issues if you were to name your wine 'Mickey #7', am I right?" I leaned forward awaiting the response from Mickey.

"Bingo, you got it, wow! You must be a Yankees fan or something. Usually I have to divulge the answer after multiple tries. Here you go Kevin," Mickey reached below the table and pulled out a bottle of Mickey #8.

"Thanks Mickey, I appreciate it." I looked at the backside of the bottle and noticed that Mickey had signed it.

"Keep Smiling, your friend Mickey Kelleher," I read the inscription aloud for everyone.

I got up from my seat and walked over and shook Mickey's hand. He gave me a big smile. He was proud of his wine.

"Excuse me guys, I'll be right back," I placed my glass on the table and walked back toward the house.

"Restroom is through the door to your left Kevin," Paul yelled over to me.

Although that's what I wanted them to think, I had no plans to use the restroom. I walked right past it and proceeded out the front door to the porch where the rocking chairs were located. I grabbed a seat and that was it. Tears started running down my face. I doubled over in the rocking chair placing my hands over my eyes. I could feel the tears slide down my hands and then to my wrists and drip off onto the wood floor below. My emotions got the best of me. Seeing Mickey in his condition I started to flash forward and I just couldn't hold it in anymore. All of the guys looked at him like "poor old Mickey". They weren't able to separate his illness from the fact that he was an outstanding guy. The fact that the guy was sick took center stage. All I kept thinking was that is how things are going to turn out for me. I know that sounds selfish, but it was unavoidable. Mickey is living his last days. It's clear that he has accepted that and frankly he seems very happy. I don't know if I'll be able to be as strong as he is. I'm scared, just plain scared. I don't want to die, it's just way too soon. How can Mickey accept it, how? I won't be able to do that. I'll be fighting until the last breath comes out of me.

"Oh, there you are," Sylvia nudged open the screen door and made her way over to where I was sitting.

"Yeah, I was just enjoying the view from here and rocking away for a few," I knew when she looked at me it was obvious that I had been crying.

"Kevin, are you OK?" Sylvia placed her hand on the arm of the rocking chair and bent down to my eye level.

"Sylvia, to tell you the truth, no, I'm not fine," I said as my eyes began to tear up again.

"Kevin, let me tell you something. Mickey's been sick for a while. You're not the first person and certainly won't be the last to have your emotions get the best of you when meeting him. Now, I'm not sure if that is why you are upset, but I have a hunch that's why." Sylvia was on the right track, but not 100% accurate.

"I just feel bad for him. He seems like such a good guy. It doesn't seem fair that he's being taken away," I stood up from the rocking chair and began to compose myself.

"It's been a roller coaster ride for him, me and Paul, but after all of the heartache, the pain and the countless sessions of pleading with God to produce a miracle, we had to turn the page and accept it. Paul and I owed it to Mickey and we owed it to ourselves to enjoy the time he has left and put the crying and pain aside," Sylvia grabbed my left hand with both of hers and gave me a little squeeze.

I could see the pain hiding behind her eyes. I know she believed every word she was saying, but deep down she was still hoping for that miracle.

"Now, let's get back out there with the guys and enjoy ourselves," Sylvia led the way back through the house to the backyard.

What was supposed to be an hour-long stop at the Kelleher Winery turned into two hours and then to three. The Kelleher's didn't host many tastings anymore and without Alvin I doubt this one would have ever happened. They were enjoying themselves just as much as we were. Paul and

Sylvia saw how much fun Mickey was having and that was all they could ask for. Their desire now is to have their son live out his days with a smile on his face. Right now, that smile was impossible to wipe off. Sure, he was getting a little bit drunk, but so were the rest of us. This visit was cathartic for not just Mickey, but Paul and Sylvia too. They don't leave their home very often anymore as caring for Mickey is their number one priority. Their once vibrant social life has died down to almost nothing. Visits from friends and family, along with visits from new friends like us, are the extent of their socializing now.

By the time the third hour was rolling into the fourth we were all completely saturated. It was time to shut down this little impromptu party and pile back into the Suburban. We were running way behind schedule and missed our windows at the other wineries on our tour. Alvin had already called his contacts and canceled our visits. An hour late may have been acceptable, but three hours called for a cancellation. None of us minded. This stop was worth it and was one of our best experiences on this crazy trip so far.

We all slowly rose out of our seats and felt the buzz from the wine. Actually, "buzz" was not the appropriate term for what we felt. We were drunk, plain and simple.

"Let's get a picture." Frank grabbed his Nikon from his bag. He was a bit of a photo geek and had this expensive camera that required you to manually focus. Way too advanced for my point and shoot digital skills.

"Alvin, can you take a shot of all of us," Sal waived Alvin over.

"Not necessary, we'll use the timer. We need Alvin in this shot too." Frank found a spot to place the camera and lined everyone up accordingly.

We all huddled around Mickey. I decided to kneel down to get to his level. Sal followed my lead on the other side of him. Frank, being the picky photographer that he is, didn't accept the first shot. We kept shooting until he was satisfied.

We said our goodbyes to the Kelleher's, exchanged email addresses and of course, suggested that we look each other up on facebook and become friends. We were there so long that the day was turning into night. The air was a little crisper and a nice breeze was coming through the valley rustling the leaves on the trees. We piled into the Suburban and Alvin honked the horn. Paul, Sylvia and Mickey waived and the dust kicked up behind the Suburban and we were on our way back to the Heritage Inn. Surprisingly, none of the guys even asked me about my disappearing act earlier in the day. After all, with all the food and alcohol we've been ingesting it had become common for one of us to disappear to sit on the toilet for a while. If it comes up, that's the answer they'll be receiving. No need to share the details of my breakdown. That is something only Sylvia and I need to know about.

The ride back to the Heritage Inn was only about twenty minutes, but that was plenty of time for Sal to take a nap. The guy had the knack of being able to fall asleep anywhere, at anytime and in any position. He was seated in the back row of the Suburban and if he wasn't snoring, it would be impossible to tell that he was sleeping behind his sunglasses. He was sitting perfectly upright, looking straight forward, but completely conked out. Sal is quite the odd duck, but he always keeps us laughing.

"Sally, rise and shine buddy," Frank nudged Sal's shoulder.

"Alvin, you're the best. Great day, thank you so much," Nolan grabbed Alvin's hand and placed a nice chunk of cash into it and patted him on the back.

"Next time you're here, let's do this again. We'll hit those other wineries next time. They are great stops as well," Alvin said as he made the rounds shaking our hands.

"You bet Alvin. You can count on it," Nolan replied with what was obviously a lie.

It was just before 7pm when we arrived back at the hotel. It was obvious that no one had the appetite to keep going. We didn't even have to say anything to each other. We all knew this night was going to end early. One by one we peeled off into our cottages. Some of us went through our normal routine before bed. Brushed our teeth, took the necessary medication, which was primarily cholesterol meds for all of us, changed our clothes and shut it down. Others simply walked in our rooms and crashed on the bed fully clothed. Yes, the "others" was just Sal. What a mess.

I dozed off around 8pm. Going to bed that early would mean that I would be up extra early the next morning, but I couldn't fight it. My eyelids were heavy and I was drunk. I didn't even make an attempt to get under the covers. I fell asleep on my back, which meant two things. One, I was drunk and two, I'd be snoring so loud that I'll probably wake myself up. Anytime I'd fall asleep on my back at home I could count on Lisa nudging me, well more like pushing me, until I turned over to my stomach. Lying on my stomach was the cure-all. Not a peep out of me after that maneuver was successfully completed. Another odd byproduct of me falling asleep on my back was the propensity for me to dream. As I understand it, we dream every night, but simply don't remember all of them. It is a fact that when I fall asleep on my back I dream and I dream hard remembering most details. Sure enough, this night wouldn't fail in the dream department.

Occasionally, I'll find myself so wrapped up in a dream that I wake up and know that I was just dreaming. I'm so groggy that I can't stay awake, but I'm able to put two and two together knowing that I don't want to fall back asleep because I'll be transported back into a place I don't want to be in. It takes me two to three times of fading in and out of sleep to get out of the dream I'm in. It's more appropriate to call these nightmares, rather than dreams. If they were dreams I would want to continue enjoying them, but I don't want anything to do with these nightmares. I just want to wake up.

It was around 4:30am when another one of these
episodes took place. This nightmare didn't seem
lengthy, but the content was shocking and intense.
The setting was at a winery, which of course,
seemed appropriate. It wasn't a winery that I had
ever been to and much like a lot of my dreams
and/or nightmares there are always things that don't
seem to quite make sense. For example, in this
episode, instead of vines lining the vineyard
property, there were orange trees. Now where that
came from I don't know, but maybe it had
something to do with my Florida roots. All of the
guys were there with me, plus a few others that I
didn't know. We were sitting around a table
drinking wine, much like we did earlier in the day.
For some reason, I was the focal point of the group.
Everyone was looking at me with what appeared to
be fake smiles and I felt uncomfortable, but didn't
know why. All of the sudden the table started to
move away from me. I reached out to no avail, it
just kept moving further and further away.
Something didn't make sense. The table was
moving, but the people around it weren't. I realized
that it wasn't the table moving. It was me. I was
being pulled backwards, but smoothly. It was
almost like I was floating. I couldn't feel anything
below my waist. I kept reaching forward and
started yelling. Everyone was looking at me and a
couple of the guys raised their glasses and smiled,
but I kept being pulled further and further away. I
put my hands to my head and came to the shocking
realization that I had no hair. I panicked and started
looking side to side and then I fought to turn around
as far as I could to see behind me. That's when I
saw it and everything came together. I wasn't

floating. I was being pulled away and the person that was pulling me was Mickey. No, not the frail cancer stricken Mickey, it was the fit, tri-athlete Mickey. He had a serious, almost sinister look on his face as he kept wheeling me away from my friends. All of the sudden the chair stopped. I tried to scream, but nothing would come out. I had no control over my arms anymore. They were like jelly. I attempted to wheel the chair myself, but I couldn't. My hearing was the sense that was heightened for some reason. I could hear Mickey walking through the grass. He unlatched a door and came walking back over. He grabbed the handles of the chair and continued to pull me backwards. My friends were still looking over at me without a care in the world. Mickey pulled the chair over a small bump and we were in what appeared to be a barn of some sort. The only thing I could move on my entire body was my head. I tried to look back at Mickey, but it was impossible. I could only see to my left and right and couldn't muster up the energy or strength to turn all the way around in the chair like I did earlier. The chair stopped. Mickey was behind me. I heard a spray bottle dispensing a liquid and then crumpled newspaper glided across the surface. I thought the room started to spin, but it was Mickey spinning the chair around. When it came to a stop I looked up and saw a person that I barely recognized in the mirror that was placed in front of me. A frail, bald man that must have weighed less than one hundred pounds was staring back at me. The only thing I could recognize were the eyes. The light brown eyes staring back at me were my own. My heart was pounding so loud that my heightened sense of hearing could hear it beat. I could see Mickey standing behind me. He leaned over and whispered in my ear.

"You see Kevin, you don't have to feel bad for me anymore. Feel bad for yourself. You're the one that's dying, not me."

I woke up in horror. I was sweating. My heart was racing. I put my hands to my head and felt a little better knowing that I still had hair. I sat up in bed and let that terrible nightmare sink in. My emotions quickly went from being scared to being angry. I grabbed the closest thing I could find and threw it across the room. The lamp shattered against the wall, glass went everywhere. I didn't care. I'll pay for it.

After a nightmare like that it was impossible for me to go back to sleep. We have a long drive down to Phoenix today. I'll get plenty of sleep on the cruiser. The four of us checked out of the hotel. I settled up with the Heritage Inn on the lamp. Not one of my finer moments and I decided to keep that incident to myself. Anthony had the cruiser ready to go and was waiting for us outside the lobby entrance.

"Off to Phoenix, I have some boys down there that played for the Cardinals," Anthony was waiting outside of the cruiser ushering us inside to get moving.

"What is that, about ten hours away or so?" Frank asked.

"About that, but I'm going to head down along the coast for as much of the ride as possible. It's too beautiful to pass up, then we'll push east," Anthony was right. We all remembered driving down the Pacific Coast Highway twenty years ago and it is gorgeous.

"I realize that. We're going to Phoenix and that's as far South as we're going. I'm telling you we have a deal," Nolan was on his cell phone with someone that was clearly annoying him.

"Fuck my life," Nolan hung up the phone and climbed into the cruiser.

"Attorney?" Frank asked.

"Of course and just so you know, he informed me that the authorities think I'm a flight risk. He asked me if I had any plans to head into Mexico. The truth is, I had thought of that, but I'm not going to do anything stupid. I'll take my medicine like a man when we get back. Oh, and by the way, he let me know that we've been followed this entire trip. Awesome, right?" Nolan was surprisingly calm about this news.

"Holy shit, really?" Sal was wide-eyed, thinking that this was pretty cool.

"Yes, Sal, really. Is that fun for you?" Nolan responded.

"Truthfully, it's kind of cool," Sal patted Nolan on the back as if to say thanks.

Chapter Nine

Anthony fired up the engine and we were on our way to Phoenix. Our trip is about halfway through. Once we leave Phoenix we'll continue to head east. Granted, we have a few stops along the way, but the reality of the trip coming to an end is making me nervous. I've yet to tell the guys about my situation. The right moment hasn't presented itself yet, but I doubt that perfect moment will ever arise. I just need to do it.

"Holy shit you guys, did you see this?" Sal was looking at his iphone.

"What is it?" Frank asked.

"Scott Carmichael, he died yesterday," Sal turned his phone so that Frank could see it.

"That's terrible. I knew he was sick. Brain tumor, right?" Frank asked.

"Shit, the guy was only in his late forties, right?" Nolan joined in on the conversation.

"Yep, he was a senior when we were freshmen," Sal confirmed.

I didn't know Scott that well and the other guys didn't either. I remember him being a pretty cool guy, but not much else. We crossed over at Florida State for a semester. Frank and Sal were friends with him on Facebook and that's how they learned of his illness.

"Man, that's brutal to go that young. He's married and has three kids. Awful, just awful." Sal continued to provide us with additional details.

"You know who saw him a few months ago? Mason did. They used to work together and Mason kept in touch all of these years later. He said the poor guy looked terrible. The chemo was killing him. Come to think of it, if I remember correctly, Mason said that Scott had decided to stop the chemo and see how things progressed without it. I guess that plan didn't work out too well for him," Sal didn't mean for it to come across as a smartass remark, but that's how I took it.

"Come on man, that's brutal. How can you joke about something like this?" I shot back at Sal.

"Who's fucking joking? I just said that it obviously didn't work out since he died. Relax." Sal defended himself.

"You know, that's how I'd do it," Nolan proclaimed.

"Do what?" I asked thinking that I knew where he was going, but I wanted him to elaborate.

"Fuck that chemo shit. It rips you apart. Why live out your final days suffering like that?" Nolan was adamant about how he would handle fighting cancer.

"Maybe because that is the treatment to beat it you idiot." Of course, I was thinking of my own situation as I defended what I thought was the proper way to fight cancer.

"I'm sure if Scott could go back and do it all over again he would have bailed on the chemo and just enjoyed the little bit of life that he had left," Nolan somehow felt he had a direct line into Scott's mind.

"First of all, how the hell would you know that? You didn't even know the guy. Second, that's just giving up and I would imagine going against doctor's orders," I was getting animated on this topic. The reasons of which were only obvious to me at this time.

"Kevin, when you have cancer I promise that I won't give you any advice on how to handle it. You can have all the chemo you want until you have no hair and can hardly move. Will that make you happy?" Nolan laid on the sarcasm pretty thick.

"Fuck you," I walked to the back of the cruiser. I was finished with this conversation.

"Come back Kev, come back!" Nolan laughed as I walked away.

I decided to lie down in my bunk for a little while. My intention was to nap, but I found it very challenging to do so after that conversation. I lay there staring up at the ceiling just thinking about Scott and the family that he left behind. It was a very surreal moment for me. I'm sure Frank, Sal and Nolan won't even think about Scott anymore. The news broke on Facebook and it's now just another post in a long line of crap that flows through there. Piles of "I just made cookies"; "Sunday Funday"; "Date Night" and all of the other meaningless posts that I see on Facebook all day long will push this news to the back burner quickly. Is that going to be me? Will I be a post that gets about five minutes of attention and then fades away? I don't want to be meaningless, but other than Lisa, the kids, family and a few friends I've done nothing to make a mark while I've been on this Earth. Sure, I've had a successful career, but what else? I guess it's better late than never, but when I get back I'm going to start giving back as much as I can. Maybe that'll give me seven minutes on Facebook.

My parents followed my sister to Phoenix about eight years ago. My brother-in-law landed a job there and they did what a lot of grandparents do, they moved to be around their grandkids. My niece and nephew are now in their teens and don't have much to do with my parents anymore. All I hear from them now is how they want to move back to Florida and can't stand Phoenix. The reality is that they won't ever be moving. They're too old now and moving away isn't an option. Of course, they don't agree with that line of thinking. They tell me often how they don't want to die in Phoenix. It's been pretty challenging for my sisters and I. We know they want to leave, but their health just won't allow for it. My mom has early signs of Alzheimer's and my dad has emphysema. We have a nurse that stops by each day to administer meds and help my sister out with caring for them. The nurse can administer the meds, but unfortunately she can't do much about the verbal abuse my sister receives on an almost daily basis. They've decided to blame her and my brother-in-law for their Phoenix "jail cell", as they put it. It's unfair, as my sister doesn't deserve it. She's tired of it and would love for them to move back to Florida. I know that sounds terrible, but it's the truth. We love our parents, but unfortunately they aren't the same people they were years ago. Not just because of health reasons, but their attitudes about their lot in life have made them bitter old people. It's sad. I've learned a lot from their situation and if I'm fortunate enough to live into my eighties like them I'll know what not to do.

Our family along with our extended family has seen a number of changes recently. We once had a wonderful close-knit group of aunts, uncles and cousins that spent all of the holidays together. Our dinner table would stretch through a couple of rooms just to fit everyone. We'd enjoy our multiple course dinners and then sit around the table listening to the many stories from my uncles as we sipped our coffee or after dinner drink. One of my aunts, that I still speak to often, refers to it as the "good old days". She's 100% right. Those were the good old days. Now, Lisa and I are lucky to even see my sisters for Thanksgiving or Christmas. Our once largely attended Christmas dinner is now Lisa, the girls and me. I blame myself for allowing this to continue on. I've just made excuses for not spending time with my family throughout the years. There always seems to be something. Whether it's work, time, money, there's always an excuse. The guys I'm traveling with aren't any better. Their families live all over the country too. They rarely see each other. It would be easy to say, "That's just how it is today", but that's bullshit. I hope I get a chance to fix this. I would love for Lynnie and Reilly to grow up with their cousins. I had so much fun hanging out with my cousins when I was a kid. I'd look forward to every holiday knowing that I'd get to see them. We were tight for a long time, but of course, that's faded away too.

It all crumbled from a meaningless disagreement that my parents had with my aunt and uncle. I don't even remember the details and at this point, neither do they. A lot of nasty things were said about me, Lisa, my sisters, my cousins, and their kids. No one was safe from the barbs that were being exchanged. All of the family values that our grandparents had instilled in my parents and my aunt and uncle were flushed down the toilet. An outsider would think that some type of family fortune was at the root of our problem, but no, it was just a stubborn group of four people that acted selfishly driving a wedge in between family members. Sides were taken and feelings were hurt by ignoring birthdays, weddings and other family celebrations that normally would be a cause for a fun get together, but now those dates come and go without much mention. Occasionally, a card will show up at the house for the girl's birthdays. A simple card, no gift, but I guess that's better than nothing at this point. We've done the same though, therefore, I can't throw stones. My cousin's son just graduated from high school and we put the card in the mail, that's all. I'm beginning to wonder if it will take the source of this feud dying to start reversing this craziness within our family. Knowing my parents and my aunt and uncle, that's what it's going to take. I've never met four people that are so stubborn.

My mom's Alzheimer's continues to progress. Speaking to her is like having the same conversation over and over again. Much of it focuses on how much she hates it in Phoenix and how terrible my brother-in-law is. That's unfair to him. As much as my sister does to help them out, he's right there in the mix as well. Like I said, she's a stubborn woman and if she doesn't like him there's nothing that's going to change that sentiment anytime soon. The poor guy is so nice that he chalks it up to her disease, but I know better. Disease or no disease, she dislikes him. I'm not sure why, but her feelings won't be changing anytime soon. When we arrive in Phoenix, my sister, brother-in-law, niece and nephew will stop by to visit. I hope my mom can hold her opinions to herself, but we'll see how that goes. If I were a betting man I'd say my brother-in-law is going to get abused by her, but to his credit, he'll smile and chalk it up to bad health. He's a stronger man than me.

I like to refer to my dad as the "science project". No, he's not aware that I refer to him like that, but my sisters and I get a good kick out of it. Think of it like this, every experiment has the control subject and then the other subject that gets abused with all of the bad shit. My dad is not the control. Smoking two packs a day – check. Drinking at least six beers a day – check. Eating fast food every day (or not eating much at all) – check. Zero exercise – check. Avoids going to the doctor or taking any medicine – check. All of that and the guy is still ticking. Hence, the "science project". He's watched as most of his friends have passed on. Friends that lived much healthier lifestyles than him have kicked the bucket. Every time one of his buddies passes he vows to quit smoking. This may sound crazy, but I believe that if he quit his body may go into shock and he'd be done. He'd be the only person that actually died because he quit smoking. I'm pretty sure that if a doctor attempted to take a blood sample from him all that would come out is tar or beer. Studies should be done on him. Maybe they'd find the cure for cancer by checking him out more closely. I guess I won't be the beneficiary of those genetics. I must be getting my bad lot from Mom's side.

I slept for about six hours and felt refreshed when I got up. The night before was brutal with that nightmare. My six hours were nightmare free and I was thankful for that.

"Man, and you give me the business for sleeping all of the time," Sal remarked as I shuffled into the main cabin.

"You were out man. We stopped and grabbed a bite to eat and you didn't move. We had to make sure you were breathing dude," Frank added.

"I feel good. Ready to get going again," I motioned to Nolan who was sitting next to the fridge.

"Fire it up then and have a seat. We're about three hours or so away." Nolan tossed me a can of beer.

It seemed odd to wake up and go right after a beer, but then again it was around 6pm, not 8am. The guys were looking forward to seeing my parents.

They remember the old Joe and Lorraine. The same two people that used to throw parties during the holidays when we were all on winter break. The same two people that used to buy Sal and I booze when we were in high school with the stipulation that we don't drive anywhere. They would serve as our taxi, no matter what time of night it may be.

"Are we going to throw a few back with Joe when we get there?" Nolan asked.

"What do you think?" I said, knowing what the answer was. So did Nolan.

I was going to give the guys a heads up as to what they should expect when we arrived at my parents house, but I decided that I didn't have the energy to go down that road. They knew my mom had Alzheimer's, but these guys haven't made a habit of being around people with that illness. It's a bit shocking. I hope she remembers them.

They'll also get a good dose of my dad's hacking and wheezing. Sometimes it's so bad that I wonder if he'll be able to catch his breath. He sounds like he is dying. Yep, that's the "science project". A cough won't bring him down.

"Guys, unless you like the smell of smoke, I would suggest planning on staying in the cruiser while we're visiting my parents. Their place is like a gigantic ashtray and I'm not kidding. It's hard to breathe in there," I provided a bit of advice that I know they'll take as soon as we enter the house.

"Come on, it can't be that bad," Frank thought I was being too harsh.

"OK, we'll see, but you can count on me sleeping right back there. I'll be comfy and cozy in my bunk while you struggle to breathe." I motioned to my sleeping area, which has surprisingly been a perfect little cocoon for me.

My parents reside in one of those "55+" communities. The development is a mix of single-family homes and condos. They have a little two-bedroom house that looks identical to all of the other homes on their street. I had to text my sister to make sure I had the right house number or we'd be giving someone a big surprise when the cruiser pulled into the driveway of the wrong house. Speaking of the cruiser, believe it or not, we had to get permission from the Home Owner's Association to park it at my parent's house for a couple of nights. Their HOA board is full of grumpy old men that used to have some power in their lives through whatever job it was that they did prior to retirement. Now this HOA board is the only thing in their lives that they feel they have some kind of control over. Their wives control everything else.

"Ant, my dad called ahead. We should be on the list," the cruiser pulled up to the guard gate.

"Hold on a second," Anthony said to the guard. "Kevin, we have permission to park in here, right?"

"Yes, it's done. Do you need me to speak to him?" I was getting a little frustrated already.

The cruiser moved forward and began to pass by the condo complexes in front of the development.

"OK, it's that first sub-division on the right, Falcon View," I directed Anthony.

We moved down the small street past houses that probably had about the same square footage as the cruiser. I'm sure as we drove by calls were already being made to the HOA board informing them of our presence. Not to worry though, we're official. The cruiser will be an eyesore for the next couple of days, but too damn bad.

"There's Joe in the driveway. Look at that, a beer and a cig. That's our man," Sal laughed as my dad stood on the edge of the driveway with his can of Budweiser and his cigarette.

Anthony inched the cruiser up as close as he could get it to their garage. We barely made it in the driveway. The back of the cruiser blocked the sidewalk, which will probably result in some kind of fine, but I'll pay for it if needed.

One-by-one we made our way out of the cruiser. My dad took one last puff of his cigarette and flicked it aside. Frank led the way and was lucky enough to greet my dad first. He was greeted by that last exhale that included a small cough and big billow of smoke. Maybe now Frank won't think I was being too harsh.

"Now that is a fine piece of machinery. What kind of gas mileage does it get?" My dad always needed to know what kind of mileage someone was getting.

"Not sure Mr. M., you'll have to ask Anthony, but it's not much," Frank replied.

I was the last one to make my way out of the cruiser. Every time I see my parents they look like they've aged another ten years. Their skin wrinkles a little bit more and they just get skinnier and skinnier. My dad is a pretty tall guy, about 6'3". He topped out at about 235 pounds back in the day, but now he looks like he's about 165. Skin and bones. He's swimming in his pants. The belt he is wearing is on the tightest notch and his pants are bunched up around his waist. They probably fit right about 15 pounds ago. The shirt he's wearing seems to fit fine, but that's because it's an old one of mine that Lisa sent to him. He has a closet full of shirts that are way too big for him now.

"Hey Dad," I reached out for a handshake. We aren't huggers.

"Hello there, welcome." Our greetings were always like this for some reason.

"Where are your bags? Don't you need to bring them in?" As I suspected, my parents were expecting some or all of us to stay in the house.

"No Dad, we're going to stay out here. It'll be much easier for everyone."

"OK, but your mom is going to be disappointed."

"We're just out in the driveway, we'll be fine," I said hoping that this would be the last of this conversation.

We all made our way up the path, through the screen door and into the house. Growing up my mom always kept a nice house. This was no different. Clean, homey and lots of photos of my sisters, the grandkids and me.

"Oh, you don't know how happy this makes me to see you boys. I know, I still call you boys, but that's what you'll always be to me." My mom was smiling and giving hugs to each of us as we strolled in.

My dad trailed behind us. "Who wants a beer?"

He proudly walked over to the refrigerator and grabbed four cans of Bud. I grabbed a couple for him and passed them to Frank and Nolan.

"I have dinner ready. Do you guys want to eat now?" My mom asked the question that we were all waiting for. The chance to feast on my mom's ziti and meatballs was discussed quite a bit on our trip here.

"How can we help Mrs. M.?" Nolan asked.

"Everything is ready, but I could use some help getting it over to the table," she motioned to the huge bowls on the counter.

Everything looked delicious. The salad, the bread, the pasta and, of course, the meatballs. We were all ready for this home-cooked masterpiece.

"Finish those beers guys, we have some nice red wine here to have with dinner." I grabbed the bottle and found the corkscrew.

"I'm going to stick with the beer. I don't want Mr. M. to feel lonely," Sal knew that my dad wouldn't touch the wine.

It's beer or nothing for him. It became a family joke over the years, but he never veered from it. Give him a beer and he's happy. Give him twelve and he's ecstatic.

The wine, and beer, flowed from course to course. The Alzheimer's may be wreaking havoc on my mom's memory, but apparently, her cooking skills have not been affected. She sipped on her wine and nibbled a little bit, but her priority was making sure all of us enjoyed the meal. That was not an issue. Four full bellies pushed away from the table. All of them very satisfied.

It was about 10 o'clock when everything was cleaned up and the few items that were left over were placed in the refrigerator. I'm sure they won't last through lunch tomorrow, possibly breakfast. We all crowded on to the tiny screened in patio that was just off of the kitchen. A few more beers and a couple of glasses of wine and the group dwindled down to just my dad and me. As suspected, the guys all decided to sleep in the cruiser. Hopefully,

I'll be able to do the same without hurting anyone's feelings.

To say that my dad and I have a great relationship would be far from the truth. Unique or odd might be the correct way to describe the way we interact with each other. I guess it has to do with the fact that he wasn't a part of my life growing up. When I was about eight years old my parents decided that living with one another was not a good idea anymore. It wasn't officially a separation or a divorce. They simply chose to live in different places. Those different places happened to be New York and Florida. I was so young that I didn't understand what was going on. I was given the story that my dad couldn't find work in Florida. His job was so good in New York that it didn't make sense to leave it. Like I said, I was just a kid. I bought it, hook, line and sinker.

It wasn't until I was in college that my parents decided to get back together. Yes, they actually got back together or is that even possible? How does a couple get back together if they never admit that they were apart in the first place? I was a kid trying to decipher this odd relationship. I'm a man in my forties now and I still don't get it. There are so many questions that I'd like answered, but I just haven't had the courage to ask them.

I sat across from my dad on the little patio with plenty of thoughts running through my mind. Both of us had been drinking for several hours and the alcohol was taking its toll. We both have a pretty good tolerance. I guess that is what genetics is all about. My grandfather must have been a lush.

Maybe this was the right time to ask all of the questions that have been haunting me for years. Maybe I should tell him I'm sick. I didn't know what to say and was very nervous. That's a very bizarre feeling to have sitting across from the person that has known me all of my life. The tragic part is that he doesn't know me at all. Those years he was away from us were the years that made me who I am today and he missed it all. There are days that I wish that he had stayed away forever. The fact that he decided to come back after I had already grown up is frustrating. He conveniently skipped the most challenging years of my life. From eight years old to twenty years old he was missing, well except for the occasional visits that always ended too soon. I still remember the time that my mom and I drove him to the airport. I was nine years old at the time. He left the car and I said goodbye. I got back into the car and tears began rolling down my face uncontrollably. I began sobbing and screaming to my mom that I wanted him to come back. She stopped the car and yelled to my father. He came back to the window of the car and looked at me with a sad face of his own. He turned and headed to his plane. That was the last time I ever drove him to the airport with my mom.

I've never spoken of that incident since it happened. Lisa doesn't even know about it and I tell her everything. I know what she would tell me. She'd say, 'why don't you two sit down and talk about it'. The "it" she'd be referring to is about the twelve-year void in my life where I didn't have a father figure around. Of course, she's absolutely correct and that's what we should do, but it's a little bit more complicated than that. Or is it? Our family has a terrible way of dealing with problems. The strategy is to ignore the issue and hope that it will go away. That's exactly how our close-knit family fell apart after the big feud. No one will apologize or even acknowledge that there was a fight. Some of us speak to each other now, but it's not the same. That's how it goes with us and this situation with my father and I is no different. Just ignore it and it will go away. I've been ignoring it for over thirty years now and it hasn't gone away. Maybe it's time to let this thing unravel for better or worse.

"So, pal, have you been paying attention to the Marlins?" For some reason, my father continues to root for the now Miami Marlins as his favorite baseball team.

"Can't say that I have," my curt answer indicates my non-desire to discuss baseball with him.

"If their pitching holds up I really think they have a chance this year," he adds to the riveting conversation.

What's funny is that I enjoy speaking with him about baseball. I don't follow it much anymore, but it was once something that helped connect us. It just seems like small talk right now and I'm more interested in diving a little deeper. I hope I can get the words out.

"Yeah, maybe." I have no idea how good their pitching is.

"They could have three twenty game winners I bet." That sounded good, but I didn't know which guys he was referring to.

This small talk exchange continued as the clock kept ticking away. I felt like I was blowing my opportunity to get this off my chest. I had all of the motivation I needed. It's quite possible that I may never see my father alive again. With both of us having health issues and living so far away from each other, this could be it.

I took a deep breath and let it out. "I gotta ask you. What happened with you and Mom?"

"Oh, she gets mad at me because I get frustrated with her repeating things all of the time. That Alzheimer's is really taking its toll," he replied to my complex question with a simple answer which was off the mark.

"No, I mean when we moved from New York and you stayed behind," I clarified my question.

The man literally squirmed in his chair. I'm sure he's been dreading this day for a long time, well at least I hope this has been top of mind for him. It has been for me.
He took a nervous sip from what appeared to be an empty beer can. He was searching for that last drop as this question hit him like a ton of bricks. I thought about getting up and grabbing another one for him, but I wasn't going anywhere. I wanted a response.

"You should ask your mother," in typical fashion he pushed the responsibility over to my mom. A cowardly answer at best.

Part of me wanted to give up on this conversation after hearing that response, but something inside told me to keep pushing. I wasn't going to let him off that easy.

"Mom? How is she going to answer it? She was the one in Florida, not New York," I was showing my frustration a little bit now.

My dad got up from his chair and grabbed his pack of cigarettes. He walked toward the sliding glass door. He was going inside.

"Wait a second," my voice rose as I sprung out of my chair. The beer can that was at my feet fell over and beer started running across the floor of the tiny patio.

I positioned myself in between him and the door. He grabbed the handle to slide it open and I held it closed. So much rage began to flow through my body. I had to do everything in my power to not knock him down.

"Get away from the door" he yelled.

"No, answer the question. Answer it!" I screamed in his face. We were about four inches apart battling for the door handle.

I looked him straight in the eye and in a calm voice I said, "I need you to answer it, please give me an answer."

He let go of the handle. His cigarette had fallen to the ground. He bent down to retrieve it and didn't come back up. He was sitting on the floor with his back against the wall with his knees up in front of him.

It's sad to say, but I now had him trapped. I was standing in front of the door and had no plans on moving until he gave me some kind of answer.

He took another puff of his cigarette and along with an exhale of smoke, the answer came out.

"I don't believe in divorce," he responded and then looked down at the floor.

A devotion to the Catholic religion is what fucked up my life. Because the Catholics say people can't divorce I had to live without a father figure in my life and my mom had to be alone and miserable. What a crock of shit.

"You don't believe in divorce?" I had to clarify the statement even though I heard it loud and clear.

He just looked at me. I could tell it was going to be like pulling teeth to get much more out of him. This was pathetic.

"So, let me get this straight. Because of a fucking religion, I grew up without a father?" He hated cursing, but I didn't care. I'm sure I also offended his precious religion too.

"Watch your mouth," he fired back.

"No, you don't get to tell me what to do. You lost that privilege a long time ago," I was furious.

He continued to sit there without engaging in this conversation, but if this had to be a one-sided conversation, then so be it.

"What you did was wrong. Down to the core, it's absolutely wrong. You felt like you were being a dad by calling me after every one of my baseball games, but that's a cop out. You should have been there, like everyone else's dad. Instead, I had to tell the story that I believed to be true. 'No, my dad is still in New York because of his job'. You know how ridiculous that sounds. OK, maybe for about a year, but not for twelve." I was laying it on thick and he just sat there.

This was like a boxing match where one fighter has knocked out the other, but the referees don't step in and the victorious boxer just keeps pummeling the other guy while he's laid out on the mat. I intended to keep swinging.

"Then, you come back. That was convenient. You wait until I'm in college to move to Florida. What the fuck was that about?" Again, another question that wasn't intended to illicit an answer.

"Was it me? Could you not stand living with me? I don't get it." I took a deep breath and continued my rant while pacing back and forth.

"There is a silver lining though. Yes, you failed miserably, but you know what? I'm the type of person who learns from other's mistakes. So, in your own twisted way, you've made me a better father. You showed me exactly what not to do. So, thank you, thank you for that. You can go to your grave knowing that by not providing any parenting you actually taught me an important lesson. My girls come first and I'm a great dad. You are not and that can't change now. How does that feel? You're just a fucking failure."

I had never seen my dad cry until that very moment. I know it shouldn't have felt good, but it did. Seeing him slumped over, feeling some of the pain that I've been carrying around for thirty-plus years felt good. It's terrible to admit that, but that was how I felt at the time. A huge weight had been lifted off of my shoulders. I wanted to call Lisa. I knew she would be proud that I finally said something, but she'd probably be disappointed that I was so harsh. Right now, I didn't care. I knew I hurt him and he was just going to have to deal with it. He thought he was going to have a pleasant conversation about baseball, but much to his surprise, we discussed something with a little more meaning. Now take it, take the pain, the humiliation and the sadness. I've been carrying it around too long. It's your turn.

I walked passed him, slid the door open and shut it behind me. I was done listening to the pathetic sobbing. It was 3:30 in the morning, but I wasn't tired. I had so much adrenalin running through me. I finally did it. Finally.

I quietly made my way to the front door and much to my surprise, I found my mom standing in the foyer.

"What's wrong?" She asked as she grabbed my arm gently.

"Nothing, it's time for bed, been a long night," I casually said, hoping that she didn't hear my rant.

"What happened?" She continued to press. My mom has always had a knack for knowing if something was bothering me. It's impossible to fool her, even with the Alzheimer's.

"Can we talk tomorrow? I'm wiped out, but I'm OK," I continued to do my best to end this conversation.

"Where's your Father?" She looked me in the eyes and I motioned to the patio.

She began to slowly move through the kitchen until she turned the corner to the sliding glass door.

"Oh my God, what's wrong, what happened?" She slid the heavy glass door open slightly and made her way on to the patio to find my dad slumped over.

"Kevin, what did you do?" She was screaming back at me while trying to help my dad up off the ground.

I walked over to the patio to witness this performance that my dad was putting on for my mom.

"He's fine. Just let him be," I said.

"What happened? What did you do?" My mom continued to accuse me of doing something to my father, which sounded ridiculous to me.

"Why don't you ask him what he did? He knows." I turned my mom around and escorted her back inside.

"Look at me. Please calm down. I'm telling you, he is fine, just let him be," I begged her to leave him alone.

"We should take him to the hospital." Now she was taking this too far.

"He doesn't need to go to the hospital. I promise you, just let him sit there. He'll get up soon and go to bed." I didn't have much sympathy for either of them at this point.

"Can you help him to bed?" I had no interest in helping him do anything, but I couldn't do that to my mom. She'd probably end up trying to do it herself and then both of them would be lying on the floor out there.

I walked out to the patio and grabbed my father's hand.

"Come on, let's go. Time for bed."

He looked up at me. His eyes were red and watery. He looked miserable.

He slowly got up leaving an empty can of beer on one side of him and multiple cigarette butts on the other side. I walked him into the living room and guided him on to the couch. That's as far as I was going to take him. It's not like he wasn't accustomed to sleeping on the couch. He'd be fine right there.

By the time the drama ended it was approaching 4:30am. Still, I wasn't tired. I know I'd be paying for this late night tomorrow and probably the next day, but I felt good right now.

"Good night Mom. Don't worry he'll be fine." I gave her a big hug and a kiss on the cheek.

I quietly opened the door to the cruiser. Unfortunately, it wasn't very quiet in the cruiser. Nolan's snoring was unbearable. He sleeps all the way in the back room, but his snoring can be heard all the way up front. Luckily, Anthony bought a bag of ear plugs that we've all been using on the nights that we've slept in the cruiser, granted there have been a few that everyone was so drunk having ear plugs didn't matter.

Lying in my bunk, the reality of everything that just unfolded hit me hard. It's amazing how many times I've played out that confrontation in my head over the years. It felt incredible to get it off my chest, but I couldn't help feeling bad about how it all went down. My vision for how it would unfold was different. I suppose I may have been a bit naïve. I thought we'd have this big heart-to-heart followed by an apology and a big hug, but, of course, that didn't happen. I know I could have handled it better, but all of the emotion just poured out. I've always provided advice for friends, colleagues, and employees to never hold anything in. Holding things in only makes the situation worse. I was quick to dole out that advice, but I never thought about taking it when it came to my own personal issues. The reality is that I should have met this head on years ago. I don't know if the outcome would have been any different than right now, but at least the burden would have been lifted off of my shoulders. I've been carrying it around too long.

Something else that hit me hard was the idea that the conversation I just had with my dad may be the last face-to-face conversation we ever have. The combination of both of us being sick will make that an almost certain outcome. Is that how I want it to end? Right now, my answer was an emphatic yes. I know I am being selfish, but I'm more concerned about how I'm feeling right now. He had the control all of those years to fix it, but he didn't do anything about it. I was just a kid and had no control over the situation. I stopped crying about it a long time ago and I don't have any plans to cry about it now.

I finally dozed off around 6am. My sleep wouldn't last long. Around 8am the sound of Frank and Nolan conversing awakened me. Our plan was to grab some breakfast and then continue heading east.

We weren't sure of our next stop, but as long as it was on the way to Atlanta it didn't matter.

"What time did you finally get to bed?" Frank asked.

"Oh, probably around 6 or so," I raised my arms in the air and stretched out.

"So, are we gonna get one of Lorraine's famous breakfasts before we head out?" Years ago, while visiting on Spring break, Nolan was able to partake in one of my mom's signature breakfasts.

"Sure, but remember that was a long time ago. It may not be quite that elaborate now, but I'm sure it will be damn good."

"Were you up with Joe all night drinking?" Frank asked.

"You could say that," I smiled.

"You must be exhausted," Frank added.

"Kind of, but I'm sure it won't hit me until later. Besides, all we're doing is grabbing breakfast and getting back on the road. I can sleep then."

Frank was right. I should have been exhausted, but I wasn't. The adrenalin was still rushing through me. I knew that going into the house was going to be awkward. My mom still didn't know why my dad was slumped over and crying outside and it's unlikely that she knows yet. I'm sure my dad is still sleeping on the couch. He'll be there until someone wakes him up. I wasn't in a big hurry to get inside, as I knew a confrontation was on the horizon. The buzz from the beer had worn off and I was completely sober now. An uncomfortable situation was going to get even more uncomfortable as soon as I walk in that door. No one else knew anything was wrong. Only my dad and I knew that a monumental conversation took place last night. A conversation that was more of a one-sided rant, but nonetheless, it was monumental. I never thought about it until just now, but is it possible that he has been carrying the same burden throughout the years? Seeing him cry was surprising. Seeing him sob was shocking. I have to believe that everything about this situation had been pent up inside and that's how it flowed out from him. At least, that's what I want to believe. I want to know that it has been challenging for him and he cares. Up until last night, I never saw any emotion out of the man. Yes, I've seen plenty of angry rants, but nothing emotional like last night. It was nice to see that he had that in him. I didn't think it existed.

"Give me a minute inside before you guys come in. I'll come back out and get you," I said as I moved toward the front of the cruiser.

The walk from the cruiser to the front door was about sixty steps or so. With each one my heart began to race more. It wasn't hot outside yet, but I began to sweat. I felt a strange warmth run through my body. I didn't know what was waiting for me beyond that door.

"Mom, we're up." I opened the front door and the smell of bacon filled my nose. Lorraine was at it early this morning. She always enjoyed cooking for my friends and me. She'd never eat much, but she made sure everyone was full and happy before they left the table.

Apparently she didn't hear me as the sizzle of the bacon was drowning out my words.

"Mom, good morning," her back was to me at the frying pan flipping the bacon.

"Hi honey, I didn't hear you come in. Where's everyone else?"

"They'll be right behind me. I just wanted to make sure you were ready for us." I took a closer view of the stovetop where four pans were sizzling away. The bacon, plus eggs, pancakes and her famous spicy hash browns. The guys were in for a treat.

"Where's Dad?" I glanced over to the couch and didn't see him there, much to my surprise.

"He was still sleeping, but I think I heard him moving around in there."

That was my cue to go get the guys. I didn't want to confront him without them around. It would help diffuse some of the awkwardness.

I walked back outside and before I could open the door to the cruiser the guys starting filing out.

"Well boys, you're in for a treat. She's got all four burners going right now. You name it, she's got it." I was very proud of my mom at that moment. The fight against Alzheimer's has been a terrible one. This is the first time in a long time that she seems to be herself. These simple things, like cooking breakfast, make her feel like her old self. Unfortunately, those skills will soon fade away. Some afflictions affect your heart, your lungs, your pancreas, as I can attest to, but the ones that affect your mind are so challenging. It's frustrating for her. She walks in a room and forgets why she went in there. She's having trouble remembering names. She forgot my nephew's, her grandson's, name the other day. The doctor told my sisters and me that it's only a matter of time now. Slowly, but surely, her mind will completely fade away to the point that she doesn't even remember our names. I'm glad I'm here. I'm enjoying seeing her, especially seeing her smile. Having my friends around always seemed to do the trick.

"Good morning Lorraine!" Sal gave my mom a nice peck on the cheek and made his way to the kitchen table.

"Anything we can help you with?" Frank asked.

"You just have a seat. That's all you'll need to do, well, eat of course," she smiled as she began placing the hash browns on to a serving dish.

We all grabbed our places at the table. Everyone but my dad.

"Don't wait for him. Dig in," my mom directed us. Not one of us hesitated.

I took a few bites, which were delicious and out of the corner of my eye I noticed the door to the master bedroom open.

"Joe, you made it," Sal exclaimed as my dad approached the table.

"Yes, I did and looks like you guys survived last night," he motioned to my mom for a cup of coffee. That's how their marriage is. He motions, she does.

The head chair on the opposite of where I was seated was open for my dad. While I was happy that he was as far away from me as possible, it was awkward looking him straight in the eyes across the table.

"Kevin, I looked up Manero's stats last night. He never hit over .300 in the minors like you thought," My dad's fork rose up to provide him a serving of eggs.

My fork dropped to the side of my dish as I heard that nonsense from him. I was shocked. Not only does he make a comment that shows he proved me wrong, but he did it as if nothing happened last night. Another thought went through my head, when the fuck did he look up those stupid stats for some non-factor baseball player? It was either after he woke up from lying on the couch or sometime this morning, but he had to do it. He had to prove me wrong. After everything that went down last night, this is how he chooses to start the day. I don't understand him and I suppose I never will. I lost my appetite, which pained me because my mom was so excited to feed us. Once again he took a nice moment and flushed it down the toilet. I couldn't wait to leave.

"So what, the guy's a bum," I responded sharply.

"Maybe, but I knew he never hit over .300," he continued to prove how smart he is.

That was it for me.

"Oh yeah, what did I hit my senior year? I bet you remember that too, right?" I was going to a dark place with this question and my dad had no idea that I was reeling him in.

"If I recall correctly, it was .317, right?" He was very proud of himself for getting it correct.

"Wow, very good. You know what I else I remember from that season?" I paused before I dropped that hammer.

"You saw one game of mine. One game, that was it. We played over thirty that season and that's all you could do. Of all the games, that's the one I remember the most. Three for three, with a walk, a double, two RBI, including the game-winning one in the last inning." I saw the look on the guys' faces as I continued down this road. Frank and Nolan weren't very familiar with the issues I had as it relates to my dad, but Sal knew everything.

Sal tried to diffuse the situation. "Yep, we wouldn't have needed those two runs if I didn't misread that line drive in the gap." Sal was referring to a play where he took the wrong line to the ball and it rolled out to the fence. It wasn't an error, but he always believed he could have caught it.

That was it for my dad. He got up from the table, gave me a stern look and walked outside to slowly kill himself with another cigarette.

Seeing him leave helped me get my appetite back.

"Mom, you've done it again. Thank you." I shoved a big chunk of pancake in my mouth.

"Well guys, time to hit the road," Frank grabbed his dirty plates and rinsed them off.

"Oh, I hate this part," my mom put her hand on Frank's arm. "Can I go with you?" She joked.

Frank was right. It was time to go, but I had one more thing I needed to do. I walked out to the patio to find my dad sitting in his chair smoking away.

"We're leaving now," I stood in front of him as the smoke billowed above him.

"OK. See you soon," his words were short and his emotion was non-existent.

I bent down next to the chair and proceeded to whisper in his ear.

"This is goodbye. I'm dying, you'll never see me again."

I rose back up. Looked him in the eyes and walked out. I don't know why I decided to say that to him, but it just came out. I guess I wanted to hurt him. I wanted him to feel some pain. It was wrong and I knew it, but I wasn't going to take it back now. Who knows, he may not have even taken me seriously. After all, who says things like that without elaborating on the situation? If anything I confused the hell out of him. He'll know soon enough that I was serious.

"Let's do it guys," I rounded up the guys and it was time to go.

"I'm going to say goodbye to your dad," Nolan popped outside with Frank and said a quick goodbye.

The emotions of this part of the trip ran the gamut. Seeing my mom was special. She'll never know how special this visit was and that's fine with me. Seeing my dad was stressful, but at least I said my peace. I'm leaving here with that issue still unresolved though. He didn't provide me with any of the comfort that I so naively was expecting. I wanted a happy ending, but instead I just got a slap in the face.

My mom walked us to the front door and took a few steps outside. The guys said goodbye and I was left alone with her.

"Mom, thanks so much for everything."

"Oh, you know I love when you and your friends visit," she smiled.

"No, that's not what I mean. I mean thank you. Thank you for being such a strong woman. Thank you for raising me by yourself. You mean the world to me and I don't say it often enough." The reality that this may be the last time I see her hit me hard.

Tears starting rolling down my face and I grabbed her and hugged her frail body so tight. So tight that I thought I might break something.

"I love you Mom."

Her eyes started welling up.

"No, don't do that. I shouldn't have and I'm sorry. I gotta go now."

I grabbed her hands one last time and gave them a squeeze. I walked down the driveway and didn't look back. I couldn't, it was too hard. Anthony started up the cruiser. I stepped in and we pulled away. It was obvious that I was crying, but the guys didn't know the magnitude of the situation. The reality is that I'll have many goodbyes to come as things progress with this disease, but none may ever be as hard as that one.

"You OK," Sal asked.

"I'm good, no worries," I replied as I walked to the back of the cruiser.

Sal got up and followed me back. I felt a hand on my left shoulder.

"Look, I know you're not fine and I'll give you your space, but just know that when you want to talk about it, I'm here," Sal whispered as he looked me in my bloodshot eyes.

I didn't even have to respond to Sal and frankly, he wasn't expecting one. He knows me too well. I'd want to talk about it with him. He understands the dynamic situation that I just walked out of. Having a friend like him is a blessing. Little does he know that I'm harboring a lot more than just the issue with my dad. That conversation will come in time. We keep heading east and I can't muster up the courage to speak to these guys. I'm running out of time. We'll be home in a few days.

Chapter Ten

Nolan had been up front with Anthony giving him directions to the next stop. It would be a surprise to us, but that's how this trip was supposed to play out. Just like it played out twenty years ago, we had no plan, no agenda, just kept driving.

"I got it guys. It's a bit further than we'd probably want to make a leg, but I got it," Nolan was thrilled with his idea.

"Whatcha got 'Nol?" Sal asked as if he were ready for anything.

"Are you ready? Here it is, Tupelo, Mississippi," Nolan did a little happy jig of some sort.

"What?" Frank was dumbfounded.

"Yeah, home of our boy big Ant," Nolan responded.

Now it seemed to come together for all of us. We've all grown to like Anthony so much that this idea to visit Tupelo was right on the money. None of us disagreed. In fact, we were all very intrigued by the idea. This should be fun.

"Ant, you're going home buddy!" Nolan yelled up front.

"Woo hoo, that's what I'm talking about!" Anthony pounded on the horn a few times to express his jubilation.

Once again, this trip has taken a bizarre turn. Who would have thought that we'd be stopping in for a visit to our driver's hometown? That's the spontaneity that we loved about this trip twenty years ago. Being spontaneous had become a rare thing for all of us. Everything was always planned out. After all, when you're part of a family that's what needs to happen. When you're four, well make that five, guys traveling cross-country in a gigantic bus, well, you can do what you want and right now, we want to go to Tupelo.

As the West began to disappear into the East many thoughts began to run through my head. To say that I was emotionally drunk would be an understatement. It's an accurate assessment for all of the guys at this point. I don't plan on making it any easier with the grand finale that I have planned. There have been so many distractions on this trip so far with Nolan's attempt to kill himself, Sal sharing that he's getting divorced, my confrontation with my dad and let's not forget everything that happened in Reno. We've packed a lot into just a few days. I laugh to myself at what we thought were problems twenty years ago. The biggest issue we had on that trip was the fact that Sal's dad had just found out that he piled up about $200 in campus parking violations. He almost made Sal stay home, which would have canceled the trip for all of us. Cooler heads prevailed and Sal was able to join us. Now, here we are twenty years later with a few more issues than unpaid parking tickets. I wish it were still that simple. The funniest part about that story was that Sal didn't end up paying for those tickets until about three years ago. After he paid them Florida State sent him his diploma.

Leave it to Sal to finally receive his diploma seventeen years after he graduated. Knowing him, it's still in the little cardboard cylinder that it came in. Rolled up for another seventeen years. No, probably forever.

"Hello?" My sister Patricia was calling.

"What happened with you and Daddy?" Word had traveled quickly.

I got defensive as the tone in my sister's voice seemed to suggest that I did something wrong.

"I finally gave him some long overdue medicine, that's what happened. Why, what are you hearing?"

"He sent me an email this morning, really early. He asked me to call you," Trish replied, her voice sounding more concerned now than accusatory.

"Oh yeah, what for?"

"He didn't say. It just read 'please call your brother. He's leaving here soon'. I didn't look at my email until just now, so I'm calling," she sounded very confused.

I wasn't in the mood to rehash the entire confrontation, at least not yet. It was too fresh in my mind and I'm not even sure how I feel about it. Part of me is proud that I got it off of my chest, but part of me is also embarrassed for treating him like that. After all, he is still my father. I should have shown a little more respect.

"Trish, I appreciate you calling me, but I can't do this right now. It's too fresh. I need a little time to digest it. You know I'm on the trip with the guys right now. I'll call you when I get home in a few days, OK?"

"I understand. I'll write back to him and tell him that I left you a message, but you have to promise we'll talk about this when you get home," as I expected, Trish was supportive.

"You got it. I'll call you then. Say hello to everyone for me."

I will call her and I'm looking forward to it. She knows that I've been carrying this around for a while. Lisa will receive the play-by-play first, then Trish. Now, only if I can figure out how I feel about it. It wasn't supposed to play out like this. I'm frustrated. The vision I had was my dad and I embracing after he apologized, but of course, that didn't happen. All I wanted was a little closure, but instead, I'm left with more questions.

The excitement of going home to Tupelo gave Anthony the adrenalin to push through miles and miles without stopping for anything but gas. The four of us sat around a little, napped a little and continued to enjoy each other's company. We were about four hours away from Tupelo snacking on some McDonald's when Frank made his way out of his bunk to find the three of us hanging out in the main sitting area.

"Frankie, how was your nap?" Sal asked.

"Um, I wasn't napping," Frank appeared very serious.

"Frankie, you know, you don't have to be ashamed about spanking the monkey. I've done it a dozen times so far on this trip," Nolan figured that if Frank wasn't napping there was only one other thing he could be doing.

"Jesus Nol', a dozen times? We've been gone for less than two weeks?" I made it clear that his activity seemed to be a bit overboard.

"Hey, I've got a drive that I need to suppress and that's the only way I know how. Don't worry, I didn't use any of your socks," Nolan laughed hysterically.

Sal and I joined in on the laughter, but noticed that Frank didn't find any of this amusing.

"Frankie, you alright?" Sal asked.

A silence fell across the cabin as we waited for Frank to respond.

"No guys, I'm not. I'm really not OK. I need to speak to you guys in confidence." Frank paced back and forth a few times and planted himself down towards the front of the cruiser.

The three of us wiped the smirks from our faces and hung on every word that was coming out of Frank's mouth. The tone of his voice and his body language were clear. This was not just your run-of-the-mill attention getter. He had something serious to lay on us.

"I know you guys must think that I've really got my shit together, right?" The question didn't require an answer. Frank continued.

"Well, I still believe that for the most part I do have it all together, but my life has changed dramatically over the past year and a half. Changed in a way that was long overdue." Frank grabbed a bottle of water and took a big gulp. The suspense was killing us.

"I've done something to Erica that I can never forgive myself for." Frank's eyes began to water up.

"What, are you having an affair?" Nolan being his typical self couldn't let Frank just speak to us without butting in.

"Damn it Nolan, just let me finish," Frank lost his composure, but quickly gained it back.

"I'm sorry, I'm sorry. I didn't mean to snap at you. I'm the one that asked to speak to you guys, I'm sorry." Frank was visibly shaken.

"To answer your question, I wish it was as simple as an affair, but it's not. The fact is that I've been living a lie for years and I just can't do it anymore."

Now, for the three of us listening to this it was a bit déjà vu. Nolan had proclaimed that he had also been living a lie and proceeded to pull a gun out and then shared that he's going to prison for the rest of his life. I'm not sure any of us can take another story like that, ever.

"Frank, whatever it is, I'm sure you can handle it. So, what is it?" I asked.

"Erica is going to hate me. Her family is going to disown me. The kids are going to be embarrassed," Frank continued as the tension in the cruiser increased.

Once again, Frank went silent. Then it happened, Sal decided to take an educated guess as to what was bothering Frank so much.

"Frankie, are you gay man?" And just like that, the cat was out of the bag.

Frank pulled his head out of his hands and raised his watery eyes in Sal's direction. He looked at Sal in astonishment, but really looked at him in a way to say "thanks". Sal had helped get the secret out. We could see the weight lifted off of Frank's shoulders immediately.

"I am guys, I am," Frank nodded up and down.

Wow, another shot between the eyes on this trip. Another one we just didn't see coming, although, it wasn't the most shocking thing to hear from Frank. To say that we had our doubts about his sexuality would be an understatement. Granted, once he married Erica and popped out the kids, we all thought our doubts were just nonsense and haven't thought much about it since.

"I've been with someone for a year and a half now. His name is Brian and we met on a case about two years ago," Frank started to share more with us.

"So, what's his story? Married too?" I asked.

"No. He's never been married. In fact, he's never been with a woman in his life."

"He recently gave me an ultimatum and that's why I needed to share this with you guys. If I'm going to go through with this I'll need your support. Brian has been suffering through this double life for too long. I either need to end things with Erica or continue to live this charade. I know what I need to do, but I need you guys to help me," Frank was caught in an awkward situation. If he stays with Erica, he loses Brian, but more importantly continues to live as something he is not.

"I won't have any family to turn to once I reveal everything. I'm not just talking about Erica either. I know that my parents will lose their minds and obviously, Erica's parents will go off the deep end." Frank is right. His parents are very old school and while they'll most likely come around because they love him so much, it's going to take awhile. Erica's parents are even more conservative. Hurting their daughter, of course, is unacceptable and hurting their grandchildren is unfathomable. He's in for a tough go with this. He'll need his friends.

"Frank, let's call a spade a spade here. This isn't shocking to us. We always thought you might be leaning that way, now you've just confirmed it." Nolan was blunt as usual.

"Frankie, I think what our friend Nolan is trying to say is that you're our friend no matter what. We're here to help," Sal chimed in and summarized the feelings of the group in a simple manner.

"So, what's your game plan?" I asked.

"Well, it's Brian. Brian is my game plan. Now, I have to muster up enough courage to tell Erica when I get back. I need to get a few things together before I tell her, but I'll do it soon." Frank's statement sounded like he wasn't sure of his next steps.

"Frank, with all due respect, if you're going to do this, you need to do it right away. Like a band-aid, pull that sucker off. The longer you wait, the more likely you'll continue to wait. Haven't you been waiting long enough?" Nolan was giving great advice for once.

"Trust me. From a guy that's screwed up more lives than anyone I know, get out of the lies. They'll only lead to more lies and more people will get hurt. I know you love everyone involved. You need to do it for them and you need to do it for yourself," Nolan continued to speak first-hand about hurting others and tried building Frank's confidence.

"He's right you know Frankie, he's right," I added.

"Yep, on the money," Sal offered his two cents.

"I know guys. I just needed someone other than Brian to tell me that. Thank you." Frank stood up and walked over to each of us and gave us big hugs. Nolan was the furthest away and he and Frank embraced last.

"Hey now Frankie, watch those hands!" Nolan couldn't resist the joke. It was a good one that cleared the tension. We all laughed and then followed it up with a big deep breath. What else could we be in store for on this trip? Little did they know.

Frank walked to the back of the cruiser and entered Nolan's room shutting the door behind him, presumably, to call Brian to let him know what had just transpired. This was a life-changing moment for Frank. What he just did can't be easy and this is just the start. He has many hurdles in front of him, but telling Erica will be his most challenging.

"Holy shit," Sal whispered.

"I know, how about that? I wasn't expecting him to drop a bomb like that," I added.

"Agreed, but when it's all said and done, are you really shocked?" Nolan was right.

There had always been suspicion when it came to Frank's sexual orientation. He seemed a bit out of his own skin when he was with women. Once he met Erica and they got married everyone believed that our previous assumptions were out of line, but they weren't. Of course, Frank didn't roll out of bed one morning, stand up and declare that he was gay. He is gay. He didn't become gay. Chances are he's been battling this for a long time and Brian coming into his life prompted him to make a decision to put his fears behind him and live the life that he was meant to live. The road ahead for him is long and it won't be easy. This was a gigantic step for him and I'm sure he's relieved that his three best friends are being supportive. I wasn't sure where Sal and Nolan stood on the subject. To my surprise, Nolan is supporting Frank more than I would have ever imagined.

"Of course, we're not shocked, but it definitely caught me off guard," Sal continued.

"I know. I thought he was going to tell us he got fired or he was getting a divorce," I suppose the divorce part is accurate though.

"Man, what else do you guys have hiding in your closets?" Nolan smiled, as he knew his closet was full of skeletons and we only knew the half of it.

"I'm clean man. My divorce was the only thing hanging over me," Sal tapped his hands together the same way the dealers do in Reno when they leave the table.

"What about you Kevin? Got anything you want to drop on us? I'm not sure we can take much more on this trip, but you may as well pile it on," Nolan was half-joking.

"No guys, I'm good."

I suppose that was as good an opportunity as I've had so far on this trip, but it didn't seem right. We were still in Frank's world right now. Throwing my fuel on the fire wasn't the right thing to do.

The door opened to Nolan's room. Frank emerged with a big smile, but it was obvious he had been crying.

"How ya doin' Frankie? Everything alright?" Sal asked.

"Well, as you can imagine, Brian was thrilled. I'm pretty sure he figured I'd never drum up the courage to do it, but I did. This is just the beginning though." Frank recognized the challenges he'd face moving forward.

It would start with telling Erica when he got home. Although I'd like to think that his conversation would go well, that is an unlikely scenario. Erica comes from a very religious family. Her grandfather was a minister and her father is a deacon at his church and sings in the choir. Erica introduced Frank to church. His family is not religious at all. As a matter of fact, other than attending weddings and christenings, Frank never set foot in a church. His life with Erica and the kids was different. Not only do they attend church every Sunday, but they are also active in the various church events that take place throughout the year. If I were to predict how this whole thing will go down at the church I'd say that Erica will get a ton of support while Frank will be ostracized. It's sad that it will come to that, but its reality. His employment situation shouldn't be as challenging.

There are a number of openly gay men and women working at the firm. It'll be nice to have some support from them. I hope he has some friends he can lean on.

Chapter Eleven

We were on our way to Tupelo for what should be a memorable stop. We were about five hours in. Another twenty hours lie ahead. It's funny how parts of this trip are mirroring our trip from twenty years ago. Twenty years ago we got to a point on the trip where we just wanted to go home. So much in fact, that we drove straight through from San Francisco all the way to Atlanta stopping for food and bathroom breaks only. If memory serves me correctly, that was just about forty-four hours of driving, counting all of the stops along the way. Now, the trip from Phoenix to Tupelo isn't quite that long, but twenty-five hours is still a long stretch. Of course, we don't expect Anthony to pull a clip like that without getting some sleep. We'll find a place to park the cruiser and get some rest at some point. We need our guy to be fresh when he arrives for his big homecoming.

None of us had ever been to Tupelo, as a matter of fact, I don't think any of us had been within 100 miles of Tupelo. Anthony comes from a huge family, not just in stature, but also in numbers. He's one of nine kids. He has a younger sister, two older sisters and five older brothers. While his siblings were all athletic, none of them had the career like Anthony. He was a football hero in Tupelo. Normally, offensive linemen don't get a lot of attention, but Anthony sure did. He started every game from his freshman season through his senior year collecting a couple of state titles in the process. When Ole Miss came knocking on his door to see if he'd like to play football for the Rebels it was a no-brainer. Oxford, where the campus is located, was about an hour away. Staying close would allow for his family to watch him on Saturday's, and that they did. Anthony was recruited by a number of big name schools and the recruiting visits were always comical. He was such a stud in High School that the head coaches of the various universities always conducted the actual visits. That doesn't happen unless you're a five star recruit like Anthony. The big guns came calling on him. You name it, they were there. Lou Holtz, Bobby Bowden, Nick Saban. They may as well have placed a "take a number" dispenser at the front door. What made the recruiting visits comical was Anthony's mom or "Momma". I'm sure these big time coaches expect to walk in the door of these households and spend most of their time speaking with the recruit's father, but not in Anthony's house. Sure, his dad was involved, but Momma ran the show. If a coach wanted Anthony, they had to go through Momma first. The same way Anthony protected his quarterback, Momma protected her baby boy, her 300lb plus baby boy. Ed Orgeron was the head coach for Ole Miss when Anthony was being recruited. He recognized that to get Anthony to sign on with Ole Miss he had to win Momma over. Sure, the proximity of the campus to Tupelo was a huge advantage for him, but Momma wasn't going to be sold that easy. Having nine kids and a husband to take care of provides a person with certain "smarts" that most people don't have. A skill that Momma has is that she can see right through the bullshit. As a matter of fact, she had the stones to end her visit with Nick Saban about fifteen minutes in. The man traveled over from Baton Rouge, Louisiana to meet with her son and after fifteen minutes he was sent packing. After he

left Anthony was puzzled and a bit upset. Nick
Saban had recently won a national championship
with LSU and his program was one of the best in
the country. So, why did Momma shoo him out the
door after only fifteen minutes? Well, Anthony
asked the same question and what did Momma tell
him? She said, 'that man sat on my couch, in my
living room and lied to my face'. Now, Anthony,
his father and the rest of his siblings thought
Momma was nuts. Who tosses a national
championship football coach out the door?
Anthony, of course, asked Momma for some
clarification as to what Nick Saban had lied to her
about and she was very clear with her response.
She said, 'that man won't be your football coach.
He said he'd be around, but I know better. He's
ready for the next best thing, just you watch'.

Well, she read Nick Saban like a book. Momma
was 100% accurate. Sure enough, a few months
after that recruiting visit he left LSU for a job with
the Miami Dolphins. Needless to say, Momma ran
the show for all future recruiting visits. What she
said was gospel. In the end, Ole Miss was the big
winner. Anthony ended up having a great career,
starting every game in his Junior and Senior
seasons. The San Francisco 49ers made him a 5th
round draft pick and he was on to his next
challenge. Unfortunately, the NFL game was just
too much for Anthony to handle. A little too fast
for him and he couldn't cut it. His career lasted one
year. Even 5th round draft picks usually hang
around for more than a year, but not Anthony. He
was invited to the St. Louis Rams training camp
after the 49ers cut him, but that didn't last long
either. He bounced around in the arena league for a

little bit, but let's face it, that's not football. He hung them up and planned on using his degree to start a career, but it's never happened, unless driving four forty-something's around in a big bus is a career.

Anthony's family doesn't know what he is doing now. He's come up with some elaborate story that he works with NFL prospects at a training facility in Atlanta. He grooms them for the NFL combine and works with them after they are drafted to assist them with the financial rigors that come with being a professional athlete. In theory, this is a great idea, but it's a complete lie. Sure, Anthony has assisted at times with programs like this, but for his friend's company, not his as he has told his family.

We're now a part of this charade as Anthony spilled his guts about this lie and has asked us to play along. Reluctantly, we decided to do it, to the point that Nolan volunteered to pose as the driver of the cruiser. In essence, he's the new Anthony. Nolan will do fine in this role as he's been a professional bull-shitter for most of his life. Sal, Frank and I on the other hand, don't feel great about deceiving his family and we can't get the Nick Saban story out of our heads. If that guy couldn't fool Momma, how the hell are we supposed to?

"Hey Ant!" Nolan yelled up to the front. "If we're going to pull this thing off I have to get some lessons driving this thing you know."

"You got it. We'll find you an empty parking lot and you can take us for a spin. It's easy. If you like it enough you can drive us back to Atlanta," Anthony followed this up with his big belly laugh.

Tupelo, Mississippi, the birthplace of the King of Rock n' Roll, Elvis Presley. That's about all we know about Tupelo and not all of us even knew that until Anthony told us. It's big enough, about 35,000 to 40,000 residents that everyone doesn't know everyone else's business, but it's also small enough that everyone knows the local football hero and that guy is Anthony. He called his brother and let him know that we'd be stopping in for a quick overnight visit. His entire immediate family still lives in Tupelo plus a bunch of extended family members. Anthony is kind of a black sheep when it comes to an allegiance to Tupelo. Everyone just comes back. If they go to college somewhere, they come back to be with the family. If they go into the military, they come back. Anthony has chosen to live his life outside of Tupelo, something that hasn't gone over very well with his family members. Of course, they still love him to death, but they've made it clear that they'd like him to come home.

It was just before 4pm when Anthony yelled back to us.

"The exit is coming up, just about two miles up the road. Nolan, I'll pull off into a gas station and we can make the switch. Are you ready?" Nolan had his practice session late last night in some old strip mall parking lot we found. Let's just say that I hope the trip from the gas station to Anthony's house is short without a lot of turns.

"Let's do it," Nolan was excited to get behind the wheel again.

It was hard to be inconspicuous in the cruiser. It looked just like the tour buses that big-time musical acts ride around in. We pulled into the gas station, an old Marathon station with a few pumps and a small convenience store. There were several cars pumping gas and a few teenagers hanging around outside the convenience store. The cruiser managed to turn heads. The teenagers were pointing and snapping pictures with their phones. They were all curious as to why this gigantic vehicle chose to make a stop in Tupelo. On occasion, musical acts do stop in to Tupelo. Many of them want to see where the King was born. If they're in the neighborhood they'll make a quick detour to see where it all started, the tiny house where the King was born.

There would be no photos taken today of the occupants of this cruiser. Our driver switch didn't require opening a door. Anthony stepped aside and Nolan found his way into the driver's seat.

"Ready boys, here we go!" Nolan started to pull away and then stopped. Oh boy, did he already hit something?

We heard him talking to someone and then he started to pull away again.

"What the hell was that? Did you hit something?" Frank yelled up to the front.

"No, it was one of those kids," Nolan yelled back.

"What? You hit a kid?" Sal yelled up.

"No, you idiot. The kid wanted to know who was in here. So, I told him we had Rascal Flatts back there!" Nolan laughed. "You should have seen this kid's face!"

We were now heading down the main road toward Anthony's house. We were a couple of miles away. Nolan's little lie wasn't helping us out. It turns out those kids decided to follow us on their bikes to attempt to get a peek at the members of Rascal Flatts. They were riding their bikes and texting as they went. After the first mile the group had grown. Social media was turning this ruse into a pretty funny joke. There must have been about twenty kids following us. Oh well, it's all in fun. Sure, they'll be disappointed, but it's still pretty funny.

"Nol', you got about twenty of them behind you. Every time we hit another block it seems like a few more gathered. Uh oh, now there are a couple of cars back there. They are snapping pictures of the cruiser outside their windows.

By the way, who the hell is Rascal Flatts, is he famous?" Frank made an inadvertent joke, which got us all laughing.

We made the big turn on to Anthony's street. The cruiser was so big tree limbs were scraping the top of it.

"Right up there on the left," Anthony was guiding Nolan to his house, although it was impossible to miss.

I'll give Anthony's family a lot of credit. Anthony gave them about eight hours notice that we'd be coming and it looks as if they had a year to plan this. It was a hero's welcome. Anthony's front yard was decked out in balloons, a bounce house for the kids, a couple of tents and a massive BBQ smoker that was churning out a delectable aroma already. Wow, his family knew how to throw a party.

Nolan guided the cruiser into its resting place right across the street from Anthony's house. There must have been at least fifty people, friends and family, waiting outside already enjoying food, music and their beverages of choice. Not to mention the additional thirty or so in tow from the Rascal Flatts prank. It didn't matter. Anthony's family knew most of the kids anyway. They were invited to stay, although they were a bit disappointed when the five of us exited the cruiser. No Rascal Flatts today.

Anthony led the way out of the cruiser. Sal, Frank and I were posing as his business partners/friends, while Nolan was his driver. We felt a little funny about it, but it was the least we could do for Anthony. Anthony was met by a multitude of hugs and kisses from all of his relatives. He got lost in a sea of people, leaving us to fend for ourselves. We all started making the rounds introducing ourselves. It was a complete blur. We met cousins, neighbors, aunts, uncles, sisters, brothers and it didn't seem to stop. One thing was consistent though, these people were as genuine as it gets. It was nice to witness this southern hospitality. Sure, I live as South as a person can get in this country, but South Florida isn't known for being the most welcoming place on earth. As a matter of fact, a lot of the people are down right rude. This was a welcome change.

"Guys, guys, come over here," we located Anthony again after all of the greetings had taken place.

We made our way toward the front of the house where the tent was set up. It was obvious who Anthony wanted us to meet. There, sitting in her favorite chair, was a woman with gray hair and a big smile on her face. Her reading glasses were barely hanging on to her nose. She had a crinkled legal yellow sheet of paper in one hand, which we assumed was the guest list for this bash, as she always liked to know who was in her house and a glass of sweet tea in the other. A gigantic man, a couple of inches taller than Anthony, flanked her left side. That was James, Anthony's dad. By looking at the two of them it was easy to see where Anthony got his size. Momma was not a small woman either. The genetics from Anthony's parents were running wild around the front yard. We all felt tiny.

Anthony made a beeline over to his mom and dad. He gave his dad a quick handshake and a big hug, and then he focused his attention on Momma. She slowly pushed her way up from her chair. James grabbed the guest list and the sweet tea for her. She wasn't going to sit down to greet her son.

"My baby, my baby is home," Momma was tearing up as she struggled to rise from her chair.

Anthony helped her with the last push and then went in for the big hug. She was so happy to see him. It's been tough without him around. She knows she's fortunate to have so many family members still living in Tupelo, but without Anthony, something is missing.

We let the two of them enjoy their embrace and introduced ourselves to James. He crushed each of our hands just like Anthony did when we met him. Not on purpose of course, but when you're that big it's hard to be gentle.

"Momma, meet the guys. This is Sal, Kevin and Frank," Anthony omitted Nolan, although he was right there with us.

I put my hand out to shake Momma's, but that wouldn't suffice.

"How were you brought up son? We hug around here", Momma said with a laugh, which was similar to Anthony's, but not quite as deep of course.

I went in for the big hug and just about disappeared in Momma's big bosom. She swung me back and forth and said, "Now, that's how we do it Tupelo style."

Hugs ensued for Sal and Frank as well and then Nolan was introduced. Momma hugged him to.

"I hope you boys came hungry because your brothers have been preparing a feast for you," Momma motioned over to the huge BBQ which was loaded up with ribs, chicken, hot dogs, hamburgers, corn and baked beans. This had the making for our best meal yet on this trip and we've had some good ones so far.

We each grabbed a plate and made our way over to the table next to the grill and began to load up. It was quite the balancing act to keep everything on the plate for the walk over to the picnic table, but we made it.

The afternoon turned into the evening and we were having a wonderful time listening to stories about Anthony. Some were about his football prowess, but others were about some embarrassing moments for him as well. For instance, the time when he was playing pee-wee football and he was just too big for the uniforms. Nothing like having your pants split down your butt crack in the middle of the game. It didn't stop Anthony though. He finished the game with his fruit of the looms showing for the remainder of it. He scored two touchdowns with his drawers showing. Yes, touchdowns. Back in pee-wee ball Anthony was a fullback, not a lineman. I can't imagine what it must have been like having that guy running toward you with the ball.

Another comical occurrence that was also taking place as we took in all of the stories about Anthony was how Nolan the "driver" was being treated. Anthony took advantage of this situation. He had Nolan go back and forth to the cruiser to grab miscellaneous items for him. None of these items were very important, but it just showed that Anthony had an underling to boss around. He was showing off and we loved it. Nolan on the other hand was a good sport for a little while, but when Anthony sent him back to the cruiser with a plate of food to eat by himself he reached his limit. Frank calmed him down before he made a scene and blew Anthony's cover. It's mean to say, but Nolan should get used to other people telling him what to do.

It was hard to believe that this was our last night on the road together. Tupelo is just five hours from Atlanta. We'll get up tomorrow morning, grab some breakfast and get on the road. So far, this trip has been everything I thought it was going to be. We've experienced a lot of great moments, a few scary ones and some eye-opening and emotional ones. I have one thing left to do and I'm almost out of time. I either do it tonight or save it for the drive home tomorrow. I've procrastinated long enough and my opportunities are dwindling away.

"You boys don't stay up too late now," Momma pushed herself up out of her chair. Anthony jumped out of his to give her a hand.

"Oh, my bones, they're not what they used to be. Thank you baby," Momma held on to Anthony's arm as he walked her up the steps on to the front porch.

"Good night Momma," Anthony gave her a kiss on the cheek.

"Anything left in the tank fellas?" Anthony stood at the top of the steps and stretched high in the air and grabbed on to the porch overhang.

"That was good Ant. You know what my favorite part was?" Sal asked.

"Had to be the ribs. My brothers don't mess around with their ribs," Anthony responded.

"Sure, the ribs were great, but you sending Nolan back to the cruiser to eat had to be the best part of the night!" Sal laughed loudly at first, and then realized he should tone it down since it was so late.

"He didn't like that too much, did he?" Anthony smiled.

"No, I didn't you fucker," Nolan walked up without any of us noticing.

"Easy Nol', he was just messing around," I knew Nolan was pissed off, but he wouldn't cause a scene. That was wishful thinking.

"No, shut the fuck up Kevin. That was bullshit. I get stuck sitting in the fucking cruiser looking like some kind of peon while you guys sit around all night enjoying your fucking bar-be-que and beer," Nolan stood at the bottom of the porch steps directing his comments up to Anthony.

"Settle down, people are trying to sleep," Frank stood up and grabbed Nolan's arm to prompt him to sit down.

"Get your fucking fag hands off of me Frank,"
Nolan always knows how to cross the line.

"Come on Nolan, what kind of comment was that?"
I asked.

"Did it hurt your feelings Frank? Well, fuck you.
No one gave a shit about my feelings," Nolan was
still staring at Anthony while speaking to Frank. It
was like he wanted to get physical with him. That
would last about two seconds.

Anthony hadn't said a word. That was his style.
He was always calm. Nolan was trying to get under
his skin, but he wouldn't let him. Some big guys
would have walked down the porch steps and put an
ass kicking on Nolan, but Anthony just let him vent.

"I'm the driver, right? Right?" Nolan's voice rose.
He wasn't expecting an answer.

"OK, if I'm the driver, then I say we're leaving
right now. Without this fucking asshole." Nolan
directed his finger in Anthony's direction.

"Who fucking needs him now. He can stay here in
this shit town and we'll head home. I'm driving.
Let's go assholes. Pack it up, trips over," Nolan
was embarrassing himself now.

Nolan stormed away toward the cruiser. He was
acting like a child.

"Let him go. What a dick," I said.

"That's fine, but if he takes that cruiser it's my ass. I'm responsible for that thing," Anthony said his first words after taking blow after blow from Nolan.

All of the sudden the lights turned on and the engine roared. If Nolan was bluffing, he was doing a pretty good job of it.

Anthony jumped down from the porch, skipping the steps and started running to the cruiser. Nolan saw him coming and you could see it in his eyes. This is what he wanted to accomplish. Anthony was panicked and Nolan was the source. He loved it. The cruiser started to pull away while Anthony was pounding on the driver side window. Nolan wasn't going to stop. The rest of us ran over to grab Anthony before he did something stupid, like jump in front of the cruiser.

It was almost comical watching the three of us try to hold Anthony back, but we were able to do it. Nolan drove in the direction the cruiser was facing. Anthony, of course, knew his neighborhood well while Nolan didn't. The street he was going down would circle him back and he'd have to come out about four houses down Anthony's street in the opposite direction. Anthony started walking in that direction. The three of us followed.

"Give it about two minutes and he'll be coming right down this road," Anthony pointed to the crossroad.

Sure enough, we saw the cruiser's lights in the distance. Rather than slowing down to stop at the intersection, it was clear that the cruiser was speeding up.

"Anthony, get outta the way!" Frank yelled. The cruiser was barreling down on us.

Anthony stood his ground in the intersection. The three of us realized that when we pulled Anthony away just a few minutes earlier it was because he let us, not because we overpowered him. He wasn't budging. We were involved in a game of chicken, a bus versus a guy almost the size of a bus. As big as Anthony is, he wasn't going to win this one. The bus was about thirty feet away. The four of us were all now in harm's way as Sal, Frank and I attempted to push Anthony out of the path of the cruiser. It was like we were pushing a blocking sled, but this one was stuck in the mud.

All of the sudden we were jolted and the four of us hit the pavement hard. All of us including Anthony were in a daze. What the hell just happened? Did Nolan just run the four of us over? I felt a burning sensation on both of my knees. I grabbed one of them and my hand came up bloody. I looked over at Frank. He was writhing on the ground. It was clear that both of his hands were bleeding. Sal was sitting up with his head in his hands, both elbows bloody. Anthony was also sitting up and didn't appear to be injured in any way. Then another person came out of the shadows.

"Everyone OK?" A big hand reached out to help me up. I grabbed it.

"Anthony, you good?" It was Anthony's oldest brother Joe. It turns out rescuing people from danger was something that this family was used to doing and they were pretty darn good at it as well. It was kind of ironic that Anthony had saved Nolan from blowing his brains out in the kitchen just a few days ago and now Joe had saved all of us from Nolan's crazy stunt.

"Where did he go?" A groggy Sal asked.

"He blew right through the intersection and made a hard left. I thought he was going to flip that thing", Joe responded while pointing to the tire marks in the road.

All of us were thinking, 'what else could happen on this trip'?'

"Come on, let's get in the house. Looks like you guys are just scraped up a bit. We'll get you set up on a couple of couches and sleeping bags for the night," Joe ushered the four of us back to the house.

When the commotion stopped it was about two in the morning. Another night had passed and my story went untold. At this point, I don't know what will happen. The cruiser is gone and Nolan tried to run all of us over. Now, I think I've gotten more than I had bargained for on this trip. I just want to get home in one piece at this point.

Anthony contemplated calling the police, but decided to chance it. He was praying that Nolan would come to his senses and bring the cruiser back.

The morning came quickly as Momma was an early riser. It was just before 6am when I woke up to the rattling of frying pans and dishes in the kitchen. Sure enough, Momma was preparing a morning feast for us. She was a bit surprised to see the three of us sleeping in her living room, but she didn't think much of it. She hadn't looked out the front window yet. If she had, she would have noticed that the cruiser was gone. That would have raised a red flag, but no matter where her mind went with it I'm sure she wouldn't arrive at the notion that Nolan tried to run all of us over last night. I was there and I still can't believe it. He's a twisted individual and has done everything possible to ruin this trip for all of us. I hate to say it, but I just want to get it over with now. It's time to go home to Lisa and the girls. Right now, we're not going anywhere.

I pushed myself up from the couch. I was sore. The road burn on my knees was painful. Sal was sleeping a few feet over from me on the floor. One of his elbows was sticking out from the covers. It was scraped up pretty good too. I saw that Frank's eyes were open. He was on the other couch with one hand up in front of his face inspecting the damage from last night. My knees, Sal's elbows and Frank's hands, we all had pretty harsh road burn. Anthony was also on the floor. He sat up with a groan. I couldn't see anything wrong with him, but it turns out his back was hurting from the tumble. I'm sure sleeping on the floor didn't help too much.

"Hey, don't say anything to Momma about last night," Anthony whispered to me.

"What the hell is she gonna say about this?" I pointed to my bloody knees.

"Horse play, that's what happened. All of it was horseplay. Is the cruiser out there?" Anthony asked.

"Nope. Nothing," I was nervous. We all knew that Nolan was not in a good place mentally.

"Rise and shine boys," Momma stepped into the room.

The smell of the bacon was all we needed to get in gear.

"Anything?" Frank whispered to me as we made our way into the kitchen.

"Nothing," I said.

"What has he done?" Frank asked the question while looking up to the ceiling.

It was good to know that despite everything that occurred last night, we all still had our appetites. I think it was a combination of nervous eating and plain old hunger, but we downed several helpings of eggs, bacon, sausage, grits, biscuits and gravy and a couple of pancakes for good measure. The meal came and went, but still no sign of Nolan and the cruiser. Scary thoughts continued to go through my head. What if he killed himself? Could we have done more last night to find him? At the time, none of us cared, but as our heads cleared we were all concerned.

"We need to get in the car and start searching," Frank said.

"I know, but I tell ya, I'm a little bit scared of what we may find. We should have gone after him last night," Sal said what we were all thinking. As much as Nolan does to distance himself as our friend, we all still care for the guy. It sounds nuts, but I guess we are forgiving that way. He has a problem. That is very clear and if he doesn't have his friends to help him, who does he have?

"Let's go. We can jump in Joe's car," Anthony was ready to take a ride, bad back and all. It would be easy to say that Anthony's primary motivation was to retrieve the cruiser, but that wasn't accurate. Sure, his ass was on the line for the cruiser, but he also felt a little guilty. He felt like he may have pushed Nolan over the edge by making him eat alone in the cruiser.

"Hey, wait a second. Where are you boys goin'?" Momma walked into the family room wondering why we were all leaving so quickly. She knew it wasn't to go on a coffee and donut run.

"We need to stock up for the ride Momma. We're going to Wal-Mart. Need anything?" Anthony told a white lie.

Momma gave Anthony a look, a look that he knew all too well. Just like Nick Saban couldn't fool her,

Momma wasn't being fooled now, but she let Anthony carry on without prying.

We all hustled out of the house as best we could with our variety of bumps and bruises. Just as we made it down the steps of the porch, we could hear a loud engine. It was the familiar sound of the cruiser. It wasn't in site yet, but Anthony knew the sound.

"That's him!" Anthony ran to the curb.

Sure enough, the cruiser was headed our way. We stayed on the curb.

Nolan pulled the cruiser up in front of Anthony's house. The hydraulics on the big vehicle lowered it accordingly and around the front came Nolan.

"Ready to go? We're gassed up and I grabbed some stuff at the Wal-Mart too." Nolan said as if last night never happened.

He had lost his marbles. We were dumbfounded. The four of us looked at him and then looked at each other.

"Let's go. Anthony you drive," Nolan said with a strange smile and flipped the keys to Anthony.

I could see that Sal was getting angry and he was about to say something until I grabbed his arm and mouthed the words 'let it go'. That's what we needed to do right now. There was no sense in blowing this thing up even more than it had been already. We had five more hours with the guy and then we'll never see him again. Although that thought ran through my head quickly, it made a significant impact. We'd never see him again. It's true. Five more hours and it's possible that they'll never see me again. This goodbye was going to be the toughest I've ever experienced. Five hours.

"Let's go say thank you to Momma," Frank led the way back up to the house.

Momma was waiting on the porch for us. Anthony was in the cruiser prepping it for the trip. Momma hadn't seen Nolan toss him the keys.

"We can't thank you enough for your hospitality," Frank said to Momma as he gave her a big hug and a kiss on the cheek.

Sal and I proceeded to do the same. Joe, the hero, was standing by her side. We gave him a handshake that turned into a hug. These are just good people. It was a pleasure to have them as a part of our lives even though it was just for a brief moment. The memories will last forever.

The three of us turned toward the porch steps and Momma had a couple of parting words for us.

"Boys, you're good friends. You're good sports too, taking part in that ruse that my boy put you up to. Tell him to drive carefully," Momma smiled.

Just like that, we were called out. Momma did it in a subtle way, but she made sure we knew. She was on to us the whole time, but played along for Anthony's sake. Sal, Frank and I would keep that little comment to ourselves, no need to burst Anthony's bubble. I guess we have more in common with Nick Saban than we thought.

It was about 8:45am when we got to the edge of town. Nolan drove us out of Anthony's neighborhood just like he drove us in. Thankfully, not like the way he almost ran us over. Anthony hopped back into the driver's seat and we were on our way. This time, we didn't have any kids on bicycles in tow. Rascal Flatts was leaving town without their entourage.

Chapter Twelve

The last few hours of the trip were upon us. For some reason, I had always remembered the final few hours of our trip twenty years ago vividly. I drove that leg of the trip and recall it being oddly quiet for the majority of it. I think we were all spent at that point. After all, we had been driving for almost two days straight with food and bathroom breaks only. The car stunk, as it should. We stunk, as we should. Come to think of it the car didn't stink at all, it was just us. I was nervous as the hours ticked off of the clock. I remember thinking that this was it. Next stop work and careers, then marriage and family. It all played out just like that. The four of us took different paths along the way, but our new lives started as soon as that trip ended.

Now, all of our next steps are much more complicated than they were twenty years ago. Everyone hopes that as their lives go on things get a little bit easier, but that's not the case. All of our lives have gotten more complicated. Granted, for the most part, we've made our beds and now we're laying in them. I guess the only thing we can do is handle what is thrown at us the best way possible and let the chips fall where they may.

As this trip comes to a close I can say that I'm happy, just like I was twenty years ago when that trip ended. I'm not sure why I'm so happy. It's probably because I feel that we accomplished something. Twenty years ago we set out to see a bunch of places across the country that we'd never seen before and we did it. Now, the goal was to simply take the trip. We didn't stop anywhere on this trip that we hadn't been or seen before. Well, none of us had ever been to Tupelo, but that was the exception. The goal was simple – just take the trip. I never thought it would happen, but we did it. For that, I'm happy.

"Frankie, you're staying over tonight right," Sal asked.

"Yeah, my flight leaves at 8:05am tomorrow," Frank replied.

"What about you guys?" Sal turned his attention to Nolan and me.

"Nope, getting on the road. Gotta couple of things to do, if you know what I mean." Nolan's life was about to be turned upside down even more than it has been. He estimated that he'd be taken into custody any day now. He'll probably post bond, but who knows. I think if the prosecutor had any idea as to what when on during this trip he'd lock him down immediately.

"Me too. I'm gonna head out as well. I'll probably drive through Tallahassee. I'll grab a room somewhere if I get tired." I added.

"Alright, Frankie we'll just stay in my apartment. When we get to the house I'll let Katie know that we don't need to carry on the charade anymore." Sal sounded relieved, as he knew Katie couldn't stand having to act like she enjoyed his company.

Not like I needed a reminder, but all of this talk about what we're doing when we arrive in Atlanta made it clear that time was running out for me. If I was going to tell these guys about my situation I only had a couple of hours left. I sat there without saying a word. I was sure that the guys could tell that something was eating at me, but come to think of it, that was just my paranoia. I had gone over this moment in my head so many times during the trip. I had my game plan ready word for word, now all I had to do was muster up the courage to let the words come out. I was struggling with that for a bunch of reasons. One, there's been so much drama on this trip already I didn't feel like adding to it. Two, I was battling with the idea of telling these guys before I told Lisa. She's my wife and I owe it to her to discuss it with her first. But, the main reason, the reason why I couldn't get the words out of my mouth was that I just didn't want to accept it. I'm sick and I'm going to die soon. I don't want to accept that lot and by saying the words it seems like I'm accepting it. It's hard to explain, but I just don't want to say it.

I continued to sit there fidgeting with whatever I could find, my phone, an empty beer bottle, anything to calm me down. I kept looking at my watch and saying to myself, 'OK, in fifteen minutes just blurt it out'. Fifteen minutes would go by and I'd plan on doing it the next fifteen minutes. As I sat there chickening out Frank decided to take the floor.

"Guys, before the trip ends I just wanted to say something," he was very serious, just like when he made his last announcement.

"When we took this trip twenty years ago it was me that declared that we better enjoy it because we'd never do it again. I believed those words and I was willing to accept them until about ten years ago when Kevin started clamoring about a twenty year reunion." Frank looked at me with a big smile.

"Admit it, we all thought he was nuts. Granted, we loved the idea, but all of us knew better. We knew it would be almost impossible to pull off." Frank continued as Sal and Nolan nodded their heads in agreement.

"Well, here we are. The trip is almost over and we have more stories than we ever thought we'd have on a trip like this. Some that we'd like to forget soon, but others that we'll tell to our kids and our grandkids someday – the PG-13 versions of course." Frank motioned over to Sal to take over almost like this was rehearsed.

"Yep, so Kevin we decided that we wanted to do something for you to recognize the fact that you never gave up on this idea and provided us with a special time that we'll never forget. If you didn't keep pushing, this never would have happened." It almost felt like an award ceremony of some sort.

"Your birthday came and went while we were on this trip and we raised our glasses to celebrate, but never gave you a gift. So think of what we're about to give you as an early birthday gift for next year. Nolan." Sal let Nolan bring it home.

"Next year, for your birthday, you and Lisa will be enjoying a 7-day cruise to the Western Caribbean. Everything is booked, all you need to do is get yourself to the port and get a passport, if you don't have one already." Nolan smiled. He didn't have anything physical to present, but he didn't need to.

I was floored. I wasn't expecting anything from them, nor did I feel like I deserved anything.

"Wow guys, that's too much. That's just way too much."

"Don't worry, Nolan paid for it. Think of it as funny money." Sal laughed.

"We split it three ways and my third was clean, don't worry about it." Nolan jumped in.

"Well, thanks guys. Lisa will be thrilled." I rose from my seat and made the rounds with handshakes and hugs for each of the guys.

Not only did their gesture mean a lot to me, but it also gave me an out. Call it a convenient excuse. Call it what you want, but now I didn't have to spill my guts about my problem. How could I? These guys just bought a 7-day cruise for me to take in a year and I'm going to tell them that I'll be dead by then? Not a chance.

Chapter Thirteen

It was about 2:30pm when the cruiser made its final big turn into Sal's driveway. Hannah, as cute as ever, was standing outside with Katie as we pulled up.

"That's a wrap fellas. It's been a good one." Anthony said as he walked back to the sitting area.

"No doubt Ant. You better stay in touch." Frank said.

"Yeah Anthony, don't forget about us now." I said.

"You can forget about me and I'll do the same about you." Nolan said in a serious tone and then reached out to shake Anthony's hand. The two of them smiled at each other and the handshake turned into a hug. What a bizarre relationship.

We gathered all of our things. It was easy. We just took all of our dirty clothes and shoved them into our bags. Frank began to gather all of the empty beer bottles, fast food wrappers and any other garbage he could find.

"Frank, let it be. I got it. I'll have this thing looking brand new for the next group." Anthony said.

I led the way out of the cruiser. One by one we filed down the stairs. Hannah was there to greet us as we stepped off.

"Daddy!" She screamed and jumped up into Sal's arms.

"Hi honey. Did you miss me?" Sal said with a big smile.

"I drew a picture of you. Mommy, show Daddy my picture." Hannah wriggled out of Sal's arms and ran over to get her picture.

The mind of a child is one that sometimes takes the simplest things and recognizes them in a way that an adult just can't do anymore. Sure, we all had the ability to do that years ago, but we've gotten a lot more complicated since then.

Sal grabbed the picture from Hannah and we all peeked over his shoulder to take a look as well. It was better than any photo that we could have asked for during the trip. The picture was of the four us standing in front of the cruiser on the day we left. We didn't take a picture that morning, but what Hannah presented us with was much better. The cruiser was gigantic in proportion to the size of the four us, but that's how Hannah saw it. She even drew Anthony's head peering above the window in the driver's seat. We were all waiving with our right hands and had our luggage in our left. I felt like she drew me a little short, but who am I to complain? She made her father's gut gigantic, which had us all laughing. Nolan's biceps were huge, which of course, got him to comment on the accuracy of the picture. It was special and it captured the moment for us. I wanted to take it home myself.

"I think that's it fellas. It looks like you got everything." Anthony walked over to us as we were still huddled around Hannah's drawing.

"Anthony, what can I say, we can't thank you enough." Sal said.

"Yeah Ant, helluva trip buddy, thank you." I added.

"You better accept my friend request Anthony. Everyone needs a gay guy on their friend list!" Frank was making jokes at his own expense. Katie's eyebrows rose when she heard Frank's comment, but she brushed it off as a joke. Word would travel quickly on this one, but hopefully not too quickly, as Frank needed to be the one to tell Erica in person.

Nolan walked over to Anthony and put his hand out. "No hard feelings, OK?"

"Life's too short to hold grudges. Don't worry about it. You take care of yourself and stay strong my friend." Anthony replied and then pulled Nolan in for a hug.

Anthony turned toward the cruiser and started to make his way up the steps.

"Ant, hold on!" Sal yelled and jogged over.

"This is for you. You deserve it more than you'll ever know." Sal handed Anthony an envelope. It was a little extra tip. It was the least we could do for the guy after everything he did for us along the way.

Anthony popped back out of the cruiser and raised the envelope in our direction.

"Thanks guys, thank you. I'll be waiting for that call." Anthony was referring to the idea we had thrown around about making this trip an annual occurrence, minus Nolan of course.

The cruiser fired up and pulled away. Anthony had become our friend along the way. All of us had plans to stay in touch with him. After all we had been through together it felt like we had known him for years. It's interesting how people come in and out of your life. Some leave their mark, while others come and go without notice. Anthony left his mark. I'm a better person for knowing him and I feel blessed that our paths crossed. I know I'll stay in touch with him. I hope he can meet Lisa and the girls some day. Lisa will get tired of me talking about him and will demand to meet him just to put the face with the name. I'll point his head out to her in Hannah's drawing. That should suffice.

Nolan had been going back and forth to the trunk of his car throwing his clothes and other items in one by one. What a mess. He slammed the trunk shut indicating that he was finished packing and then proceeded to get into the driver's seat. He turned the ignition and started to back out. Sal, Frank and I all looked at Nolan and then at each other. Was this guy going to leave so abruptly? The Mercedes began to back out of the driveway while all of us looked on with amazement.

"What the fuck is that all about?" Sal directed his question to Frank and me.

"Doesn't surprise me in the least." I said as Nolan's passenger window began to roll down.

"Hey, don't look so sad you fags. You know I'm not a goodbye guy, so hug each other if you're looking for a hug." Nolan laughed as he leaned over the center console to shout out of the window.

We didn't return the laughter. After everything this guy had put us through he couldn't muster up a simple goodbye.

"Just think how boring your trip would have been without me? Love me or hate me boys, that's what I'm all about. I know you love me though. Love you too. See you on the other side!" Nolan accelerated into the road and peeled out for good measure. With a couple of honks and the smell of burnt rubber he was gone just like that. The Mercedes disappeared down the road.

No one said it, but we were all thinking it. That may have been the last time we'll ever see Nolan. It was all so surreal. It's a wonder how anyone could like a pain in the ass like him, but what he said is true. He's the kind of guy you either love or hate. Surprisingly enough we still love him, even after everything he put us through. He has a long, tough road ahead of him. He'll drive that big Mercedes back to Tennessee and then surrender to the authorities. Chances are he'll go straight to jail and he may not even be allowed to post bond. I hope they let him, but time will tell. I'll pray for him every day. I miss him already.

After Nolan's bizarre exit it was just Frank and I that were left to say our goodbyes to Sal. Since Frank's flight didn't leave until tomorrow, it was my turn by default. I went inside to use the restroom and what was about four minutes felt like a lifetime. So many thoughts were going through my head. Nolan had just left and I was pretty confident that I'd never see him again. That realization was starting to sink in. I also wondered if I'd ever see Frank and Sal again. I failed to tell them about my situation and I was very disappointed in myself. Finding the courage was impossible. I kept procrastinating and procrastinating thinking that timing was a viable excuse. That was bullshit though. Timing had nothing to do with it. I chickened out. Frank showed what true courage is all about. He did what I was hoping to do. He made up his mind that he was going to share something so personal with us, his best friends. There were plenty of reasons along the way that Frank could have used as excuses not to tell us, but he pressed on. I'm proud of him. I'm proud to call him my friend. He'll have many challenges ahead while he settles in to his new life. Many people that are close to him won't be supportive. He knows that and says that he is prepared for it, but I'm sure there will be a few surprises along the way. Some of his friends and family members may support him and some may not. The question will be, who lands on which side of the fence? That's what will surprise him. At least he's off to a good start with the three of us.

We love the guy, no matter if he's gay or straight. We'll always be there for him.

Sal and Frank were still outside sorting through their luggage making sure they each had everything they started the trip with.

"Alright guys, I guess it's my turn." I said as I grabbed my bags.

"I can't believe it's over." Sal looked up at me as he zipped his bag closed. He lost a couple of things along the way, but it would have been odd if he hadn't.

"Well, we did it. I never thought we would, but we did it." Frank added.

"Yeah, and we almost died a few times along the way." We all did the only thing we could do in response to my comment. We laughed.

It was a strange trip to say the least, but we all made it back in one piece and learned a few things about each other and ourselves along the way. I'd like to think that we are all better people because of this trip. I think the guys, including Nolan, would agree. Heck, we even made a new friend along the way.

"So, are you driving straight through?" Frank asked.

It was after 3pm and my trip would take at least ten hours.

"No, I'll stop somewhere tonight." I figured that stopping in Tallahassee would be a good idea. I could take a stroll around campus and reminisce a little bit. I hadn't been back there in years and who knows, I may not get another chance.

"OK, good idea. I'm sure you're exhausted just like us. No need to push it." Frank approved.

"Frankie, come here." I motioned for Frank to come over with my arms wide open. He came in for a big bear hug. A true hug, not the couple of pats on the back kind of hug that we greeted each other with when the trip started.

"Promise me that we won't let so much time pass again." Frank said as we separated.

I knew in my head that it was impossible for me to make that promise, but I did it anyway.

"Definitely man, definitely." I reassured him.

"You take care and stay strong. Remember, if they don't accept you, then fuck 'em." I said with a smile.

"Sally, get over here my man." I yelled over to Sal as he was still fidgeting with his bags.

"Thanks again for pushing for this, I mean it. It never would have happened without you being a pain in the ass. It meant a lot to me, more than you'll ever know. Thank you." Sal pulled me in from a handshake to a hug.

"You're a good man Sal. Take care of that little girl, she's gorgeous." Hannah was by his side.

"Goodbye Uncle Kevin, I love you!" Hannah said as she bounced up and down and then wrapped herself around Sal's thigh.

I grabbed my bags and tossed them in the back seat. I made my way around the car to the driver's side and hopped in. I turned the ignition, rolled down the windows and started to back out.

"See ya guys. Talk to you soon!" I yelled out the window as I continued down the driveway.

I turned the wheel, put the car in drive and I was off. A couple of honks of the horn and that was it. I didn't even manage to get out of Sal's neighborhood before my eyes started tearing up. Tears began to roll down my cheeks. I'm terrified. I'm terrified because I may not ever see my friends again. I'm terrified because I know I'm only a few hours away from turning my family's life upside down with my news. I'm terrified because of the thought of the physical toll that I'm about to go through.

I wish this was just a bad dream, a terrible nightmare, but it's not. This is my life. For better or worse, these are the cards that I've been dealt.

Chapter Fourteen

I heard my phone buzzing and thought that I must have forgotten something. I looked down and saw that it was Lisa.

"Hi honey."

"Hi baby, did you leave yet? Are you OK?" Lisa could tell my voice wasn't sounding like it usually did.

"I just left, no I'm good. A little emotional, but I'm good." She knew I was crying. I didn't have to spell it out for her.

"I'm gonna put you on speaker. The girls want to say hi." I could hear Lynnie and Reilly in the background.

"Daddy! We miss you!" Reilly shrieked.

"Come home Daddy, come home." Lynnie added.

"Oh my babies, I miss you so much. Daddy will be home tomorrow and we'll do whatever you want." I'm sure Lisa would have something to say about that.

"Can we go to the park?" Lynnie asked.

"If that's what you want to do then that's what we'll do."

"OK girls, say bye-bye", Lisa held the phone up for the girls.

"Bye-bye Daddy", they said in unison.

Lisa took the phone off of speaker.

"Are you stopping in Tallahassee for the night?"
She asked.

"Yeah, then I'll get on the road around six. I should
be home around 1."

"OK, be careful. We love you."

"Love you too. I have lots of stories for you."

"I bet, I bet. Love you."

I have a ton of stories. Some that she probably
won't believe, but I have witnesses to prove their
validity. Of course, I have several stories that I
won't be sharing with her either. Some things are
better left unsaid.

It was around 7 o'clock when I arrived in
Tallahassee. I'd have about an hour before daylight
would disappear. With that in mind, I decided to
drive around campus rather than walk as I had
originally planned.

For the most part, the campus remained the same as
I had remembered it. The major changes were
around the football stadium. I spent a lot of good
times in that stadium. It was fun to see it again.

The campus was quiet as the spring semester had just wrapped up and the summer session hadn't started yet. Most of the students were out of town.

I drove past the dorm I lived in my freshman year. It looked exactly the way I left it. I hope they've renovated the inside since then because the outside hadn't been touched.

I was just about finished with my brief driving tour, but had one final stop. I decided to pull up and take a peek inside my old fraternity house. I lived in it for two years. It was an old, beat up house when I lived in it. By the looks of things, nothing had changed. It was still the dump I remember. I recall bringing my parents there for the first time and to say they were shocked was an understatement. The furniture was beat up, the walls were in need of a paint job and the outside deck looked like it was about to sink into the ground. My room was a mess – clothes everywhere, a loft that had me sleeping about a foot away from the ceiling and a dingy old love seat that my roommate and I picked up from a thrift store. Yep, it was a complete train wreck, but I loved it. My parents were happy as long as I was happy and safe. Now, I'm not sure how safe I was in that rattrap, but I was happy.

I squeezed my car into what I thought was a parking space and walked around to the front of the house. The door was wide open, as usual.

As I walked in a guy entered behind me. It looked like he had just finished working out. He was about 6'1", lanky, but fit with brown hair, shaved almost all the way down. I remember my college days. I could eat almost anything and still keep a physique like this guy. My metabolism was outstanding. It's quite a different story when you're north of forty.

"Hey, how's it goin?" The young man greeted me.

"Good thanks. I'm just stopping in to look around. I used to live here." I responded as my eyes wandered around the foyer.

"Cool. What years?" He asked.

"94 and 95, down hall one year and up hall the next." I said.

"I'm Trent, nice to meet you," Trent extended his hand.

We refrained from taking part in the silly fraternity handshake. As a matter of fact, I don't think I've ever done that.

"It's amazing, not much has changed. I'm not sure if that's a good thing or a bad thing." I laughed, as did Trent.

"That's true, that's true. Well, feel free to look around. We restored a lot of the composites. I think you guys are in the up hall. I'm the treasurer and my room is right over here. If you need anything, just knock. Make sure you come back in the fall for the alumni weekend. By the way, I didn't get your name."

I introduced myself and made my way over to the stairwell to take a walk into my past.

The stairs creaked just the way they used to. One by one I climbed up and made it to our section of photos. It was amazing to see all of our baby faces. There was Sal, Nolan and Frank. It's a good thing that Nolan no longer has hair. He didn't know what the hell to do with it when he had it. Boy, was his picture hysterical. What a disaster. I'm not sure what he was trying to do, but it looked like part mullet, part butt-cut and some kind of wavy thing in the front. I'm pretty sure that wasn't stylish back then. I guess he was just happy to have hair to play with. I found my photo too. I realize it was twenty years ago, but wow, time takes its toll. Not to mention stress and another twenty years of adult beverages. Yep, that'll do it.

I enjoyed looking at all of the photos. There were a bunch of guys that I've kept in touch with, but there were a lot more that have become just a memory. Sadly enough, I also spotted several guys who had passed on from different tragedies that I either heard about or unfortunately, was around when they happened. I've found it almost impossible not to bring death into everything that I'm doing lately. Even reminiscing at my fraternity house is not immune to my depressing thoughts. The way things are going now I'll probably die from stress before this disease gets me. I could stand around here all day, but not because I want to gaze at the photos. The minute I walk out this door and get in my car the clock starts. Seven hours until I get home. Seven hours until I have to face Lisa and the girls. As much as I miss them, part of me wants to get in the car and drive in the opposite direction, but I know I can't hide this forever. It's time to go to battle against this thing. My first step is telling someone about it and that someone is going to be Lisa.

I walked back down the stairs and exited the house. Hopefully these guys will get a new house some day. Either that or it will crumble to the ground at some point.

I spent a sleepless night at the Doubletree in downtown Tallahassee. I'd say I was able to get about two to three hours of actual sleep. I got on the road around 6am as planned. Tallahassee was behind me. The minutes and the miles began to click away. It was hotter and more humid than usual for a day in May. Seven hours alone provides a person with a lot of time to reflect. I expected that the guys would all know about my situation by now and that would have helped me prepare to tell Lisa. Unfortunately, I blew it. My trip to Atlanta, while stressful, was full of anticipation since I was about to see the guys and we were going to have some fun. Now, my trip back home is full of anxiety and I've had to pull in to the rest areas to calm down. I feel like I'm going to have a panic attack. I just want to get home. I shouldn't be behind the wheel, but I've decided to keep pressing on. What am I supposed to do, call Lisa and have her come get me? That's not an option.

I tried to take my mind off of what was waiting for me at home by thinking about all of the hilarious events that took place on our trip. It helped me crack a smile. I even laughed out loud a few times. Although it was a bizarre trip, in the end it was a lot of fun and that's just what we wanted.

Chapter Fifteen

There it is, my exit off of the turnpike. I was gone for a couple of weeks, but it feels like I haven't been home in months. I've never been away from Lisa or the girls that long. This is it, no more hiding.

I hit the button for the garage door and the girls heard it opening inside.

"Daddy, Daddy, Daddy!" Reilly ran through the house to our master bedroom to find her mommy.

"OK, OK, let's go outside," Lisa took Reilly's hand or actually it was just the opposite.

Lisa opened the front door and Reilly led the way with Lynnie right behind her. I opened the door to the car and turned back to see my two precious little ones running toward me. Lisa didn't even have time to throw sandals on their feet.

"Hi girls", I grabbed both of them and held one in each arm. Simultaneously they both gave me a big kiss on the check. That's the type of stuff that will make a man melt. These are my babies and I'm so blessed to have them. My two little blondies with their blue eyes must have gotten those looks from Lisa's Swedish side of the family. There's no Italian in these girls at all, well at least not by the looks of them.

Lisa trailed behind and snuck in for a kiss. I walked a few more steps and then put the girls down. I stopped and grabbed Lisa's hand. I brought her in for a gigantic bear hug that took her by surprise.

"Whoa, you just cracked my back. That felt good." Lisa pulled her head back to make eye contact with me and give me another kiss.

"I missed you." I whispered.

"Come on, let's get inside before the girls feet turn black. I know Daddy doesn't want to be on bath patrol right now." Lisa grabbed the girl's hands and led the way inside.

It was good to be home. Our trip was a blast, but it's always nice to come home. There's nothing like it. Everything seemed so perfect right now, but I knew better. I decided that today would not be the day. Seeing the three smiling faces before me made that decision easy. We would go to the park as planned, just like the girls wanted. Lisa and I will have to speak tomorrow. I get one more day. One more day to enjoy my family without this black cloud hanging over us. One more day to feel normal.

I was ready to go as soon as I walked in the door, much to Lisa's surprise.

"Really, you don't want to relax for a few minutes and then we'll go?" Lisa asked.

"No, let's do it. I can rest when we get back. Come on girls, time for the park!" I sent them into a tizzy.

My girls have always enjoyed the simple things, like the park. Some kids would insist on going to a water park, Chuck E. Cheese's or something like that, but my kids just love being in the park on the swings or simply running around.

When we arrived the girls made a beeline to the swing set. As expected, my services were requested. I spent some time pushing them on the swings and chasing them around the park, but then it was time to rest. I joined Lisa on one of the benches as we watched the girls make friends with other kids in the park. They aren't shy.

"Look at the two of them, just a couple of social butterflies." I said as I watched the girls hold court by the swings. I could only imagine what was coming out of their mouths.

"Yes, another fine trait that they picked up from yours truly." Lisa laughed as she flipped her blonde hair back.

"I won't argue that. I'd be over there playing by myself if that was me." I was a shy kid.

We continued to watch the girls and discuss the trip a little bit. I shared some of the funnier moments with Lisa. She knew the guys pretty well, but not great, therefore some things came as a surprise and others didn't. For example, the Nolan story about bedding Carrie and his rude comments afterwards. That story did not surprise her. I kept this conversation light-hearted rather than go into the more emotional parts of the trip. I'd save those for another conversation. I didn't have the energy to talk about Nolan's scam unfolding, Frank coming out of the closet and Sal getting divorced. It made me tired just thinking about it.

A few hours passed and the girls were still going strong, but it was time to go home. I started to get up and Lisa grabbed my hand. "We're lucky aren't we?" She said as she looked into my eyes.

I felt warmness inside that was uncomfortable. I felt flush. Those four words had been so true, but our bad luck has arrived in the worst possible way.

"We are, we are." It was all I could muster up. One more day. We'll be lucky for one more day.

We got home and I took a shower. Chasing the girls around worked up a bit of a sweat. I think I finally sweated out the last of the booze from the trip. Lisa prepared a nice dinner and then we watched one of the girls' favorite shows before putting them to bed. It was around nine o'clock and I was fading fast. I wanted to stay up as long as possible knowing what tomorrow would bring. I made a pact with myself that after we sent the girls off to school in the morning I was going to sit down with Lisa. I managed to stay awake until about 10:15 and then my eyes would have no more.

Surprisingly enough, I slept through the night. I woke up early and went to my spot on the patio for some alone time. The girls would be up shortly to get ready for school. A light rain was already falling making the day a bit more steamy than usual.

The patio door opened and Lisa stepped out. "Hey there, I couldn't sleep. I'm going to make coffee, want some?"

"No thanks. Are you OK?" I asked.

"I think so, just couldn't sleep. I had a few nightmares." She said.

Before too long the girls were up as well. We got them ready to go and off to school they went. I wasn't going back to the office until tomorrow, therefore, Lisa and I had the day together. It would be very easy for me to put off talking to her another day, but I made up my mind that I wouldn't hold off any longer. She deserves to know.

Chapter Sixteen

It was about 7:45am when Lisa and I stepped back on to the patio. She had her coffee in hand. I had a glass of sweet tea. I'm a sucker for a good sweet tea. I guess all of those years in Tallahassee got me hooked. Some chitchat ensued between us. We talked about what we had going on for the upcoming week, nothing too out of the ordinary. Then, I made a decision to stop stalling.

"Honey, I went to the doctor the other day." I was fidgeting and couldn't even look Lisa in the eye. My heart began to race. This was it.

"I know we already talked about it. He was going to get back to you, right?" She asked.

"No, I went again. He did get back to me and asked me to come in again." I continued.

"When?" Lisa looked concerned already as she could see that I wasn't very comfortable.

"I went in the day before I left on the trip." I looked at her briefly and then turned my head away.

"Why didn't you tell me?"

"I didn't want you to worry. I figured it was nothing, just stress." I got up and began to pace.

"Well, what was it?" Lisa became very concerned and stood up and walked over to me.

"The scan came back. Apparently I have a small tumor."

"Where, what is it?" Lisa interrupted me and began to panic a bit.

"My pancreas." I said and pointed to my stomach area for some odd reason, like she didn't know where a pancreas resided.

"You're going to be OK, right? Right?" Lisa's voice elevated. She wanted me to stop beating around the bush.

"No, honey. I'm not going to be OK." I grabbed her hands and looked her in the eyes.

"Kevin, stop, tell me what's going on. Please tell me." Lisa's eyes began to water up.

"I'm sorry honey, I'm sorry." I began to tear up as well. "It's bad". I couldn't get the words out. I couldn't tell her that I was dying. All I could keep saying is that it was bad.

"What does that mean? Tell me!" Lisa's voice rose and the tears stopped.

"A year, a year, that's what it means!" I yelled back at her. "I'm dying".

I don't know why I did it, but I broke free from her hands and stormed inside the house. I went straight to our bedroom and collapsed onto the bed. Lisa was right behind me.

"No Kevin, no!" Lisa was shrieking now.

I was lying on my back with my red eyes looking back at her. This was worse than I had imagined. All of the anxiety leading up to this conversation and the terrible feelings of guilt just poured through my body. I didn't know what to expect from Lisa, but seeing her like this is awful. She's such a strong woman. I guess I thought she would have a different reaction. I thought she'd look me in the eyes and tell me everything was going to be OK, but maybe that was just me trying to stay positive. She was collapsing before my very eyes.

"The girls, what are we going to tell the girls!" Lisa was on her knees next to the bed grabbing my leg.

I felt like I was being yelled at for being sick. I felt like she believed that I did this on purpose. I tried to stay calm, understanding that this may be just a knee-jerk reaction from her, but my patience wore thin quickly.

"Stop yelling at me!" I sat up in the bed and moved her hands off of me.

"Why, why!" Lisa was hysterical and it was all I could handle.

I bounced up off the bed and grabbed the nearest thing I could find which happened to be the lamp on the nightstand. I threw it against wall and it shattered all over the place. I stormed out of our room to the garage, jumped in my car and pulled out of the driveway in a hurry. I was in no shape to be driving. I didn't even have shoes on. As a matter of fact, I was wearing boxer shorts and an undershirt. What the hell was I doing?

I made it out to the main road just outside of our neighborhood and turned around. Running away like this wasn't going to help. I pulled back into the garage much calmer and decided that no matter what Lisa said I was going to take it and not lose my cool. To my surprise a much different Lisa greeted me in the garage. My short trip out of the neighborhood and back provided a calming effect that we both needed. We could now sit down and have a discussion like sensible adults.

We sat down at the kitchen table and started over.

"I'm sorry, I really am", I said.

"Me too, but let's talk about this." Lisa wanted to get to the point.

"I'm in trouble Lisa. The prognosis is not good. I have another appointment tomorrow. Can you come with me?" I asked.

"Of course. I insist as a matter of fact." Lisa squeezed my hand tight and gave me a comforting look. We were now in this fight together and that's the way it should be. We've faced challenges before and we've come out on top. Sure, this is different, but we're a great team. I'm so lucky to have her.

"I love you. I love you so much." I gave Lisa a kiss.

"I love you more and I'm not letting you go."
Lisa's face was serious and then turned into a caring smile.

And so our fight began. Lisa not only accompanied me to this doctor visit, but she never missed one at all. Everything I heard from the doctor, she heard. In addition to her role as wife and mother, she now added nurse. Just as I suspected, this woman would not go down without a fight. We had plenty of ups and downs along the way. Telling the girls was the most challenging. They are still babies and they didn't quite understand what we meant. Of course, we didn't share all of the details with them, but we did let them know that Daddy was sick and it wasn't just the sniffles.

The first time I had chemotherapy I thought I was going to die. Talk about getting the energy sucked right out of you. It makes you so weak it's scary. I've played sports my whole life and there were times when I was so exhausted I didn't think I could keep playing. The byproduct of chemo is much different because it mentally drains you as well. In sports it's easy to stay focused when you're tired and push yourself along even if your body doesn't want to respond. The chemo just drains you physically, mentally and emotionally. After my chemo treatments I didn't like to see anyone. I even asked Lisa to keep the girls distracted until I felt like I recovered a little bit. I didn't want them to see me like that.

The days turned into months and as much as I prayed and hoped for a miracle, it didn't come. The toughest day I ever had was the one when reality set in. Lisa and I had gone in for a doctor's visit a few days after my latest chemo treatment.

"Hi Kevin. Hi Lisa." Dr. Peters entered the room.

"Hey Doc." I responded as I sat on the table in my stupid hospital gown.

He did the usual checks with his stethoscope and then stepped back.

"Kevin, Lisa it's time to have a tough conversation." He looked at both of us as I picked my chin up off of my chest.

"You see, we're striking out here. We've tried and tried, but nothing is working." Dr. Peters continued.

"I was hoping for some progress, but we've gotten nowhere. My fear is that we keep putting you through chemo and draining the energy out of you. It's just not fair." Doc said as he reviewed my records on his tablet.

"So what are you saying?" Lisa began to get defensive.

"What I'm saying is that it's my opinion and recommendation that Kevin lives the rest of his life as best he can." He and Lisa seemed to be having a conversation with each other forgetting I was in the room.

"Hey, I'm right here you know. I'm part of this process too." I interrupted.

"Give up, that's your recommendation, right?" Lisa was showing her frustration.

"Don't look at it that way. Look at it as embracing what Kevin has left. You see what the chemo does. It's taxing and if it's not producing results I can't recommend with a sound mind that we keep doing it. It's not fair." Dr. Peters was being as direct as possible and he did it in a way that showed this isn't the first time he's had this kind of conversation.

"We'll get another opinion then." Lisa was defiant.

"Lisa, you have every right to get another opinion and you are free to do so. I'm just telling you that this doctor can't justify continuing. This isn't supposed to be an easy conversation and your reaction is exactly what I thought it would be. I try as a doctor to leave my emotions out of situations like this, but I can't. With that, I can tell you I'm not acting on emotion. This is the right thing to do. I pray every day that Kevin will beat this thing, but I can't allow it anymore. It's just not fair." Dr. Peters said his peace and we appreciated it. Now the ball was in our court.

The drive home from the doctor visit was fairly quiet. Although I felt defeated, I did have a sense of relief. Maybe I was starting to accept the fact that I would be dead soon. I'm not sure, but something allowed me to feel relief. Who knows, it could be that I know I won't have to go through chemo again. That's a relief.

Lisa cooled down, but not enough for us to avoid pursuing a second opinion. The second opinion was the same as the first. She had a lot of hope with this other doctor, but I didn't. I know what's to come.

Chapter Seventeen

The fall came and so did football season. Although I wasn't doing well I asked Lisa to help me get to the alumni weekend football game at Florida State. That was special. It was impossible for me to hide that I was sick and I got those looks from old friends who hadn't seen me in awhile. You know those sympathetic, I don't know what to say kind of looks. Those are all part of the territory now. I even got to see Trent, although, he didn't remember who I was. After all, we only met for a few minutes and I looked nothing like I did back in May.

Thanksgiving and Christmas came and went. I surrounded myself with family and friends as much as possible. I thought about so many of the previous Thanksgiving's and Christmas' that I didn't do that. What a waste. Lisa and I would spend those holidays with each other and the girls. Of course, we enjoyed that time together, but it's not like we don't have big families that we could have been with. I knew this was my last holiday season and it was obvious that all of my family and friends did too. I can't remember the last time, or if ever, we had such big holidays. It was a little hectic for Lisa since she had to play host for both since I wasn't going to travel anywhere. We had a good time. I drank, but I wasn't supposed to. I ate food that I wasn't supposed to. I even smoked a couple of cigars. Did it matter anymore?

The holidays passed and it was back to just the girls and me. I didn't know how long I had left. I hoped that I could squeeze another birthday in, but May was a long way away. The cruise that the guys bought us was also on the horizon, but of course, that wasn't going to happen. I figured out a way to donate it to a cancer awareness charity as an auction item. It helped raise a few bucks for a worthy cause.

It was time for me to get everything in order so that Lisa and the girls wouldn't have to worry about life after me. I took all of the financial steps necessary. I had always been a saver, therefore, the combination of what I had saved through investments and my life insurance policy should provide enough security for the girls. College funds for the girls – check. A roof over their heads – check. Funeral arrangements – check. So, the monetary part was taken care of, but what about the other important things? I'd sit alone and cry just thinking about the girls going to their senior proms, starting college and eventually getting married. I wouldn't be there for any of it. It breaks my heart. This is the part that keeps me up at night and makes me feel like I've failed. What about Lisa? Sure, we've had light-hearted conversations about what she'll do when I'm gone, but we've kept it light-hearted for a reason. Neither one of us wants to think about it. I don't want her to be alone for the rest of her life, but I can't fathom someone else coming into her life and the girls' lives. The reality is that it will happen and at the end of the day, I just want her to be happy.

As January rolled on I decided to start creating a video diary for Reilly and Lynnie. Sure, I didn't look so great, but I wanted them to have something to watch as they got older and could better understand everything. It was also my way of being able to give my two cents from the grave. Ha, dear old Dad always having an opinion. I'm sure that's what they'll be thinking. I'd leave it up to Lisa as to when to show them the videos. She'd know best. The hardest part about taping them was keeping my composure. I could have gotten emotional, but why would I do that? I wanted them to see me in a happy state. I even told a few stories about some of the hi-jinks that I had gotten into growing up. Most were rated PG-13, but a few were for mature audiences. I gave a warning before those stories allowing Lisa to stop the video until the girls got a little older.

January also brought the end to my charade of trying to work. My employer was so gracious though. They would not take my resignation. They kept paying me even though all I was doing was sitting at home.

February brought Valentine's Day, which also doubled as Father's Day. Lynnie and Reilly were a little confused by that, but Lisa thought it was appropriate. We knew it was unlikely that I'd make it to June. Friends and family would visit often and I soaked up every minute of it, although there were a few days that I wasn't the most pleasant person to be around. I had mood swings, but that was to be expected. No one cared. They just wanted to spend some time with me. If I was an asshole for some reason they chalked it up to a bad day. I was entitled to a few of those.

In March, we got a scare when jaundice set in. My insides were a mess and I was warned that this may happen, but it was still strange to see a pale yellow face staring me back in the mirror. The doctors were able to clear the blockage for me and I wasn't yellow anymore. It was another sign that the end was near. Lisa and I would go to bed each night wondering whether I would wake up the next morning. I don't think I've ever seen a woman so strong. She's been the rock in our family. The girls continue to ask questions and Lisa is there with a smiling, positive face providing the answers. I'm so blessed to have her in my life. The only regret I have is that I put her aside for too long while I was chasing my career. If I had it to do all over again I would put her where she belongs, first. I've told her that plenty of times since I've gotten sick and she always tries to make me feel good by telling me not to worry about it, but I know better. It hurt her. Being second fiddle to a career is not fun and she deserved better.

As April came along it was no longer a battle to just survive. It was a battle to survive while staying at home. I wanted nothing to do with hospice. I wanted to die at home, around my family. Lisa was on board with the idea, although there were times that she thought it might be best for me to go into hospice. She did her due diligence and met with a hospice provider, but she didn't have any intention of making me leave the house. Whatever it took, she was going to see that I died peacefully in our home. Hospice care would happen in our house, not at a facility.

May arrived and this was a milestone month for a couple of reasons. It had been almost a year since I received my grim diagnosis. The doctor said, 'maybe one year'. That one-year was approaching rapidly. May was also important since my birthday was just a few days away on the 18th. Lisa had thought about making big plans for my birthday, but as much as she wanted to do it, she knew better. I was a mess and a quiet celebration with her, Lynnie and Reilly was the wise alternative.

May 9th was the day that was on my radar. Why was May 9th significant? That was the day the previous year that Dr. Peters told me 'maybe one year'. Being the stubborn son-of-a-bitch that I am, I wanted to prove him wrong. The 9th came and went, but not without me phoning Dr. Peters to bust his chops a little bit. It was all in good fun. He was the compassionate guy that he had always been and told me that if anyone were going to prove him wrong it would be me. I told him I'd give him another call in a year.

Of course, that wouldn't happen. In the early hours of May 15th my life came to an end. I fought the gallant fight, but this disease got the best of me. I made my way to the bathroom in pain like usual and collapsed on the floor. It was 2:03am when the last breath left my body. I wasn't able to hold on for another birthday. I tried, but it was just my time. Lisa slept through the night and noticed immediately that I was not in bed when she woke up around 5:45am. She figured I had gone out on the patio like usual. She looked out the window, but didn't see me. She took a few steps and then noticed my foot poking out of the water closet in the bathroom. She rushed over to find me lying on the floor. She shook me, but could feel that my body was already cold. She knew I was gone. She lay on the floor next to me giving me one last hug and a kiss on my head. Tears began to roll down her face uncontrollably. She had worked so hard preparing herself for this day, but it didn't matter. All of that preparation was useless. Emotions ran through her that had never run through her before. Our love was so strong. It was like a part of her was dead lying on that cool tile floor. She knew she had to pick herself up and go into mom mode. She needed to get Lynnie and Reilly out of the house as soon as possible. Lisa called one of her girlfriends, Monica, who had been there for us through thick and thin. She came over right away and took the girls out for a donut at Dunkin Donuts. It was still early and the girls were groggy. They hadn't put two and two together, but did think it was a little odd to be up and out the door so early on a Saturday.

Lisa wanted to grieve, but she didn't have time. She now had the difficult job of calling family and friends with this awful news. She made a few calls to immediate family and asked another friend, Kristy, to help make a few calls to friends, including Frank and Sal.

Of all the days on the calendar, my funeral took place on my birthday. When people die young like me it makes for a big crowd at the funeral. Mine was no different. Tons of friends and family, former co-workers, current co-workers were all in attendance. It was good for Lisa as she was able to put a few faces with their names. People that I had talked about a lot in the past that she never met were there to share their condolences. Two people that were missing shocked a lot of people, but it wasn't a surprise to Lisa. My parents were just not healthy enough to make it all the way from Arizona, plus I don't think they would have been able to handle it. I couldn't imagine Lynnie or Reilly passing away before me. My parents were living that nightmare now.

Sal was there. Solo, of course. I think he's been scared off from marriage for a while. Not a bad idea for him. He continues to spend a lot of quality time with Hannah and his relationship with Katie has turned civil. They've put their issues aside in the best interest of Hannah and that's the way it should be. Sal and I spoke a lot after he learned I was sick, but he never came to visit. That didn't surprise me because he told me he wasn't going to. I thought it was kind of strange, but he kept telling me that he's choosing to remember me from that day I drove away in Atlanta as our trip ended. I accepted that and he called me a few times a week. Our conversations always provided a good diversion from my reality. He was a good friend. No, he was the best of friends. I miss him already.

As we figured, Frank had a tough go of it after he came out. Erica and her family made it hard on him by threatening to take the kids away and only allow supervised visits. They called him a pervert, a fag and every other derogatory name possible. Erica's brother even confronted Frank and threatened him with violence if he ever came near Erica and the kids again. They went so far as to file a restraining order. It was all complete nonsense of course, but nonetheless it hurt Frank to the core. Their custody battle is still going on. He gets to see the kids on the weekends now without supervision, but Erica is not giving up. If she gets her way Frank will never see them again. It's a sad state that they're in and the end result will be that the kids suffer which is unfair. Frank's relationship with Brian ended a few months ago. Frank will always have a place in his heart for Brian, as he helped him come out, but Frank needed to move on. He goes on dates, but has yet to find someone, but at least he found himself through this.

Nolan was sentenced to thirty-three years in a federal prison. It turns out that he did everything he could to reduce his sentence, as it was originally fifty-two years. One way he got it reduced was by ratting out some organized crime figures that were involved in his scams. Because of this, he is in a prison somewhere being protected. No one knows where he is, but news did get to him that I was sick. He was unable to contact me though. He probably doesn't even know about the funeral. He'll find out soon enough. I wonder if he'll ever see the light of day again? I suppose he has a chance. He'll be about seventy-six when his sentence is up. What a waste. He threw his life away for a few bucks and left countless numbers of families devastated, including his own.

It was very challenging for Lisa to make her way around and say hello to everyone. Most people came to her, many of which she was meeting for the first time.

"Hello Lisa, I'm very sorry for your loss." A big black man standing about six and a half feet tall put his hand out.

Lisa embraced his giant, but gentle hand. "Thank you for coming," she wasn't sure who this person was, but had an idea.

"I'm Anthony. I spent some brief, but great times with your husband. He was a good man and will be missed."

"Oh, Anthony." Lisa smiled as I told her a number of stories about him and did show her a few photos of him, but that was a while ago. She had a few other things on her mind today.

"Kevin had so many good things to say about you. I'm sure he is very happy that you're here." Lisa smiled, one of her few for the day.

"Well, I just wanted to say hello and again, I'm so sorry for your loss." Anthony gave Lisa a hug and walked away.

After our trip Anthony never drove the bus again. He figured it was time to get his life together. He's now an assistant offensive line coach at Ole Miss. Momma is thrilled that he is so close to home now and Anthony is just happy to have a purpose. A light bulb went off after our trip. He decided that he owed himself a little bit more and decided to go back to what he's loved for so long, football. He had been so afraid to try and go back to Ole Miss thinking that he'd get rejected, but of course, they took him in with open arms. Now, don't get me wrong, no one is just handed a college football coaching position. He works his tail off and also helps on the recruiting front. Ole Miss was much improved this past season and a lot of the credit goes to the improvement of their offensive line. Anthony is on his way. Who knows, maybe he'll be a head coach some day? He made a few fans for life with the four of us.

After the funeral, family and friends began to get back to their own lives. Lisa had so many people around to comfort her during the days leading up to my death and for several days afterward. Slowly, but surely people began to leave town or just get back to their daily routine. This was the hardest part for Lisa. She had to go back to our house without me. It was just she and the girls. The house seemed so empty. Everywhere she turned there was something to remind her of me. Simple things like the coffee table in the family room. I must have stubbed my toe on that damn thing about twenty times over the years and that always gave Lisa a good chuckle. She loved how I would do everything in my power not to curse in front of the girls. I'd make up some interesting words that would serve as replacements like 'momma-poppa-mints'. What that meant, I have no idea, but it just came out of my mouth.

She'd drive by our favorite restaurant on the water, Max's. We spent anniversaries, birthdays and any other excuse we could come up with to go there. Her eyes were never dry after driving by there and she had to do it quite a bit as our bank was near there and there were still loose ends to tie up.

Nothing was worse than the first night she spent in our bed alone. Sure, I had been gone on business trips before and that was OK, but this was permanent. She'd find herself rolling over in the middle of the night to touch my back, but I wasn't there of course. She'd wake up in a panic and then realize where she was and more importantly, where I was.

It is said that time heals all wounds. I hope that is true for Lisa. I never wanted to leave her, but I guess that wasn't my decision. Time will march on and Lisa will move on without her husband while Lynnie and Reilly will move on without their father. I tried. I really did. I fought hard and lost. Sure, there came a time when we decided that further treatment wasn't in my best interest, but that didn't mean that I wasn't still trying. Accepting this disease was never an option for me. I died on that cold tile floor and up until I took that last breath, I never accepted it. I didn't have to and I wasn't about to. I realize that may sound defiant, but that's not it. All I wanted to do was live. I just wanted to grow old with Lisa and see our girls grow up. I don't think that was too much to ask. A lot of people get that chance. Why didn't I? I guess I'll never get an answer to that question.

I left an envelope for Lisa in a spot that I knew she'd eventually come across, but not before I passed on. The video diary was strictly for Lynnie and Reilly, but this note was for Lisa only. It took her about three weeks to find the envelope. On the front it simply read 'Lisa' with a little squiggly line under her name. I always did that for some reason. She grabbed the envelope and gave it a strange look. She probably wondered why she hadn't come across it before. She opened it with anticipation and it read:

My Dearest Lisa,

I'm sure you're surprised to find this and I'm not sure how long it took you, but if I were a betting man I'd say about three weeks. I'm sure all of the dust has settled and it's just you and the girls doing your best to cope. Our girls are so fortunate to have a mom like you. I know it won't be easy, but I have no doubt that our babies will grow up to be outstanding young ladies, just like you.

We've shared so many memories over the years and unfortunately, the last one we spent together wasn't how we had envisioned it. I want to thank you for so many things, but there's one that stood out over all of the rest. The way you handled my illness was extraordinary. You were my rock through it all. I made it as long as I did because of you and only you. Do you know that you never cried in front of me other than the first time I told you I was sick? That is the definition of an unselfish act. It was always about me and never about you. Even the times when I tried to turn it around and profess my guilt for getting sick and eventually leaving you and the girls you stopped me dead in my tracks. I thought I knew everything about you before this, but I saw you soar to new heights that I don't think others have the ability to even come close to. I know I certainly couldn't.

Well, that's enough of that depressing stuff. I'm sure you're full of tears already and I'm sorry about that. If it makes you feel better, I was full of tears while I was writing this too. I look back on our life together and I know that from the day we met I was the happiest that I had ever been. You were able to do something that was so powerful. You made me smile all of the time. I'm sure I made you smile all of the time too, but it was usually at my expense. Case in point, that damn coffee table! Do me a favor and get rid of that thing, OK? Or how about when I was pulling the hose around the pool and fell in fully clothed? I know you loved that.

I realize there are so many things that we didn't get to do, but on the other hand we were blessed to enjoy a lot of things that others will never have a chance to. No matter what the experience the most important part was that we did it together. Let's just think that our times together are not gone, they certainly aren't forgotten and let's hope they aren't over. I'm looking at this as a temporary stop, not an end. Someone has hit the pause button, but we'll get to push play again some day. Until that day know that my love will continue to grow for you. I miss you so much and I'll be counting the days until we see each other again. Live a wonderful, glorious life and I'll see you on the other side.

Thanks for being the best wife, mother and friend a man can ask for. You deserve only the best that life has to offer and I know you'll get it. Forever and always, I love you dearly.

Kevin